BRIGHT'S CROSSING

Bright's Crossing

Short Stories by
ANNE CAMERON

HARBOUR PUBLISHING

HARBOUR PUBLISHING
P.O. Box 219
Madeira Park, BC Canada V0N 2H0

Edited by Mary Schendlinger
Cover design by Roger Handling
Printed and bound in Canada

CANADIAN CATALOGUING IN PUBLICATION DATA

Cameron, Anne, 1938–
 Bright's crossing

ISBN 1-55017-022-8

I. Title.
PS8555.A5187B7 1990   C813'.54   C90-091298-7
PR9199.3.C35B7 1990

For Alex
Erin
Pierre
Marianne
Tara

and especially
Eleanor

Contents

Pat

Pat Fleming believed Joe when he said he loved her. She believed him when he said he wanted to marry her. She believed the part about forsaking all others, she believed the sickness and health, she believed the richer or poorer, she believed till death do us part. She left behind her other name and her other life. She went from spinster to matron with a smile on her face, wearing something old, something new, something borrowed, and something blue. She was in love with Joe. He said he loved her and she believed him. She believed every word he said, especially five years later when he told her he was going to kill her. She believed he would. Believed him totally.

Joe felt life passing him by, and he resented it. There he was, only thirty-two, and tied down the same as if he were sixty-five. Thirty-two, and tied by a wife and four-year-old son to a job he knew was a go-nowhere grind, a mortgage that would hang around his neck for another twenty years, and a secondhand car that would fall apart before he had finished paying for it.

His brother Jim was two years older and immeasurably freer. No wife, no mortgage, no relic of a gas-guzzler, and no job working in a shake-and-shingle mill with the noise making his ears numb. Jim kept a job only as long as he wanted it, and as soon as it started to pick him, he packed 'er in and went on Unemployment Enjoyment until he felt like getting up in the morning and slogging off in the rain. Jim drove a good car, and with it he impressed teen-agers in tight jeans who loved to ride around showing off to their friends. Jim gave them stuff to smoke, or bits of blotter to chew, or pills to wash down with their beer, or powder to stuff up their noses, or whatever it took to get their firm little bodies out of those tight jeans. Jim got more than a body could believe and it hardly cost him anything.

"Try it," Jim said. "you might like it."

Joe tried it, Joe liked it. He liked the way grass made him giggle, he liked the way hash smoothed him out, and he wanted to try more. So Jim got Joe some high-grade acid.

They said they were going on a fishing trip. They said they'd be gone a week. They were gone two and a half weeks and by the time they came home Joe didn't have to worry about his job any more. So he took a holiday. He took one helluva holiday. Then he and Jim both took a six-month holiday across the pond in the Crowbar Hotel, busted good and proper.

By the time they got out, Pat had started putting her life together. She had a job in the shake-and-shingle mill. Little Matt was in kindergarten half a day and with a sitter until Pat got home from work. She even had her babysitting arranged around her shift work.

Joe was out of the pokey on Wednesday, home Wednesday night, and in a foul mood within two hours. He had expected certain things to be the way they always had been. But when he showered, shaved, put on after-shave, and went to bed grinning with anticipation, Pat went into the bathroom, showered, brushed her teeth, and went to the spare room.

"What in hell are you doing in here?" Joe demanded.

"Getting ready to sleep."

"You're my wife!"

"You should have remembered that a few months ago instead of whoring around with your brother."

"What do you mean?"

"You know what I mean." She sat up in bed and looked him in the eye. "You and Jim and those...kids."

"Ah, for..." He slammed the flat of his hand against the door frame, turned away in anger, and went back to bed by himself.

Joe went to his old boss and apologized for acting like a pimply-faced nose-picker, and got his job back. But he was on probation, same as any snot-face, and that griped him. He'd lost his seniority and that griped him, too. Pat had almost half a year more seniority than he had, and that griped him most of all.

"A wife's place is in the home!" he roared.

"Is a husband's place in jail?" she asked.

"I paid my debt to society."

"And me? I should quit my job and become totally dependent on you, even though you've proved to me and the world you aren't dependable? Then what do I do if you goof up again?"

"I won't. I promise."

"You promised me a lot and broke every one of those promises. Once bitten, twice shy."

"You're my wife and you'll damn well . . ."

"I'm not quitting my job."

"What about Matt?"

"You weren't worried about Matt when you started acting like a teen-ager, why worry about him now?"

"Don't you get smart with me," he raged.

"I wouldn't think of it," she laughed, "I know it's beyond you."

So he hit her. Several times. Bounced her off the wall to let her know who was boss in the house, then headed off to the pub for a few beer. While he was sipping suds, Pat phoned the police. When he got home he was all set to teach her what for all over again. Instead, he was put in the back seat of a police car, taken down to the pokey, and informed he had been charged with assault. The judge reamed him out, explained to him life had progressed well beyond the caves and warned him what a bad idea it would be to break the peace bond or in any way repeat his offence.

Joe was so angry he could hear every beat of his heart echoing in the space behind his ear. He really thought his head might explode with fury. But he gritted his teeth, apologized to the judge, the court, his wife, and society in general. He paid his fine, he posted his peace bond. He promised to clean up his act, straighten up, and fly properly.

Then he went around to the house and told Pat he wanted to talk to her.

"What about?" she asked through the locked door.

"About us, of course."

"There is no 'us,' Joe," she said.

"What do you mean?"

"You don't live here any more. Go away."

"I need my clothes, don't I? And my shaving gear and . . ."

"I'll send them to you. Let me know where you're living and . . ."

"With Jim," he interrupted.

The taxi cab arrived halfway through Hockey Night in Canada. Not all his stuff was in it, but his clothes, his shaving kit, his work boots, his lunch pail, his hard hat, and more stuff than he'd have room for in a two-bedroom ground-floor apartment was packed in boxes and black garbage bags.

A month later he got a notification from Family Court. Pat had applied for a legal separation. He had half a mind to let her go ahead with it, but there was the kid to think about.

"Man's got a right to bring up his own son," Jim growled, sucking on a beer.

"Yeah," Joe agreed moodily.

"Alternate weekends," Jim scorned. "What do they think they're doing?"

"I'll show 'em," Joe promised. "Her and that smart-ass lawyer of hers."

When Pat went out the next morning to drive to work, her windshield was smashed and her tires slashed. She knew it was Joe. She knew it the way you know where the sun comes up and where the sun goes down, but the young cop explained to her that without proof there was nothing he could do. She got the car towed to the garage, got the windshield replaced, got new tires, and waved goodbye to her next two weeks' pay. The next morning the back window was smashed and an old battery lay on the back seat, dripping acid all over everything.

Pat got the message. If Joe could vandalize her car and get away with it, he could start in on the house and get away with it. If he could crack open a battery and spill acid on the inside of the car he could crack open a battery and rearrange her face.

She thought about it at work, she thought about it at home. She woke up at night in a cold sweat thinking about it, especially after she found a dead rat in her lunch bucket. She stood in the kitchen listening to Matt tell her about a song he had learned in school, and she nodded in the right places, she said uh huh and that's nice and it sounds like fun, but she stared into her open lunch kit, her sandwiches still in her hand.

The rat had not been there when she'd washed the lunch kit after supper the night before, and the rat hadn't got itself in there, even though it's well known a rat will pick the most goddamnable place possible to die. Someone had been in her house. Someone had come in while she and Matt were asleep, padded around silently, found the lunch kit, opened it, put the dead rat inside, closed the kit, put it away, and left again.

She knew who. She also knew there wouldn't be a fingerprint to be found. She started to shake. She knew he could just as easily have slit her throat from ear to ear and left no proof.

Then he phoned her and told her he was suing for custody of Matt.

"And I'll win," he gloated. "You know I'll win. One way or the other. Sooner or later."

"Why?" she begged him. "Why?"

"Because you piss me off."

"I'll go to the police . . ."

"You do that," he laughed. "You do anything you want. But do it knowing that if you piss me off any more than I'm already pissed off, or if you fight me in this, or if you do anything to keep me from getting Matt, I'll kill you," and he laughed again. "You havin' cheese sandwiches today? By the way," he added, "if I was you I'd remember to get my brakes checked regularly. Real regularly."

She stood for a long time after he hung up, holding the phone and staring out the window. Then, finally, she went into the kitchen, threw the lunch pail into the garbage, and packed her sandwiches, her apple, and her small container of yogurt in a brown paper bag. She believed him. He'd kill her and he'd get away with it.

She didn't go to the police. She went to Family Court and talked to the worker there, then waited until it was time to sit down with her lawyer and Joe's lawyer. She got her divorce and half the sale price of the house. Joe got the other half of the money, and Matt.

Pat knew that wasn't the end of it, though. She knew it would be more slashed tires or broken windshields or cracked batteries or dead rats or something even worse. They were right when they said taking acid changed you completely. One man had gone off with his brother and another had come back. One man had taken the acid and another had come home after the high was finished. The first man, the one she had married, was gone forever. The second man was a stranger. A dangerous stranger.

She left. Packed her things in her car and drove off with no firm idea where she was going.

She headed for the island because water seemed to be a barrier, a moat between the island and any threat from the mainland. Just like an old castle, only instead of a drawbridge, there was the Ferry Corporation. Besides, it was one place she and Joe had never gone, never even discussed visiting. When she got there, she decided not to stay in or near Nanaimo, because of the traffic snarls, and because it was too similar to the town she had just been forced, by fear, to leave.

She could have headed north. She could have driven off on the highway that slashed into the green wall of forest. Instead, as much on a whim as anything else, she turned south, and in no more time than it would have taken anybody else, there she was, turning off the highway, taking a right past the store/post office/cafe, bouncing over the railway tracks, past the community hall and school, not even knowing when she did it that she had come to Bright's Crossing. The sign, which for years had hung on the wall of the store, was off at the time, being repainted, nothing fancy, just white background and stark black letters, as plain and serviceable as the people who had decided to live there.

Pat didn't decide immediately to stay in Bright's Crossing. She didn't park her car, step out, smile widely, and say Eureka! or Excelsior! or start to sing Free, free, free at last, great God almighty I'm free. She drove to the inn, parked her car, went inside, chose a small cabin rather than a room, and paid a week's rent in advance.

She carried her suitcases into the cabin, then went for a walk along the banks of the creek which ran behind the inn. The salal and Oregon grape glistened with dampness, the sword ferns brushed her jeans and left traces of wet. The ground was spongy with morning rain, and the clear water sprayed from large, rounded grey rocks. A jay screeched from a cedar tree and somewhere in the distance a thin-voiced dog yapped an answer.

Pat walked for three-quarters of an hour along the creek, then sat on a damp rock and stared at the ribbon of water. The remembered sound of Joe's voice mocked her, but the breeze washed from her nostrils the smell of carpet cleaner and furniture polish in the lawyer's office. When she finally got up off the rock and started back to her rented cabin, she felt settled inside, certain she had done the only intelligent thing, resigned to the realization she would have no real relationship with her son, because Joe, and the distance demanded by safety, would see to that.

She had a bath, watched the flickering TV for an hour or so, had supper in the inn, then went back to her room and slept like a hibernating bear. In the morning she went to the inn for breakfast. There, sitting in a booth, drinking coffee and reading the paper while waiting for her bacon and eggs, she overheard two men discussing all the things men discuss while sipping coffee and waiting for French toast.

Two and a half hours later, Pat was in the office of the Bright's Crossing sawmill, applying for a job.

"Don't know that we've ever had a woman here before," the clerk admitted, reading what Pat had written in the "Previous Employment" space.

"You know what they say," Pat smiled, "Better late than never."

"Stitch in time saves nine," the clerk replied, almost idly.

"A penny saved isn't worth much," Pat offered.

The clerk laughed and Pat left, smiling. Three days later there was a phone call for her at the front desk of the inn, and two days after that, Pat started work.

She stayed in her cabin for another month, then one of the men on her shift told her about a small farm for sale. "Not much to it," he admitted, "only four or five acres and a small house. There was more land once, but it got sold off when the old woman got too old to work the farm. It's got water, though. Lots of water."

"Thanks, Fred. Appreciate it."

"It's not listed with a real estate company," Fred added. "That's how we keep some kind of control over who moves into the place. Otherwise you wind up being invaded by a buncha people who come here looking for something they never had, then a year later start criticizing because they miss what they were tryin' to get away from in the first place."

The money she had from her share of the house was more than enough to persuade the bank manager to approve a mortgage. The old woman signed the papers. Pat helped her load what little furniture she was taking, and drove the rental truck the five miles to the senior citizens complex.

"You might as well make use of the rest," the old woman said gruffly. "I'll not be needing it." She looked around her small unit, smiled widely, and nodded repeatedly. "I can put the sofa here, and sit on it, and look out the big glass sliding doors, down the hillside to the beach, and across the beach to the water. Just sit here and keep warm with the 'lectric heat. No ashes to haul, no wood to split and stack, then pack into the house. No chimney to clean. There's big red buttons in every room, so if anything happens, I just get to one and push, and they come racin' over from the main office to check."

"If you get lonely for your garden," Pat said gently, "just get on the blower and I'll come and get you."

"I will miss the bulbs in the springtime," the old woman admitted. "But I won't miss the sore back I got weeding them!"

Pat did nothing to the house until she'd been in it six months. Then she repainted the walls and ceilings and got oval braided rugs at Woolworth's and put them on the floors. She got a brand new colour TV because after a hard day's work it was nice to sit and watch the flickering screen, nice to sit with her brain turned off, letting her body rest and repair itself.

She lived in suspended animation for a year and a half. The second time the bulbs started to bloom, Pat realized she had come to love the little old house. Daffodils threw green spears from the mud around the house, they marched up both sides of the front walkway, they surrounded the fence around the front yard, they sent forays into the grass patch, they surrounded the fruit trees and even wandered beyond the fenced yard to the meadow beyond. When the daffodils started to fade there were tulips, and after the tulips the come-back-forevers, most of them self-seeded. The trees blossomed, the hummingbirds returned, the cedar waxwings came back. It was time to put out tomato plants, time to plant squash and vegetable marrow, time to put in the beet seeds and four kinds of lettuce, time for collards and cabbages to be planted, time to putz and putter and think about maybe phoning for a price on a proper roof. Pat decided to go for a new metal roof, and once that was done she was so pleased with the effect she started thinking about getting some other work done on the place.

She had the back porch taken off and another two rooms added on out back. Not that she needed more room, but you never knew when you'd find use for more space. She had the front porch checked over, some punky boards removed and replaced with new ones. The old windows leaked heat and let in winter drafts, so she had them removed and new ones installed. She had the hardwood floors refinished, and before winter came again, she had the old plumbing ripped out and new pipes installed.

Tuesday nights, if she wasn't on afternoon shift, Pat went to the community hall and took the Crafts Program. She learned to make stuffed cloth dolls with appliquéd or embroidered eyes, nose, and mouth. She turned out entire wardrobes for her dolls, then began planning ahead, doing logger dolls in jeans and plaid shirts for little boys and girls who had fathers or uncles working in the bush. She made fisher dolls, male and female, for kids whose families hauled salmon from the chuck, she made doctor dolls for boys and girls, she made androgynous truck driver dolls. Then she sold them and donated the profits to the Save The Children Fund.

She bought the best material she could find and started making clothes. She soon found she couldn't possibly turn out enough to satisfy the waiting market. She spent a few months in a Painting from the Right Side of the Brain class. Then she started taking adult education courses, filling in the huge blanks in her education, reading books she wouldn't ordinarily have picked up and read.

Springtime followed springtime, and was followed by summer. Pat had neighbours and she had good friends. She even had good friends who were her neighbours. She didn't bother getting hens because she could buy free-range eggs from the Callahans. She didn't get a goat or cow because she could buy good milk from the Olsens. She bought fresh corn from the Callaways and beautiful potatoes from Grandma Amberchuk. She bought the jars, rings, and lids, then paid by the quart to have them filled with pickled beets or dill pickles, and Grandma Amberchuk's daughter-in-law Ruthie considered herself lucky to be making extra money by doing something she'd have been doing anyway. "Six dozen jars of dills or seven dozen, it's the same amount of work," she crowed.

Year after year everything just got better. And every month of that time Pat sent a hundred dollars via bank transfer to Joe for Matt. It was a way to get the money to her son without his father having any idea where she was living. It was a way to ensure she could do something for her own flesh and blood without having it beaten to a pulp or spilled on the floor. What Joe did with it was Joe's own business.

Her family understood the situation. They kept in touch with her and let her know how things were going for Matt, but they didn't see much of him, either, because Joe was as vindictive towards them as he could be without exposing to the world the extent of his assholiness. Once in a while he would allow Pat's mother to have Matt for a weekend, once in a blue moon he allowed the kid to visit for a week of summer holiday, but he always made sure everybody knew what an open-hearted gesture he was making.

It was comforting to Pat to know Matt was doing well as goalie for the soccer team, and pleasing to know he might never set any academic records but was passing regularly from one grade to another. She would have liked to see him graduate from high school but she knew what a hoo-rah that would kick off, so she contented herself with sending enough money to her own mother that Matt could graduate in a good grey suit and brand new everything else, from jockey shorts and undershirt to shiny new shoes and a carnation in his buttonhole. In return she got a colour photograph of a young stranger standing in her mother's living room, smiling widely.

Less than six months later, in the middle of a cool autumn afternoon, as she knelt on a rubber tarp to keep her knees out of the mud while she put in several dozen different species of daffodil bulbs, the same young stranger walked towards her, not smiling.

"Matt," she managed.

"Mom?" he answered.

"For crying out loud!" She rose to her feet, wiping her muddy hands on the seat of her jeans. "Oh my goodness. Oh. I never expected..."

"Hi, Mom." He smiled then, very naturally, as if he had been doing it all his life. He put his arms around her and gave her the most welcome hug she had ever had in her life.

He stayed a week. He told jokes, he talked, he showed her pictures, he dug a new flower bed and helped her plant lily bulbs. He scrubbed the vegetables for supper, he cleared the table and did the dishes, he got up in the morning when she got up, he drank coffee at the table with her, he saw her off to work, and when she came home he was there, waiting, with supper started.

When he left he took a huge part of her with him. But he left her with far more than he was taking. He phoned her at unexpected hours, he even wrote her a two-page letter. Then, in the spring, he came back to see the flowers which had grown from the bulbs they had planted together.

As before, he got up when she got up, he had coffee with her, he waved goodbye when she headed off for work, and he had supper waiting when she got home. He read her books, he ate her food, he slept in her bed, and he drank her beer. In fact, Matt drank a lot of beer.

He left two weeks later because he had a line on a job. He didn't get that job, so he came back again, then borrowed money from her for a bus ticket to some other place where he had a line on a different job. He phoned and asked if she could front him the money for work boots, work pants, work shirt, safety hat, and smokes until he got his first paycheque.

"Then, right off the top, first thing," he promised, "I'll send you what you fronted me."

"Oh, that's okay," Pat said, remembering how tough it had been for her when she first started working.

"You're an angel," he told her. "I really appreciate this, Mom, I really do."

It wasn't much of a job and the foreman was one of the world's all-time idiots, but what can you do except smile, say yessir, and hang in as long as you can. When you can't hang in any longer, you clean out your locker in the bunk house, pick up your pay, and catch a ride out with the first thing heading away from the place.

But he found another job. Then another. And one thing about it, there was no denying he was getting experience in a great number of fields. "When I'm ready to settle down," he told her, sitting in the recliner with his legs stretched out in front of him and another beer in his hand, "I'll have a real good idea of what I want to do with the rest of my life. Construction is good, it pays well and all, but it's kind of here-again-gone-again, and too much at the mercy of market fluctuations. Then there's all that union crap, like you can't join the union unless you've got a job, but you can't get a job unless you're in the union."

"I'm very strong on unions," she said quietly. "Everything we have in the way of social programs, from medical care to old age pension to welfare, we have because the unions managed to squeeze it out of the government and the guys in suits. If we'd waited for them to do it voluntarily, we'd be like Brazil or the Upper Volta or something."

"Oh, I agree totally!" He sat up straight and bent forward eagerly. "I mean it. I'm not anti-union, it's just so damned hard to get IN. I think, myself," he said, settling back again and smiling slightly, "that the bosses arranged it that way. Do you think that's an off-the-wall idea?"

"I think," she answered, "that if you went to trade school and got an apprenticeship through the union you'd have no trouble at all getting into the union."

"Yeah, but if I don't know what I want to apprentice in, there's no sense going to trade school, right?"

And since he had no idea what he might want to do twenty years down the pike, there was no use going to college, either. He went tree planting for one whole season and made good money while the job lasted, then he was working in a supermarket as a management trainee, stamping prices on the lids of cans. He didn't like that because of the long hours and weekend work, so he quit and got another job, then another, and eventually had to borrow money from her to get himself to some town she had never heard of because he'd got a line on a job there.

"You might try putting in an application at the sawmill," she suggested.

"Yeah, but there's no future in that, is there? I mean this countervail thing the Americans have slapped on is going to knock hell out of the lumber business."

"There's not much future going from job to job, either," she said. But he was full of plans, too full to listen to anything that might be construed as criticism, and off he went.

Eventually, even Pat had to wake up and smell the coffee. Matt was no more stable than a shitfly, buzzing and hovering from pat to pat but never settling long anywhere, ready to waft off on the first breeze, blown this way and that way, never still. And he drank up every cent he made.

She had to start paying attention to what was being talked about on the radio and television, about adult children of alcoholics and predisposition to substance abuse. But she couldn't do that until she had worked her way through her own guilt and stopped blaming Joe for being the cause of the problem. She reached for, grasped, and exhausted every other possible excuse before she finally let the chickens go home to roost. Matt was what he was because that's what he wanted to be. Still, he was her son, and she loved him.

Pat continued working at the sawmill. She put most of her pay in the bank, made her dolls and stuffed toys, sewed blouses, shirts, and flannelette nighties, and took them to craft fairs where they sold quickly. She counted the years by the blossoming daffodils and deliberately avoided thinking about anything she couldn't change.

Then Matt sent her a Mother's Day card and, inside the card, a couple of colour photographs of himself and a red-haired woman several years older than him. They stood with their arms around each other's waists, grinning over the heads of two young children, a boy with curly dark hair and a girl with hair the colour of arbutus bark. The card was signed Love, Matt, Gerri, Carol, and Tim.

There was no return address on the envelope, and no hint of Gerri's last name, so even though the card was clearly post-marked Burnaby, there was no way Pat could write or phone. If he'd said Gerry Smith or Gerry Jones she might have gone to the library and looked it up in the Burnaby directory, maybe even phoned all the G. Smiths or G. Joneses in the book, but she couldn't even do that, so she waited.

A few months later Matt phoned. He was on his way to Faro, where he'd heard of a job.

"How does Gerri feel about it?"

"Huh? Oh, her. I don't know how she feels about anything. Haven't seen her for a couple of weeks."

"Oh. I thought . . . when you sent the photographs I thought . . ."

"Yeah, well, you know how it is. You think you know a person, right, and then you move in and find out you're bunking in with a stranger," he laughed. "Might as well just move in with a stranger and hope you can get to know them, I guess."

One night a few months later he phoned, three sheets to the wind, to tell her he was back in Burnaby.

"And, well, Gerri'd like to say hi . . ."

"Gerry? Oh, the woman with the red hair. But I thought . . ."

"Yeah, I know," he laughed happily, "but we kinda patched it up again. You wanna talk to her?"

"All right." She heard the muffled clatter of the phone being put on a table, then picked up again.

"Hi, I'm Gerry," the voice announced.

"Hello. I'm Matt's mother. Pat."

"Hi, Pat." There was the sound of laughter running under the husky voice, and the sound of beer suds wrapped around the words. "I guess you're kinda wondering who he's taken up with, right?"

"When he phoned on his way to Faro he said you'd split up, so . . . how are the kids?"

"Oh, they're fine. Awful little rug-rats, but healthy. Can't ask for more than that, I guess. And yourself?"

"Fine. Just fine."

"You workin'?" She heard the click of a lighter, an indrawn breath as the woman sucked deeply.

Pat reached for her own cigarettes. "You know how it is," she said, "forty hours a week, four weeks a month, eleven months a year, and the first seven of those months you're working to pay taxes."

"Right on. So they can buy some more bullets for the boys."

"And yourself?"

"Thinking of getting the whoofare to sponsor me on one of those non-traditional trades courses. Gotta get some upgrading first, and then see what can be had. I don't want to spend my whole life slinging hash, you know what I mean?"

"I know what you mean."

"Well, I guess you'd like to hear from your son. So . . . nice talkin' at ya."

"Yes. Nice to hear your voice. Maybe get to see your face one day soon?"

"Yeah, well, the road's as long both ways, isn't it."

"It is. But I don't have an address."

"Jesus, and isn't that just like him! I wondered, you know. Why we hadn't had a note or something. He didn't give you an address? Sometimes he's too stupid for words. Even if he is your son."

"Even if he is my son I'll agree with you. I don't even have your last name so I could try to find you in the phone book."

"What a jerk! So, you got a pencil or something?"

Pat took it down. Gerri Hayes, and an address in New Westminster.

"We're close by the skytrain," Gerri explained, "So if you don't want to bring the car it won't be hard for you to find us. Parking's a pain in the ass," she elaborated none too elegantly.

"So maybe we'll see you?" Matt asked cheerfully.

"Maybe so," she half-promised. "And maybe you can bring Gerri and the kids over here, show them some small-town living."

"Yeah. Sure. Be good for the kids to see some real grass, eh."

She went to see them first. On the next long weekend, she left the car at the ferry and walked on, then took the bus on the other side. She got off the bus at the depot, walked across the street to the skytrain station, and sat nervously, her instructions clutched in her hand, watching carefully, almost convinced she'd miss her stop.

She didn't. She got off the train and flagged a cab, and got a dirty look from the driver because it was such a short haul. Three dollars later she was overtipping him because she felt so guilty.

"I've never been here before," she apologized, "I didn't know it was so close or . . ."

"That's okay, lady," he sighed. "I didn't figure you for a twenty-dollar trip anyway."

The red-haired girl, Carol, was four and a half and the most suspicious child Pat had ever met. She glowered from across the room, watching jealously as Tim tried to pull himself up on Pat's knee, flirting and smiling, drooling candy juice onto the front of his striped tee shirt. Pat had half a dozen small metal cars for Tim and a whistling top and Raggedy Ann for Carol, but the big hit was the large box of chocolates she'd brought for Gerri.

It was better than splitting and stacking stove wood, but it wasn't a big family breakthrough that promised warmth and cuddles, understanding and acceptance for years to come. Still, the gesture had been made, the ice was cracked, and by the time she headed back to the skytrain station, the little red-haired girl had stopped watching her for signs of betrayal.

She sent them colouring books and crayons on payday, she sent them funny slippers, she sent them frisbees. And even when Gerri and Matt split up, she sent them flannelette pyjamas and toys she had made herself. Gerri and Matt got back together again for a while, then split up again. And so it went, like a parade of prepositions, they split up, talked it over, made it up, got it on, moved back in, got snowed under, and broke it off. Pat stopped caring whether Matt was in the picture or not, it was easier to assume he was permanently entangled, and to suspect that if he wasn't there this week he'd be back next week.

She wasn't sure why. Maybe it was the closest thing she had to a link with her own son. Maybe if she didn't assume he would sooner or later return to Gerri's apartment, Pat would have to wonder where Matt was and what he was up to this time. Something wet, you could be sure of that. He would work until she almost got sucked into thinking that this time he had his head together and was growing into maturity. Then he would quit, go on a three-week binge, and, when his money was gone, move back in with Gerri and the kids.

Pat supposed Gerri was on welfare. She supposed it was probably some kind of fraud for her to have Matt there, especially when he handed her what money he still had in his pocket, then applied for and got Unemployment Insurance. But it wasn't Pat's business what other people did.

At Christmas time she sent parcels. Stuffed toys, pyjamas, cozy housecoats she had made for the kids. A warm woollen shirt and some nice wool socks for Matt, chocolates and bath salts for Gerri. She was surprised to receive a framed photo of the four of them sitting together neat, tidy, and sober, like a regular family.

Carol started school and Pat sent her a shoebox full of pencils, pencil crayons, erasers, water paints, and brushes, and several pads of doodle paper to practise her letters and numbers at home.

Then Matt phoned to say he was working in construction in Maple Ridge, and Gerri was pregnant. Pat spent hours doing her work mechanically, her mind dancing towards, then shying away from what ought to have been good news. She waited for the grandmotherly feeling to well up inside her, and it didn't. She began to hear, to really hear, things she had ignored before, stories about fetal alcohol syndrome, about children of alcoholic parents and the damage done to them before they are even born. She tried to ignore the reports of babies born with alcohol dependencies, she tried to tell herself Gerri's other two kids seemed fine, she tried to run away from it all as she had run away from Joe. Finally, when she couldn't run from it any more, she bought a book, then another, and began to read up on the things which were scaring her. Maybe if she knew more about it, she told herself, she wouldn't be so afraid. After all, everyone said it was not knowing was the worst.

But knowing was no better. Halfway through the pregnancy, Gerri phoned Pat to tell her she had split up with Matt again. Pat knew Gerri had been drinking. She could hear it in the slurred vowels, but she said nothing. After all, she wasn't really anybody's grandmother, and if Gerri got mad at her she might refuse to let Pat see the baby.

"Do you need anything?" Pat asked.

"I need someone to grab that asshole and shake his brains into gear is what I need! How did a together woman like you ever manage to raise a dip-shit son?"

"How did you ever manage to get hooked up with him?"

"Ah, you know me, I'm a sucker for stray cats, lost dogs, and anything with big, shiny eyes."

Matt moved back in again, as both Pat and Gerri had known he would. He said he'd really found out this time, really knew what he wanted and how to get it. "None too soon, I guess, eh?" he joked into the phone. "After all, pater familias and all that. Time to grow up whether I want to or not, right?"

"Right," she said, and there was no hint of humour in her voice.

"Hey, not so heavy," he teased. "Lighten up, Mom. I'm telling you, this time it's okay, we talked it all out and got some stuff worked out."

"Sure, Matt."

They called her Patricia Marie, but her last name was Hayes, like Gerri's. At first Pat thought it would bother her, but it didn't. After all, she wasn't really Pat Fleming, even though she'd never taken back her own name. And even if Patricia Marie had been a Fleming, it wouldn't have connected her to Pat's own name, which she remembered now only the way you remember the name of the kid who sat behind you in grade three.

She bought a rocking cradle and had it shipped to them, but didn't go to see the baby right away. Matt phoned to say thank you and to tell her Joe had bought a carriage and a playpen and brought them around.

"He wasn't too pleased about the Patricia part," Matt crowed, "but what could he say about it? Can't hardly expect anybody to call a little girl Josephine in this day and age, right?"

"How's Gerri?"

"Oh, she's fine. Wanna talk to her?" and before Pat could answer yes or no, Gerri was on the line, sober and subdued.

"How you feeling?" Pat asked.

"Tired," Gerri admitted. "They're gonna give me an extra allowance this month so's I can have a homemaker in to help out with the kids and such. Which means Matt has to make himself scarce during the day."

"He'd be at work anyway, wouldn't he?"

"He's not working right now."

"Oh, for God's sake, what is it this time?"

"He got sauced on the job and . . . well, they take a dim view of it, you know."

"I'll send you some money first thing in the morning."

"Thanks. I could use it. So, when you coming over to see your granddaughter?"

"I get a long weekend at the end of the month. What does she look like?"

"A baby. Wrinkled, scrunched up, and monkey-faced. Looks like she'll have red hair. Only Tim didn't get cursed, and damn if I can figure out how he managed to miss it."

Patsy was small, wrinkled, scrunched up, and still more than a bit monkey-faced when Pat finally got over to see her. Matt was subdued and looked worried, something Pat had never seen before. He watched his mother holding the baby and trying to find something inside herself to tie her to this little warm thing that smelled of baby powder and felt no more real than a stuffed toy.

"Why'd you take off on us?" he asked suddenly. Pat gaped.

"Why did I what?"

"Take off on us."

"To stop Joe from breaking my neck. Or worse."

"Him? Ah, g'wan!" her son scoffed.

"No g'wan about it," she said. "He told me he'd kill me if I tried to get custody or even access. Much as I loved you, I wasn't about to die just because I wanted to see your sweet little face from time to time."

"Hell," Matt scoffed, "he couldn't have stayed sober or straight long enough to form the intent, let alone do the deed!"

So she told him about the slashed tires, the smashed windshield, and the battery acid. She left out the part about knowing he'd been in the house when she was sound asleep.

"I didn't know that," Matt said honestly. "I thought you just . . . you know, woke up one morning and decided you didn't have much use for us and took off."

"What did he say when you asked him?"

"He said you'd fucked off and a good thing, too."

"So why did you look me up? If you thought I was that kind of person, I mean."

"I wanted to find out if you really were that kind of person," he shrugged. "Water under the bridge, I guess."

"Chickens always come home to roost," she answered automatically.

"You always do that?" he laughed. "Respond to a cleech with another cleech?"

She laughed too, remembering how, before he'd decided to expand his awareness and elevate his consciousness, Joe had enjoyed her deliberate mixing and mis-matching of cliche and metaphor, how he had laughed when she called metaphors "matadors," said "nayve" for naïve and "blayze" for blase. Nor could she keep back the memory of how, after he had joined the Now Generation, he had told her not to be so stupid.

Pat knew both Matt and Gerri were drinking, and drinking heavily. She knew that when she sent them money, they just drank more. She thought of setting up an account with the supermarket closest to their apartment so that when they were flat broke they would be able to charge groceries. But that would only give them permission to blow even more of their charity cheques on booze. So she did nothing. She sent stuffed toys to the kids until the apartment overflowed with bears, giraffes, kangaroos, and pandas. She made clothes, she mailed sneakers, and she tried to forget that every time she saw Matt and Gerri, their faces looked more haggard.

"We're having Christmas dinner at our place," Gerri announced on the phone. "We'd like you to be with us."

"Great," Pat enthused, as every instinct she had cringed away from the thought of it. "I'll bring a turkey. I can get free-range farm birds from the Williamses. Twenty pounds be big enough, you think?"

"Sounds good to me," Gerry laughed, and Pat could almost see the bottle of beer in her hand. "Kids're looking forward to seeing you."

"Great. Sounds like fun," Pat lied.

She took her car, even though she was more than moderately terrified of city traffic. The huge turkey, scrubbed, wrapped in clean cloth, and packed in layers of plastic, lounged on the back seat like some swaddled potentate on his way to his own coronation. The traffic was so bad, the streets so crowded that Pat was too frightened to pay attention to anything except what was directly in front of the nose of her car. She drove grimly, and when she finally found herself in front of Matt and Gerri's apartment, she thanked God aloud for having done the driving and navigating for her.

Then she did just about everything that needed doing for the big event. The Christmas tree leaned against the wall in the hallway, and the kids stared at Matt and Gerri with wordless accusation. Pat took the two older ones with her and walked to the supermarket, where she bought a metal tree stand and several boxes of ornaments and icicles. They went back to the squalid little flat, rearranged the furniture in the tiny box that pretended to be a living room, and crammed the tree in a corner. While the kids climbed on the back of the sofa to decorate the higher branches, Pat made popcorn. Then she and the kids sat on the floor with needles and thread, stringing four popcorns then two cranberries, four popcorns two cranberries, four popcorns two cranberries, quieting their disenchantment until it went to sleep and the spirit of whatever present began to appear.

She was up with the kids by seven in the morning. Gerri and Matt got up briefly to see the unwrapping of presents, but both were so badly hung over they went back to bed once the excitement had dimmed to a mere roar. Pat made stuffing for the turkey, she stuffed the turkey, she skewered the turkey, she wove the twine around the skewers, she put the bird in the big roasting pan, she put the pan in the oven, and when the bird was roasting, she sat down with a cup of coffee. Before she finished it, the baby needed changing. Then the baby wanted breakfast. Then the baby whined and whined and whined until Carol told Pat the baby wanted her lie-down and nap. So Pat put the baby in her crib and went back to her cold cup of coffee. When the baby woke up again she fed her cereal and smashed bananas, then bundled up all the kids in their warmest clothes and took them for a walk through the streets of New Westminster, up one hill and down another.

"It's worse than Rome," she said.

"What is," Carol asked.

"The hills. Rome is built on seven hills, a bit like this."

"Seven hills," Carol scoffed. "Hell, we got seven hills in our front yard."

"We don't got no front yard," Tim objected.

"How could we with seven hills where the yard ought to be?" Carol laughed, and Pat felt herself warming to the sullen little stranger.

"Look at all the Christmas decks," she said, pointing.

"Decks?" Tim frowned.

"Sure. That's why they sing Deck the Halls," Pat teased.

"Decorations, stupid." Carol poked his arm and he swatted her hand.

"All decked out," Pat laughed.

They found a small corner grocery and bought frozen juice and large bottles of ginger ale, a dark fruitcake and a slab of commercial marzipan. The kids wanted chocolate Santas wrapped in bright red and white aluminum foil with Santa painted on the front.

Back at the apartment the smell of turkey was everywhere but there was still no sign of Gerri and Matt. The baby needed to be fed again, and changed again, and put down for a nap again, and then Pat and the kids played with the toys, building fantastic things with little coloured bits of interlocking plastic, driving cars and trucks along the arms of the chairs and over the cushions of the sofa.

"I really like the clothes," Carol said quietly. "All of them. Not just the Christmas ones, but the others, too. And the stuffed bears. I really like them."

"I'm glad, honey. Some time you can come over to my place and I'll show you how to make them."

Finally Gerri and Matt got up. They drank several mugs of coffee, then started adding something stronger to the coffee. Gerri helped Pat prepare the vegetables and put them on to cook, and things began to seem a bit the way Pat remembered Christmas when she herself was small and believing.

She was sitting at the kitchen table, smearing half-melted marzipan on the dark fruitcake, when something, she was never sure what, made her look up at the front door. She froze. Coming through the door, smiling widely, was Joe. A huge knot formed in her stomach. She almost leaped to her feet and raced for the back door to escape.

When Joe saw her, his grin broadened. Amazed and disbelieving, she sat, knife in hand, smelling almond paste and raisins, watching as this overweight, half-bald, greying stranger who looked more like Joe's father than Joe himself, moved towards her. If I don't do something, she realized, this bozo is going to grab me, hug me, and kiss me! She jumped to her feet, dropped the marzipan-coated knife, and rammed out her hand, almost getting him in the belly. Reflexively, he took her hand and shook it cheerfully.

"Hey, doll," he blurred, "you're lookin' good! Life must be treating you okay."

"Fine, thank you," she parroted.

"This is more like it," Matt said with beery amiability, "the family all together again."

Pat wanted to say something explicit, like Oh fuck that or Up your nose or better yet Shove it sideways, stupid. Instead, she sat down, picked up the marzipan knife, and went back to trying to get the almond paste to stick to the cake.

The kids and Pat ate hugely, although she was certain she wouldn't be able to digest a thing. It was something to do, though, something to keep her hands off Matt's throat, keep her mouth so full she wouldn't say the wrong thing. All she had to do was chew, smile slightly, and nod like one of those little woodpecker carvings that sit on the edge of a glass and dip, dip, dip, dip into the water, endlessly dipping, accomplishing nothing.

By ten o'clock she was exhausted, but Joe, Matt, and Gerri were still sitting in the living room, surrounded by mess, drinking and gassing about things Pat knew nothing about. She wanted to go to bed but she didn't dare. The way things were going, she might wake up to find Joe stripping off his clothes and preparing to join her in a tender marital reunion. Pat knew that if he did, she'd kill either him or herself.

Finally, lurching and laughing, Joe phoned a cab, then had a hot rum while waiting for it to arrive. When the cabbie knocked on the door, Joe wove his way towards Pat, and again she had to do the handshake-in-a-hurry routine to avoid being smooched. The cabbie wouldn't leave until Joe proved he had money to pay the fare. As it turned out, he was five dollars short. Pat dug into her wallet, hauled out a ten, and told the cabbie to keep the change. Anything to get Joe the hell out of there.

That night she slept as though she had been slammed on the head with a tire iron. When the baby started yowling at seven in the morning, she was the one got up, made the banana-and-cereal goo and fed the little darling they had named after her. While everyone else slept, Pat sat in the kitchen spooning glup into her grand-daughter's mouth, trying to scoop up all the scattered jigsaw pieces in her mind, trying to find a way to fit the puzzle back together. But none of it fit with any of the rest of it. Especially not this red-haired kid with greyish banana goo smeared around her almost formless mouth.

"Hey, punkin," Pat laughed, "don't ever in your life expect any wisdom from your grannie, okay?" The baby scowled at her, and opened her mouth like a half-naked bird wanting more worms. Pat spooned in more glup, the little mouth closed, the glup oozed from the corners of the lips. The baby swallowed, opened her mouth, and waved her arms and legs demandingly.

"Christ," Pat sighed, spooning more slime into the waiting mouth. "Christ Jesus."

She went home the day after Boxing Day, driving through streets nearly deserted, the bright lights and decorations now looking abandoned and glum.

And that night she wakened late, convinced there was someone in the house. Cold with fear, she crept out of bed, checked every room, and found nothing at all. From then on she locked her doors and windows before retiring, and still she woke up in fear at night. She bought extra locks and deadbolts, and still she would hear creakings and groanings. Her mind knew it was just the old house responding to the cooling of the night, but her heart knew the sounds were warnings that someone—Joe?—was creeping towards her bedroom, axe in hand.

She went to the doctor, who gave her some small blue capsules that made her sleep, all right, but also made her wake up with the next best thing to a full-blown hangover. As soon as she stopped using the pills, the night fears returned. She lay for hours listening to everything and nothing, fearing at any minute the door to her room would slam open and the ogre would be there with the axe, the knife, the club, his fists.

She went to the RCMP and filled out a form, saying there were raccoons raiding her fruit trees and upsetting her garbage cans. They gave her the permit and she bought the rifle, which she kept in a wooden rack nailed to the wall beside her bed. It didn't help.

And then during a coffee break at work, she overheard a very interesting conversation.

"Bloody stupidity," Chuck growled. "The goddamn thing cost them six hundred bucks as a pup, and then they put three hundred into getting it trained and all, and now, because of a few ding-dongs and a lot of hysteria, they can't keep it because the municipality over there passed some kind of by-law outlawing pit bulls."

"You're kidding!" Henry laughed. "Hell, we've always had pit bulls. In England they call them cradle dogs because they're so good with kids!"

"But you got the English pit bull, right? My kid, that's what he's got, too. Bull terrier. But to those townies, a bull terrier is a pit bull is a menace. Sure there's been trouble, but only with those half-bred mixed-blood things they call American pit bulls. One guy, he crossed one of them with a wolf, for Chrissakes, and then the pups got given to his friends, all of whom was bikers, by the way. Anyway. . . it looks like Cuddles is gonna go to the SPCA and be put down because there's no way I can take 'er. If I bring one more dog into the place the old lady says she's leavin' home."

"Hardly blame her," Pat laughed. "You've got a pack of cougar hounds staked out in what used to be her flower patch."

"You wouldn't want a dog by any chance, would ya?"

And so Henry's son Tom brought Cuddles over in the back of his four-by-four pickup and delivered her to Pat's front door. Pat looked at the bullet-headed brindle bitch with the big white blaze on her chest and almost hoped Joe would try to come through the window some night. "Hey, darlin'," she said softly, squatting and holding out her hand. "Hey, how's the good girl?"

Tom spent the weekend in Bright's Crossing teaching Pat how to get Cuddles to do what she'd been so expensively trained to do. Come. Sit. Wait. Watch. Stay. He made a list of what the dog knew how to do and ought to be made to do, and Pat dutifully studied it. The dog could climb ladders, the dog could track, the dog could trail, the dog could just about write her autobiography and send it off to the publisher.

"Does she chase sticks or balls or anything?" Pat asked.

Tom looked at her scornfully.

"Sorry," she shrugged. "Just thought I'd ask in case the grand-children come over and want to play with her."

She slept better after Cuddles arrived. She lay in bed feeling the dog's soft woolliness closing in on her, or listening to the quiet tick tick tick of Cuddles's toenails on the wooden floors. She would tick to her bowl for a drink of water, tick to the back door to sniff the crack at the bottom of the door, tick to the living room to check out the rug and sofa, tick to the front door for another sniff, then tick back to the living room. There would be stirrings then, and the sound of the dog lying down. There would be some snuffs and whuffs, then quiet. If Pat got out of bed and padded to the door she would see Cuddles lying with her chin on her front paws, staring wide-eyed and alert, whip-tail wagging softly, resting but on guard. Pat would go back to bed, lie down, snuggle her face against her pillow, close her eyes, and sleep soundly.

She had the fence replaced with a taller, stronger one, so nobody else had to worry about Cuddles getting loose and devouring the family baby or de-balling Grandpa. Cuddles spent her days in the yard or on the big front porch, gnawing bones, ruining an endless series of lacrosse balls which she flung in the air, caught, and chewed, only to again fling the ball, catch it, chew it, and fling it again.

Things unrolled and unravelled steadily with Matt and Gerri. They had long, emotional discussions, Matt moved back in, everything was hunky-dory for a time. Then they both fell off the wagon, first sipping, then drinking, then swilling, then boozing, then bingeing until the balloon went up again.

Matt left, vowing never to return. "This time I'm not bein' stupid," he growled into the phone, "this time, by God, is *it*. I can't live with a woman who's sauced most of the time."

"Maybe she can't live with a man who's sauced most of the time," Pat suggested. "Maybe you should both take the alcohol abuse program."

But she knew she might as well speak to her gumboot. She went to Al-Anon herself, got the booklist, then sat in the evenings reading about co-dependency and enabling behaviour. And when she had read all the books she sat in her big chair with Cuddles curled beside her, thinking of how many streams and creeks of beer and whiskey had been dumped into this growing pool of stupidity. Joe hadn't been a problem drinker when she married him, but Jim had always had something to drink on him or near to hand. Their father had been a drinker, as had his father. Their mother's father was known far and wide as a man who could drink everyone in town under the table, then drink the pub dry without falling on his face. Her own father had tried to do the same, but if he had the stomach for it he didn't have the head, and usually wound up either fighting or puking. Every uncle on the horizon left part of his pay packet in the bar, and half the aunts were as likely as not to get a snootful at least once a month. And now Matt was trying to drown himself in the stuff.

What could a person do? Especially a person who had hit the road rather than winding up in a wooden box because of someone else's bad temper? Besides, all the books and all the experts said that until the person with the problem was willing to stop denying the problem and wanted help, nobody else could do anything.

Pat did her work, she collected her pay, she put most of it in the bank, and she took Cuddles for long walks along the creek. She led her own quiet life among her new friends, making occasional visits to New Westminster and phone calls to the kids.

It was Cuddles's growling woke her up in the middle of the night. She didn't turn on the light, she just rolled out of bed, hauled on her jeans, stuck her feet in her slippers, and lifted the gun from the rack. She slapped in the magazine, clicked off the safety, and moved to one side of the front door. Cuddles's growls intensified. By now even Pat could hear the soft crunch of gravel beside the road, the squeak of the front gate, the steady pad of footsteps along the walk and up the steps.

"You hold it right there," she said loudly. The footsteps stopped. "You better have one hell of a good reason for being here." She forced herself to sound rough and tough and hard to bluff. "I've got a gun." She switched on the porch light.

"Easy, Patty," said young Pete Williams, with none of the usual laughter in his voice. "It's me, Pete." He stepped in front of the window so she could see his face. He reached up, took off his hat, dropped it on the porch and put both his hands on top of his head.

"Oh, for Chrissakes," Pat muttered, feeling about as stupid as she ever had. She clicked on the safety, ejected the shell from the gun, put the gun on the sofa, and unlocked the front door. "Pete." She knew she was blushing. "I'm sorry. I get kind of proddy living alone."

She grabbed Cuddles in case the dog didn't remember Pete was the one who liked to throw the lacrosse ball clear across the soccer field for her.

"Got some heavy news for you, Patty," Pete said quietly. "You better get your smokes and sit yourself down for this one because it's a bitch."

"I'm not ready for it." But she sat in her big chair, waiting, a huge knot in her stomach.

"Got a call from the mainland. There was a fire a few hours ago. A big old apartment building."

"Oh, my sweet Christ," she breathed. "The kids?"

"Seems the neighbours saw your boy Matt come racing out of the place with an armload of kids. The little girl holding the baby, under Matt's one arm, the little boy under the other arm. He sort of dumped them on the sidewalk, then hollered his wife was still inside. He went in to get her." Pete sucked heavily on his cigarette. "He didn't come back out again, Pat. And neither did she."

"Matt? Matt didn't get out?"

"I'm sorry, Patty. The damn place hasn't cooled down enough for them to get inside and look for . . . well, for the ones who didn't get out. But the little girl . . ." He pulled a piece of paper from the pocket of his jacket. "Carol, it says here."

"Carol, yes. She's the oldest."

"She told the police to find you."

"Yes," Pat said, the tears starting.

Pete patted her hand, then got up and moved into the kitchen. She heard the fridge door open, heard the clattering of glass against glass, and then Pete was back, handing her a glass of juice and a double handful of toilet paper.

"My mom'll be over in a few minutes," he said softly. "You got friends, Patty, and don't you be too shy or standoffish to let them do for you."

"Thank you, Petie," she managed. Then it all flooded over her, all the images tumbling faster and faster and faster. Matt sitting up in his crib, arms raised for her to lift him, smiling toothlessly. Matt in the bathtub chewing the corner of the face cloth. Matt learning to walk, Matt sitting on the edge of the table while she tried to stuff his foot into his boot, Matt eating strawberries and laughing, Matt turning to smile at her.

She heard Cuddles mumbling to herself, heard the front door open, then Blackie Williams was holding her, patting her shoulder, stroking her hair, telling her to let 'er rip, old girl, get it all out, that's it. She heard more voices and found she couldn't put names to them, even though she'd known these people for twenty years. Faces more familiar to her than Joe's or Matt's floated into her vision and said comforting things which she didn't hear. Blackie's wife, and what was her name, Pat ought to know it, she spoke to the woman at least twice a week, and the name was gone, just gone.

A one-armed woman in jeans and pyjama top, one sleeve cut off and the armhole sewn shut. She put her arm around Pat's shoulders, gave her a squeeze and said, "Stubs and I'll drive you over if you want to go."

Pat nodded, and the confusion and horror began to recede. Of course someone had to go over. There would be papers to sign, people to see, arrangements to make.

"The coffee's ready, Pat," Sharon de Wytt said firmly. "Time to haul up your socks, old thing. Coffee. A bath. Ice cubes for the eyes. Dristan for the nose. Clean clothes. And then the hard part starts."

"Right." Pat stood, sniffling, wiping her nose with the sodden toilet paper. "I bet it don't get no easier," she predicted.

"No," Blackie smiled, "but you get tougher. It don't get no easier, but you do get tougher. All you got to do is look after yourself. We'll handle the rest of it."

She sat in the tub sipping the coffee they brought her. Between sips she held the ice-pack against her eyes, hoping the swelling would go down enough so that she could squint at the world. She finished the coffee, got out of the tub, dried herself, even cleaned the tub and hung the towels to dry. She checked her face in the mirror. For all the good the ice cubes had done her face, she might as well have rammed them where the sun never shone. She wrapped herself in her robe and padded into her bedroom.

They had clothes ready for her to pull on, they had her hairbrush ready to smooth out the rat's nest, they had cigarettes and more coffee. And when there was nothing else left to do but leave the house, she left.

Stubby's big limo was parked outside, and Wright was behind the wheel, not in uniform but in jeans and a soft old white shirt.

"Son of a bitchin' bad luck, Patty," he said softly. "You got nothing to do now but what you want to do or need to do. I'm drivin'."

"And we're back here if you need us," Stubby said.

It wasn't hard at all. They found the welfare office, then found the worker, and the worker got her coat, got her car, and drove ahead of them to the receiving home.

"Grandma!" Tim screamed.

Pat knelt, held out her arms and pulled him against her. He clung hysterically to her, sobbing and shaking.

"Easy on, old boy," she heard herself say. "Easy on, my fella. It's okay. Grandma's here."

And then Carol was standing in front of her, eyes dark-rimmed, face grey. Pat reached for her, but Carol pulled back.

"They took Patsy," she quavered. "I tried to keep her but they took her."

"They'll bring her back," Pat vowed. "They probably just wanted to give you a rest."

"I'm supposed to look after her," Carol said. "I'm supposed to keep an eye out for her."

"Hey, easy there." Wright knelt. "You can't keep an eye out for anything...whoever heard of a girl with one eye out? Popeye has one eye out. Girls have two eyes."

"Don't be so fuckin' stupid," Carol said clearly. Wright grinned, and nodded approvingly. "That's it, kid, fight back!"

"Fuck off," she suggested. Then she was hanging onto Pat, and shaking.

"It's okay," Pat lied.

Then there were, as she had expected, papers to sign. Arrangements to make. Questions to answer. Pat let her friends do the talking. She calmed the kids, held them, cuddled them, reassured them, and promised them over and over that Patsy would be back with them in just a few minutes.

Finally, they brought her in, and Carol grabbed for her. "I'm supposed to look after her," she insisted doggedly.

"If you want," Pat agreed. "When she gets heavy, you let us know. And nobody," she vowed, "will take her away from you again."

"All my bears got burnded up," Tim mourned. "My clo'es, and everything."

"We'll get more," Pat promised.

"And my momma," he sobbed. "And my dad."

She sat cuddling the kids and fighting back her own screams. Her friends disappeared for an hour, then came back with clothes, jackets, and shoes. When it was time to go to the funeral home to make the arrangements, the kids refused to stay in the limo. Everyone trooped in, Carol carrying Patsy.

There wasn't much needed by way of arrangements. Identification of the bodies was incomplete.

"Seven people?" Pat echoed. "Seven people dead?"

"These old buildings," the man in the dark suit sighed, "the stairwells act like chimneys."

When Joe came into the funeral home, he looked like nobody she had ever cared about in her life. The thick smell of whiskey preceded him, and she knew all too well the look on his face, the mad glitter in his eyes. He was mesatchie, for sure.

"Gone," he intoned dramatically. "Gone as if he'd never lived!" He glared at Wright. "Who in hell are you, fella?"

"Just a friend," Wright soothed.

Joe glared at Pat. "This the one you've been pissin' around with, then?"

"He's a friend, Joe," she said.

"Ah, the poor babies!" Joe stumbled towards the children, reaching out for them. Carol stepped back and Tim followed. Joe turned to glare wildly at Pat. "In like a dirty shirt, aren't you?" he slurred. "Get there first and turn 'em against me."

"Joe, please." She tried to soothe him, knowing even as she tried that there is nothing you can say to a mesatchie that will calm him down, nothing you can say that won't be twisted, turned, taken the wrong way.

"Them's my family," he raged. "He was mine, and they were his, and that makes 'em mine. I raised him, I'll raise them."

"Joe, why don't you just go home for a while," Pat sighed. "Have a sleep, get some food into you, pull yourself together, and then we'll talk."

"He ran back in," Joe wept. "He was out, he was safe, he had the little darlin's with him, and he went back in. Did you know that? He was burned getting out, he knew the stairs was on fire, and he went back in anyway. He'd already run right through the flames, and he went back in. Lookit how their hair's all scorched! He was burned; they said his shirt was gone offa his back, he was almost balded by it, but he went back in. And he was mine! And that makes them mine! And you!" He glared at her and stepped closer, his face suffused with the deep burgundy of anger. He raised his clenched fist and held it in front of her face. "I'll tell you now what I told you before, bitch. You get in my way and you're dog meat."

"Go home, Joe," she said softly. "You don't know what you're saying."

"They're mine," he gritted. "You try to take 'em and I'll kill you."

Pat knew she could turn her friends loose on Joe and there would be little left of him. She knew she could talk to him about the law and he would laugh, she could explain that threatening is assault and he would spit, she could say police and he'd fart, she could be the most reasonable person God ever made, and Joe wouldn't care a fat rat's ass.

"Joe," she said, "go home. That kind of talk only works on

someone who's afraid of it. I'm not afraid of you any more. You're bald, you're fat, and you're stupid. You try anything and I'll come down on you like a load of bricks."

"You never learned nothin'," he snarled.

"Oh, you bet your bippy I did," she answered. "You slash my tires or smash my windshield or throw battery acid on my upholstery or try any of your other cowardly stunts and I'll send the bikers to fix your knees." She turned away. He grabbed her shoulder but she shrugged him off. "Get out of my life," she said quietly, "because maybe you know where I live, but . . . I know where you live, too. I'm not afraid of you."

They left him there. Carol handed her the baby and she sat Patsy on her hip and took Carol's hand. "Come on, darlings," she smiled. "Let's go home."

"Hey, fella." Wright scooped up Tim and gave him a hug. "You ever drive a big black limo? Well, you're gonna. You push a button and the windows go up, you push it again, the windows come down . . . you can send the radio aerial up and down, you can turn the climate control on and off, and we got more lights on the dashboard than a 747 jet."

Joe's pants sagged from his belly and his shirt pulled at its buttons as he watched with mesatchie red-rimmed eyes, chest heaving in and out as he fought for breath. He licked his lips, then licked them again, shook his head like a bull driven half-mad by summer flies clustering around his eyes.

"You're gonna be sorry," he promised.

When they got home, the lights were on in the house. Supper was waiting for them, and there were people to put kids in the bathtub, scrub them clean, stuff them into new pyjamas, hold them, cuddle them, console them. Patsy fussed until her belly was full, then she was taken away for ten minutes, brought back clean and fresh for a cuddle, then taken into Pat's room and put to sleep in a crib someone else's kid had outgrown.

"Grandma?" Tim leaned on her lap, looking up at her hopefully. "You got a bear here?"

"Darlin'," she said, kissing the top of his head, "I've got half a basement full of bears. You find yourself a pal, go down those stairs, and you pick out any one you want. Pick two," she managed, "they're small."

"That's it," someone said. "That's the way, Pat."

Bobbi

*B*obbi Duncan skipped out of school just before two in the afternoon of a Thursday like most others.

Thursday afternoon was when the music teacher came and everyone had to sit quietly, hands folded, listening to tapes of symphonies written by men long dead. Each tape was preceded by the recorded sound of the music teacher's voice, telling when the composer was born, when he started writing music, how many works he wrote and when he died. Sometimes the music would stop suddenly, and the same recorded voice would tell the children to listen for some particular thing, and a minute of music would be repeated, then the symphony would continue.

And all the time the class was sitting quietly, hands folded, listening and staring at the green chalkboard at the front of the room, the music teacher sat at her desk, reading. The slightest cough, the slightest noise, and her eyes would lift, scan the room, and zero in on the culprit. One hand would reach out, pick up a pencil, and make a mark beside a name in the black-covered binder on her desk. Three marks and you were sent to the office. In the office the big book was produced, and if your name was in it, that meant you'd been sent for disciplinary warning before, and out came the leather strap. If you got in trouble at school, they knew about it at home before you got there after school. And you got in trouble at home, too.

Bobbi Duncan's name was in the big book in the office. It was, in fact, in that book several times. She had been strapped twice on each hand, then given the belt when she got home. She had been strapped four times on each hand, then given the belt and locked in her room without supper. She had even been given six stinging whacks on each hand, then given the belt, locked in her room without supper, and grounded for two weeks. So she couldn't even begin to imagine what would happen this time.

It was her nose got her in trouble. Ever since they had covered the floors of the classrooms with that new indoor-outdoor carpet, Bobbi's nose had made her life miserable. Bad enough when the carpet was so full of dust you could smell it, but worse when the janitor spent the weekend cleaning the carpets. Bobbi would have known the carpets had been cleaned even if she had been struck blind. Ten minutes in the room and she started to sneeze. Her nose would itch, first the very tip of it, and no matter how much she scratched it, the itch never stopped. On more than one occasion, she had scratched the tip of her nose until there was a little water-filled friction blister there, and still it itched and itched and itched. Then the itch moved inside her nose, and once there, it became a burn. Then the sneezing started.

Nobody believed she wasn't doing it on purpose. Nobody else scratched at the tip of their nose. Nobody else sneezed and sneezed and sneezed until each sneeze brought blood. It was some rotten habit she'd got herself into, or a tactic she'd developed to annoy the teachers. It especially annoyed the music teacher. And the buggery of it all was, the music room was the worst place of all for itching, burning, and sneezing.

So she walked out of the school, across the playground, past the canvas-sling swings with their big chains and the strong log frame sunk into the ground with concrete. Past the softball diamond, through the clipped green grass of the outfield, then over the rail fence and into the woods.

They'd know when she got home. They always knew. Her mother would point, just point, and Bobbi would walk silently to her room, then sit on the bed, shaking with fear, trying hard not to cry. She would hear the crummy as it toured through the hamlet, stopping at corners and letting out the men who had been working since first light. After the sound of the crummy faded, she would hear her father's Romeos crunching on the gravel driveway. He would take his caulk boots off his shoulder and hang them on the nail in the utility room. Her mother would start the hot water running into the bathtub.

Anywhere from fifteen minutes to half an hour later, he would come to her room, open the door, and stand there, staring at her, shaking his head with disgust. "Never learn, do you?" he'd say. And then he'd wrap one end of his belt around his huge tanned fist, reach out, grab her by the back of the neck, and bend her face down so all she could see was the floor. She could either sit on the bed and get it across her back and shoulders or she could get off the bed and stand there, getting it from ankles to waist. But she got it. Whether she cried or didn't, whether she promised to be good or gritted her teeth, whether she sobbed or screamed bloody murder, he whupped on her until he stopped.

Since nothing made any difference, and since she was going to catch it anyway, she might as well have the satisfaction of knowing she had done something for which she deserved a good shellackin'. You couldn't get pounded any worse than she'd been pounded the last time. The marks were still there, and they still hurt. The only difference was that in the week since, the bruises had gone from deep blue to ugly yellow-and-green. So if that's what you got for sneezing, and that was what you were going to get anyway, you might as well do something more, something of your own choice.

She stopped and hunkered on the bare path, watched a red-with-black-spots ladybug crawling up the hard centre of a sword fern. Her gaze was drawn to a spider web glittering with dewdrops and mist it had captured during the night. The sunlight had not entered the bush to evaporate the moisture and the spider sat on one edge, ruling over her queendom of diamonds, waiting patiently for supper to fall into the sticky trap. Bobbi reached out, carefully picked up the ladybug, and placed her on a different fern, where there was no spider web to catch her. She saw a small, bright green tree frog, her long fingers gripping the ridged bark of a fir tree. Each little finger was tipped with a brown pad, and without touching the pads, Bobbi knew they were sticky. The frog watched her watch it, then, without warning, it was gone. No visible coiling of muscles or crouching, just a flash of bright green, and the frog vanished. Bobbi turned away in time to see the spider web vibrate and the spider move across it, towards something that was caught and struggling. Bobbi stepped forward, expecting to see a fly or a beetle caught in the web. Her surprise froze her so totally she almost waited too long.

A glittering little form was trapped in the web, and the harder the fairy struggled, the more entangled it became. The spider was almost on the terrified creature when Bobbi regained her wits. She picked up a piece of twig and used it to free the fairy. All she had to do was put the twig where the fairy could grab on with her arms and legs, then pull, and the web broke, the fairy was free, and the spider, enraged, was running back and forth on her web, cursing a blue streak and gnashing her choppers.

Bobbi sat on the path and watched as the fairy picked the sticky webbing from her limbs. Bobbi would have liked to help, but the fairy was so small Bobbi was sure she'd break something. A leg bone or an arm bone or something.

The fairy wiped the last of the webbing off her face, sat back on the twig, and grinned at Bobbi. Bobbi grinned back.

As fast as the tree frog had vanished, the fairy grew. With one eyeblink she was as small as a deerfly, with the next she was at least as big as Bobbi's own hand. Two more eyeblinks, and she was as big as a tiny dog.

"Thank you," the fairy piped.

"I didn't want the spider to eat you."

"I didn't, either," the fairy agreed.

"You sure you're okay?"

"I'm fine. What about you?"

"I'm okay," Bobbi lied.

"Didn't anybody tell you that if you tell lies to a fairy your tongue will split in the middle and flap like an old snake's tongue when you talk?" the fairy laughed. Bobbi just stared. "So . . . what's wrong?"

"Oh, just, you know," Bobbi shrugged.

"If I knew, would I ask?"

"I'm going to get a shellackin' tonight, that's all."

"What's a shellackin'?" the fairy asked. So Bobbi told her. Then, because the fairy still didn't understand, Bobbi showed her.

"I wouldn't go home if something like that was waiting for me," the fairy declared.

"Where would I go?" Bobbi wasn't sure the fairy was very smart. "They don't let kids just walk around with no place to live. If you try, things happen to you. Perverts catch you, or the p'lice get you, and you wind up in juvenile court and maybe even reform school. Besides, if you don't have any money, how do you eat?"

The fairy stared at Bobbi for a long long time, then she looked at the web the spider was busy repairing. Then she looked over at the ladybug which was sitting on the fern frond, leaning against the hard centre vein, all her legs crossed over each other, listening intently. The ladybug buzzed, the fairy twittered, the ladybug answered with more buzzes, the fairy responded with more twitters. Then she turned to Bobbi again, held out her hand, and smiled.

"You could come stay with us for a while," she invited.

Bobbi didn't hesitate for so much as a minute. She reached out, took the fairy's hand, and as fast as that she was someplace else altogether.

It looked exactly like the path through the woods from the school to Timberland Road, and yet it didn't look the least bit like it. There was no sign of the pigwire fence that ran along one side of the path. And all the trees were big. They were bigger than big. They were enormous. The heavy brown trunks, thickly covered with moss, grew towards the sky, the sunlight slanting between the dark branches and boughs, and on the ground the shade dappled the surface of the pathway. On either side of the path, the bars of light dissipated and were lost in the swaying wall of green long before they reached the forest floor.

"Where are we?" Bobbi managed. "It looks like a place I know, but it's all different. Bigger."

"We like it better this way," the fairy explained. "It used to be this way on both sides of the curtain, but now it's just this side looks like this."

"Curtain? What curtain?"

"Why, the curtain. The veil. The . . . whatchamacallit." The fairy stared at Bobbi, then shrugged. "Dumb you."

"I'm not dumb!"

"Everybody ought to know. Everybody used to know. There's a whatchamacallit, an asyawish, a lace curtain, a thing, and on one side of it is us, and on one side of it is . . ." She shrugged again. "And anybody can go back and forth between the two by way of the places. The holes. The design in the lace. And things are one way on our side and things are as they are on the other side."

"I didn't know that." Bobbi didn't mind confessing her ignorance.

She'd been ignorant about too many things in her life already, to feel any ego damage admitting the obvious.

"Nobody told you?"

"No. Well, not that part of it. They told me about fairies. That's how I knew you were one. But," she admitted, "they told me you weren't real. They said you were like Santa Claus, or the Easter Bunny."

"For heaven's sake," the fairy shook her head. "That's very strange behaviour, I must say."

The fairy settlement was in a clearing in the bush, an almost perfectly round circle surrounded by ferns and flowers. Huge white flat-topped fungus grew from the trunks of the trees, and mushrooms of every size and sort were thick around the bases of the giant guardians.

"You can stay here with us," the fairy offered. "Nobody will hit you or whip you or yell or give you a shellackin'. Stay as long as you want."

Bobbi felt as if a huge and horrible weight had slipped off her shoulders. She figured she would take the fairy up on her offer to stay a while. A good, long while. 🐛

Lizzie

♥

Lizzie worked afternoon shift, from four to twelve-thirty, waiting tables, wiping counters, taking orders, and putting up with guff from bozos, truckers, and the half-fried who managed to make it down the street from the bar to the X-L Cafe. Once inside, sprawled in a booth or hunched on a stool, the beer baby or booze hound searched for, brought out, and tried to demonstrate his witty repartee while gnawing on a plate of barbecued ribs or slobberingly inhaling a hamburger and fries. The truckers sat quietly, usually at the counter. They spoke politely, ate steadily, said thank you, left a tip, paid, and moved on. The bozos wove a line somewhere between the two polarities.

Lizzie endured their har hars and yuk yuks, even managed to smile at some of the less putrid jokes, and when they finally, mercifully, hauled themselves to their feet and lurched back to the bar, she cleaned up the spilled, slopped, and dribbled messes they left behind, wiped everything carefully, pocketed the tips such as they were, and ignored her sore feet and throbbing legs.

You couldn't see the aching veins. They weren't the kind that roped and twisted under the skin like purple snakes. They were hidden, embedded in her flesh. She knew where they were, she could feel them hurting and burning, and sometimes she sat with her legs up, feeling the hard swollen lines. Ingrown, her mother said, and the worst kind, but what can you do, it happens when you spend your life on your feet, lifting, carrying, hauling, lugging. And it happens when you're pregnant four times in five years. It's the screwing you get for the screwing you got, and no use blathering about it.

Everyone had tried to talk her out of it. Her mother had wept hot scalding tears, not the polite kind you see on the big glowing screen in the Iona, where all the actress needs is a pretty little lace-edged hanky. Her mother had sobbed from the belly button, the sounds harsh and phlegmy, and it took more than a lace hanky, it took several rolls of toilet paper over several days to mop up the tears.

"He's too old for you," her mother had hiccoughed.

"He's mature," Lizzie had answered stubbornly.

"He's older than your father!"

"Yes, and he's better set up, too! He's got two houses, he's got a new car and a good pickup truck, he's got a boat and a trailer to haul it . . . and he's *nice* to me!"

"Nice? *nice*? There is nothing nice about a forty-nine-year-old man who chases after a fifteen-year-old girl!"

No matter what they did, she managed to see him. She would sneak out the window and shinny down the apricot tree, skip school to go to the river, pretend to be babysitting and offer as proof the money he had given her.

Then she was pregnant, and amazed that only she was surprised by the truth the calendar would not let her ignore. So it was quit school in grade ten, and get married in the courthouse with her mother no longer crying but glaring, and her father standing stiffly, his small gnarled hands gripping the back of the chair in front of him, as if he would rather squeeze Bob's neck but didn't dare.

Sex in the back seat of the car, or on a blanket under a willow tree, had been nothing more than the few minutes' price you pay for all the other good things about being together, the comfort, the security, the safe feeling. Sex every night for hours on end, alone in the house with a man who has the legal right to do with you what he wants, was something else. Something she couldn't talk about with her mother. You make your mistakes and you live with them, especially when you know that everyone you know will just shrug and say, Ah well, you wouldn't listen. Not that they would say that.

They didn't have to. Lizzie would rot in hell before she admitted it had all been a horrible mistake.

Being owned was not a safe feeling. All sense of security vanished before the baby was born, and any hint of comfort vanished in the roughness of Bob's idea of embraces. He seemed to enjoy hurting her. It was as if he was so big, so male, so powerful, that she, failure and idiot that she was, couldn't accommodate or satisfy him.

How do you talk to your mother about that? Or about how night after night he would turn off the television as soon as the news was over, then stretch, yawn, grin, go to the bathroom for a quick shower, and walk naked and damp from the bathroom, grinning. "Come on," he'd say. Night after night, predictably, come on. And so she got into bed knowing that for the next fifteen minutes, or half hour, or however long it took, he was going to work off something there just aren't words to describe, and work it off on her, and in her, in spite of what she did or did not feel.

Sometimes, in the middle of the day, she would suddenly remember that the news was going to come on at ten, and by ten forty-five, as predictable as the bus schedule, Bob would start in on her. And by eleven or eleven-thirty, he would be curled up around her aching body, still holding her, snoring, his body sticky with sweat, clammy and uncomfortable. She might be baking cookies or folding laundry, she might be weeding the flower beds or waxing a floor, and the realization would rise up to stare her in the face, and she would want to vomit.

Then the second baby, then the third, and people were making jokes. You guys must eat a lot of carrots. What you doing, saving on the heating bill? No wonder the guy wears a hat all the time, keeps his rabbit ears from showing.

But that wasn't why Bob wore a hat. He was going bald and it made him angry. In fact, everything made him angry. The dog made him angry. The kids made him angry. Lizzie made him angry. He beat the dog, he hit the kids, he hit and beat Lizzie, and still his baldness spread and his anger grew. He shot the dog dead and even that didn't stop his rage.

One night, instead of just standing there and taking it, taking the verbal abuse, taking the insults, taking the slaps, and then obediently getting into bed, Lizzie ran away from him.

Oh, nothing brave like grabbing the kids and heading out into the night. That would satisfy all the people who didn't know what kind of hell her life was, but who had told her there was something seriously wrong with a marriage between a fifty-year-old and a sixteen-year-old. She knew what they'd do, they'd be as nice as pie when she was around, then tell each other over and over again that they had known all along what would happen.

So what she did was run around the house, keeping just far enough ahead of him that he couldn't grab her, couldn't kick her feet out from under her, couldn't hit her. She was almost twenty and he was fifty-four, she didn't smoke and he chain-smoked, she didn't drink and he put away a half bottle of rye whiskey a day.

Maybe it was the running, maybe it was all that adrenalin mixing with all that oxygen. "You bitch," he panted, "I get my hands on you and I'll break your neck!"

"You won't get your hands on me," she taunted.

"You can't run forever."

"You can't run at all!"

"You have to stop sooner or later."

"You'll be dead before I do."

Around and around the living room, through the door and down the hallway to the kitchen, around the kitchen, through the door and back up the hallway to the living room, like two kids on a rainy day, but they weren't kids, and it wasn't a game.

"Your stinking old lungs will explode! Your rotten old heart will burst open! And when you're dead . . ." She laughed, and almost got herself caught for it, but dodged out of his way just in time. He glared at her, his chest heaving, his face congested. Then cursed her for a no-good slut and slammed out of the house.

When she woke up, he was in bed, reaching for her wordlessly. She almost pushed him away, but thought better of it. Let sleeping dogs lie, never let the sun set on your anger, never use sex as a weapon, all the articles in the magazines came to her rescue and probably saved her life.

He punished her, but only in bed and not by hitting her. Then she was pregnant again, and sick to her stomach most of the time. His car needed a new transmission and that made him angry. His ulcer was bothering him, so he blamed her cooking for his stomach-ache and drank more whiskey to ease the pain.

One night, badgered half nuts, she blew up and, half-crying, half-screaming, confirmed his suspicions. "You'll die of food poisoning," she promised, "and they'll blame your drinking, your foul temper, and your ulcer, and never look any further. And then it'll all be mine and I'll sell it and pee on the money!"

He gave notice to the tenants in his other house, and when they moved out, he moved in. "See how you get along on your own," he sneered. "Just see."

She had the baby two weeks after he moved out. Food was running low and she had no idea how they would survive. The kids went to stay with her mother, and when she came out of the hospital with the baby, the cupboards were full of food again.

"Mom," she said, her face burning.

"Oh, I know." Her mother smiled a wide, false smile. "I don't get the same brands, and I'm not as good as I should be about checking for salt and additives, but honestly, Lizzie, I don't know how you keep your wits about you to pay attention to those things when you've only got two eyes, two arms, and two legs and there are three kids—four now—pulling in different directions! Don't bawl me out for getting the wrong brands, please, I thought I'd die in the supermarket with people standing around watching and the kids playing tag up and down the aisles."

"Thank you, Mom."

Bob moved back in again as quickly as he had moved out, but something had changed. He still got up and went to work each day, he still socked as much of his pay into the bank as he could, he still grumbled and groused, bitched and nagged, and he still insisted on sleeping with her and treating her like a thing designed for no purpose in the world except his physical release. But the bluster was empty and they both knew it. Lizzie'd gone more than a month without any help from him. She'd proven something. He even quit snarling at the kids and ignored them instead. She bought groceries lavishly because it was one of the few things she got to buy on her own. She had to ask him for clothes and justify her need for them, and he never got her anything pretty or fancy. They did not go to movies, dances, or restaurants. Television was as close to entertainment as they got.

And it might have gone on like that forever, all grisly and grey, except for blind luck.

"I'm taking a job out of town," Bob growled. "The company needs somebody to strawboss and I'm going to do it."

"Oh?"

"Pay's a lot better."

"That's nice."

"I'll send you half." He forced the words past his teeth. "Figure if I don't, you'll get a lawyer and garnishee and that'll queer me with the company."

She almost blurted out she hadn't even thought of getting a lawyer, then she bit her tongue. It could only mean that Bob himself had seen a lawyer and had had a bit of cold water in the face. Division of assets or whatever they were calling it.

And he was gone. Gone with his clothes, his fishing rods, his hunting rifles, and the boat, trailer, and motor, pulled off behind the pickup truck. She was left with a house to live in, an old washing machine, a fairly new dryer, a television set, and four kids with their beds, dressers, toys, tricycles, and appetites.

She lay in bed that first night and just listened to the sound of her own breathing in the room. She stretched her arms and legs to fill up the space, felt the clean sheets against her skin, felt the blessed empty place where he had lain so many nights of her life. No hairy leg against hers, no calloused hand claiming the right to touch her any place, any time he chose. No harsh breathing. No sound of beard stubble rasping against the pillow slip. She threw the window wide open and listened to the sounds of the night, felt the cool breeze on her cheek, gloried in the knowledge nobody would jump out of bed cursing, slam the window shut, and order her back to bed.

She made half a pot of coffee at breakfast time, sipped until the kids were up, then made them pancakes with maple syrup. When they had finished eating she stacked the dishes in the sink and just left them. Instead of doing housework, she took the kids to the park, with a sack of sandwiches for lunch. Bob would have said she'd wasted the entire day, but who cared what he would have said, he was miles and miles and miles away. She didn't really wish him any bad luck, she simply prayed he would never come home again. Maybe he'd be happy living in the bunkhouse, playing cards with the other men.

There was no need for potatoes, meat, gravy, and two kinds of vegetables for supper, no need for dessert and coffee. She made macaroni and cheese, and she and her children ate it sitting on the floor, their backs against the sofa, watching television. It was fun! So was the after-supper cleanup, with everyone helping, and when everything was washed, dried, and back in its place, they walked together to the store and bought ice creams.

Sometimes all she'd do about supper was help the kids make hot dogs. It didn't seem to harm their health at all, horror stories to the contrary. No sudden epidemic of rotten teeth, no blistered skin, no rickets or scurvy or pellegra or even hyperactivity.

Every several months Bob came home for a few days or a week. "Come on," he would order, and she would do as she was told. Everybody did exactly what Bob told them when he was home. The kids ate their boiled cabbage, they ate their turnips and parsnips, they said yes sir and no sir, they sat wide-eyed, polite, and frightened. Then he would be gone again and it would be cheeky grins and jokes, games with words and what he would call talking back.

"Who, me?"

"Yes, you."

"You?"

"No, you."

"Oh. Okay. It's *you* gonna do it, right?"

"Boy, oh, boy, Boy. Boy-oh-boy for *you!*" and she would scoop him up, pull his shirt up under his armpits, and blow on his belly until he laughed helplessly and gasped, "Yes, Me. Yes, Mom, Me."

She saw the little cardboard sign in the window of the X-L and stared at it for long minutes. "Waitress Wanted." No mention of experience. No mention of references required. Just waitress. Wanted.

"I've got a chance at a job," she told her mother. "Afternoon shift."

"I'll look after the kids," her mother said quickly, almost eagerly.

Compared to the demands of four kids, the job seemed pleasant, even easy. In addition to the demands of four kids it seemed impossible. But it was a job, which she had never had before, unless you counted meals, kids, laundry, the house, and the yard, and who ever counted that. It was a job and it paid. Not well, but it paid, and what it paid was hers.

"No," said her mother. "I don't want money. I love having the chance."

"Take it," she said dangerously, "or I'll quit."

"Oh, Lizzie," her mother sighed. "Can't you ever just accept. . ."

"And you?" Lizzie asked softly. "What about you?"

When Bob came home he tried to kick up a stink about her

working, but she was learning how to handle people, how to handle strangers, and that gave her some idea of how to handle Bob's rages and fits.

"I thought a lot about it," she said quietly, "and it seemed unfair that you had to be away from the kids and all, just to make enough money to keep this show going. Seemed to me that could make life kind of grim, and then I remembered how much you like fly fishing and how little of it you get to do and. . ." She shrugged, managed a small, shy-looking smile. "I know it isn't much money, but what did I know how to do? And it is a bit. I know," she smiled again, "compared to your wages it's nothing, but. . . well, one day maybe I'll do better and then you won't have to carry so much of a load."

"I can pay for my family," he growled suspiciously.

"I know you can. You've done it all these years. I know that, Bob, but. . . let me try this little thing. You can imagine how it feels, can't you, to see you tired and to have to watch you go off who-knows-where because we need the money and. . . I know you're not one of those guys who's so insecure he has to bluster and yell and cut off his nose to spite his face."

He never really agreed to the idea, but he thought about it the whole time he was home, was still thinking about it when he left to go back to the project. And by the time he came home again it was established as part of the way things were, and he didn't protest. Silence, she told herself smugly, is as good as consent.

The oldest boy started school. He liked it so much the second boy wanted to go too and pitched a fit. How come he can go and I can't, he's not that much bigger than I am. So another precedent was established. While Brian was in school, Kenny was in half-day kindergarten, which wasn't what he wanted, but better than staying home with the babies. Then Brian was in grade two, Kenny was in grade one, and Tony was in half-day kindergarten, so all Lizzie really had to do in the morning was supervise the cereal and milk, the egg and toast, then put Marty in the special little seat-box strapped to the bar of her bike, and ride with Tony to the kindergarten. She rode home again, stacked the breakfast mess in the sink, and did the laundry, which took no time at all if you did it every day instead of saving it up. She had time for a cup of coffee, then got back on the bike and went to get Tony. Lunch together, then a nap for everyone. When her alarm went off she was up and into the shower.

By the time she was ready to go to work her mother was driving up and the boys were coming home from school.

It was only fair that she work the weekends. After all, the ones who had been there longer had taken their turns with the same shift and same days. So Friday night, Saturday night, and Sunday night, she worked. She had never put any special store on the weekend anyway, and it gave her Wednesday and Thursday with the kids, a chance to be home waiting when they came in from school, a chance to hear who said or did what to whom, a chance for supper together and homework together and bathtub play, a chance for snuggles and smooches and tickling and giggling.

At the cafe, there was the after-work coffee crowd, followed by the workies stopping in for their dinner. Then a brief lull and the others came in for supper, the ones on a date, the old folks treating themselves to a night out, the out-of-towners and sales reps. People who, for all you knew, had no real home at all, just a room to sleep in and what kind of work did they do anyway that they came in dressed in a suit, with polished shoes and white shirts, then ordered the Special of the Day.

After them, it was the bar crowd, the ones who'd stopped in for a beer or two after work instead of stopping for a coffee. The later it got, the noisier the repartee.

He came in one night at seven, sat at the counter, and ordered the stew and dumplings. Average height, average dark hair, average face, and nothing at all average about his long-fingered hands, his deep-set blue eyes, or his voice. He ate his meal neatly and quickly, then paid his tab, left a tip, and was gone. The next night he was back, and the next, and in the whole first week he said nothing smart, flirty, or familiar. He just ate his dinner, paid quietly, and left.

"You ever heard that guy?" one of the beery ones asked. Without waiting for an answer, he continued. "I gotta tell you, kiddo, that guy's goin' places! I mean, I've heard my share of bar crooners and club singers, and I'm tellin' ya, this town is too small for him."

"Quiet kinda guy," another laughed, "right up until he steps into the light and then, I'm tellin' ya, he's like someone else. Be seein' him on TV one of these days."

But for all the fuss Devon himself made of it you'd have thought his life was like anybody else's. He ate his supper at the X-L, then walked down to the bar and was singing bang on the dot at eight.

"You're married, huh?" he asked quietly, looking at the wide gold band third finger left hand.

"Yes."

"Any kids?"

"Four."

"You're kiddin' me," he grinned in disbelief. "A little thing like you. Four kids? You don't look old enough."

"Well, I had 'em," she said. "When I was a lot younger than I am now."

"Boys or girls or both?"

"Boys."

"Four boys," he gaped, "How'd you get so unlucky?"

"I've been working at it all my life," she laughed. "Most people think it's great that I've got four boys. People," and she stopped laughing, "don't set much store by girls, I guess."

"I'm gonna have girls," he argued, stirring his coffee slowly. "I'm gonna have a couple of kids, at least. And my first girl is gonna be called Chantal."

"Chantal?"

"It's French."

"Are you French?"

"Me?" he laughed happily. "Me, no, nothing French about me! Irish and Welsh, maybe a bit of something else thrown in for good measure. But I like that name. Chantal. In French, you see, chanter means sing. So I figure Chantal has to mean something about singing."

"I don't know," she shrugged, "I don't know any French. Or much singing, either."

"No? You look like someone who could sing the birds out of the trees."

"No."

"You ever listen to the radio?"

"Yeah."

"You maybe heard my sister," and he told her his sister's name. Lizzie stared. Devon laughed softly.

"Really?"

"Really."

Lizzie couldn't believe it. "I never dreamed . . ."

"You ever been to the Cougars' Lair?"

"Never been in a bar in my life."

"You're kiddin'." He stared at her, then grinned. "Well, if you ever decide to break your unbroken record, come on over and I'll buy you a drink. I expect," he teased, teasing openly, "it would be 7-Up or something. I can afford that."

"You're all heart, right?"

"You've caught on to my secret. All-Heart Devon Williams."

"Where'd you get a name like Devon?"

"From the Welsh part. My grandmother's people were Effens. And I got about sixty-'leven cousins called Evan, Even, Evon, and even Evehn. So my mom called me Devon. Said it was because I had such creamy, soft skin," he laughed. "You know, like Devon cream."

"Oh, I don't know," she teased back. "You don't look all yellow and greasy to me, and Devon Cream is but half a step from butter."

They laughed, then one of the beer bellies wanted cherry pie and coffee, and when she had that taken care of, two old people were waiting to order their pension cheque splurge. Then Devon had to pay his bill and run to be at the bar on time.

They didn't so much talk to each other after that as visit, and he took to coming in a bit early so they'd have time to talk. And finally, more than a month after their first conversation, a month and a half after he had first started coming in for supper, she dared something she had never in her life thought she would do. She got a babysitter for Wednesday night, after the kids were in bed and asleep.

Lizzie had heard music all her life, mostly from the radio, sometimes from the television, once in a while from a record or tape, but nothing like Devon's music. Her mother and father liked smooth old-timey stuff, Bob liked hillbilly or country, the radio played stuff Lizzie really didn't like or hear. Devon played the guitar as good as any Mexican or Spaniard, as good as anyone she had ever heard, except he didn't always play the chords, sometimes he played the note-by-note melody line the same as if it were a piano. He sang songs everybody knew and songs he'd written himself that nobody knew. And when he saw her sitting at a table with a Mother Superior in a tall frosted glass he grinned widely, and nodded, then finished the song he was singing and started another one right away, a happy one, with the guitar chortling beneath the words. Open the window, he sang, open the doors, catch the sun and make it yours, winter's gone and spring is showin', grass is green, and flowers growin'.

He walked partway home with her when the bar closed. The following week, she went back. That's all it was at first, one night a week for two or three hours, drinking a couple of Mother Superiors and listening to the music. But nothing stays where it started.

He was sitting on the bank of the creek when she and the kids got there with their picnic basket.

"Hi, there," he grinned at Tony. "What's that fishin' rod for? You figure there's fish here?"

"I seen 'em," Tony said seriously, pointing. "Over by that big rock. They live under it or something."

"Man, you should see the fish in the creek where I grew up," Devon confided. "They got trout in that creek like none I ever saw anywheres else. They got trout...man," he sighed, "I'm gonna catch me one of them one of these times."

"You ever catch any?"

"Small ones and some middle-sizers," Devon admitted, "but I never did catch one of those big grandpas. My dad did. Once."

"Did you get to see it?"

"And eat some of it. You know if you kill it you gotta eat it."

"Yeah. Was it good?"

"Actually..." Devon leaned closer and lowered his voice, and Tony bent his head to hear the confidence. "It tasted kind of muddy. You know how some things taste like they lived all their life in a swamp?"

"I never ate anything that tasted like mud except mud," Tony said firmly.

"Well, that big fish tasted like mud. Sort of."

"Then why would you want to catch another one? "

"It might be deeeeeeeee-licious!"

Midsummer and it didn't even start to get dark until after ten at night, but when it did get dark it was like velvet, sprinkled with stars. The meteor showers were starting and the scent of ripening blackberries was sweet on the breeze. Bob had been home for almost a week, and then gone back to his bunkhouse and his job, and Lizzie still felt used and shamed, still felt soiled and insulted, inhuman, a thing that made him feel better.

Devon had a thermos of fresh orange juice and some ripe cherries in a little green plastic basket. They sat on a hillside, halfway between the lights of town and the light of the moon, talking softly, sharing long silences, and then he kissed her. It was nothing at all like being kissed by Bob. There was no stubble of beard to scratch her face, no taste of snuff, no demanding and taking. The hand on her arm was not restraining her, not grasping her, not forcing her to submit. It was feather-light and stroking softly, her skin burning beneath it, trying to lift up and press against it, and she knew she had known for weeks this was how it would be.

"Ah, Lizzie," he smiled. And then she was leaning forward, kissing him, her hand against his face, and there was no need for words, but they spoke them, breathily, shyly, and softly. There was no pushing her on her back and thrusting in, no dry rubbing, no unwelcome invasion. There was no fumbling and no grunting impatiently, no getting it over with so that it would become a distasteful memory a few minutes later. It was hours of stroking and pressing, of soft lips and damp tongue, it was the faint taste of salt and sweat, the musky scent of eager bodies.

"Ah, Lizzie." He held her gently, his chest lightly damp against her face. "I wish I could tell you how good you make me feel."

"I love you, Devon," she said, so softly she wasn't sure he had heard her. But he must have, for he tightened his arm, moved to kiss her forehead, her nose, her lips, and then it was all folding over them again, even softer and gentler and more all-consuming.

Except for the one time at the creek, the kids never saw him. Except for the babysitter, nobody knew Lizzie wasn't at home every night. She stopped going to the bar and went, instead, to Devon's room, or met him on the hillside after he had finished his show.

"I have to be careful," she told him. "If Bob ever found out he'd . . ."

"Sssshh," Devon soothed, "Sssshh, Lizzie, it's okay."

Bob phoned to say he was coming home for two weeks and Lizzie had to tell Devon she wouldn't be able to see him for a while. He nodded, his eyes squinting at the corners, but there was no argument about it. And Bob's visit was worse than ever because now she knew how it was supposed to be. She knew she wouldn't be able to stand it for long, and so she did something she had never done before with Bob, she squeezed the muscles she had only recently realized she had. Just the same as when you have to pee and there's no place to go, so you have to tighten up and hold it until you can get home. She squeezed and Bob gasped, and it was all over, almost no time at all. And Bob didn't even know! That was the best part of all. For the first time in her life, she had some control over the thing that had dominated her life for so long.

Not long after Bob had returned to camp, she and Devon took a blanket into her back yard, under the huge willow tree whose branches brushed against the lawn. There she was close enough to hear the children if they called for her, but she was hidden, safe, and private with Devon until the sky began to lighten. Her hunger was so intense it almost frightened her. She clung to him, wanting more, and more, and more.

"I love you," she sighed, "I love you so much."

"Ah, Lizzie, sweet Lizzie." He lay on his back, looking up at her, his face bright with surprise and pleasure.

She couldn't get enough of touching him, of tasting him, of arousing him and calming him.

Two weeks later he said what she had known all along he would say. He rolled to his back, his arms tight around her, reversing their positions, his hands stroking her back, her butt, his fingers tightening on her thighs. "I've got a gig back east for two months. Come with me."

"Back east?" He might as well have said the antarctic.

"Bring the kids if you have to. Just come with me."

"I can't."

And she couldn't. Two months back east, then what? A month in Tennis Shoe? Two weeks in Gumboot? Maybe spend the winter in Aardvark, Ontario? Kids changing schools and getting left behind, kids whining in hotel rooms, kids sick on airplanes or trying to behave on a stinking bus?

She wasn't surprised when her period was overdue. You don't feel things like she felt with Devon without something wonderful happening. But she didn't want to tell Devon until she knew for sure.

Two months back east, and then he had another gig in the maritimes. But the big problem wasn't Devon's moving around from gig to gig. It was Bob, narrow-eyed and tight-mouthed, looking through her dresser and checking her clothes in the closet.

"You don't fool me, lady," he said pleasantly enough. "You don't fool me one little bit. Took me a while to catch on, maybe, but I've been with enough whores and floozies in my time to know when I'm being milked before I'm ready!"

"What?" She stared at him. "Milked?"

"You know what I mean, Little Miss Innocence! I ever find out who he is there'll be more blood outside his goddamn body than there is inside it."

She knew he meant it. She'd seen him gut a deer with one determined swipe. She'd seen the coils of gut falling to the grass, steaming in the crisp autumn air. She'd seen the eyes glazing, the blood clotting thick. He'd do it.

Bob began showing up unannounced, waiting outside the X-L, or halfway home, or sitting in the living room with the lights out, waiting. And when she started to show, he asked right out if it was his baby she was carrying.

"You're right," she shrugged. "Me and Prince Charles got this big thing going, but don't tell nobody because Princess Di'll pitch a fit. Not to mention what Mummy would do about it if she found out."

He raised his hand to slap her face for cheekiness. She didn't cower, she didn't cringe. "You do," she promised, "and the cops'll be here before my nose stops bleeding. A man as will hit a pregnant woman isn't going to look like much in court."

"So whose kid is it?"

"Mine!" she shouted. "*Mine!*" She took several deep breaths to calm herself, then continued. "You've got a bug in your ear about something and I'm not one to try to talk you out of whatever idea it is you've hatched, you'll just get mean again, and ugly again. If you want to think it isn't yours, fine, you think what you want. I know it's *mine.*"

"I never trusted adult women," he told her flatly. "I never trusted 'em at all. I either made do with whores or went for young ones who didn't know enough about anything to try something smart. You used to be like that."

"You made me what I am today," she laughed. "I hope you're satisfied."

"You slut," he said. But he grinned from ear to ear, almost admiringly.

She didn't write to Devon, and he didn't write to her. He knew Bob could intercept the letter as easily as not. The only mail she had ever got was bills and advertising flyers. The only letters she had ever written had been practice business letters in grade nine commerce class. But once in a while the phone would ring, always during the day, and it would be Devon. Once and only once, Bob was home, drinking coffee at the kitchen table when the phone rang. Bob made no move to answer it, he never did.

"Hello?"

"Lizzie?"

"Oh, hi," she said brightly. "I was going to call you as soon as I finished doing Bob's laundry."

"He's home?"

"Yes, sure, of course I've got a minute to talk."

"He's there?"

"Sure. What's on your mind?"

"What's on my mind," Devon laughed, "is your body. What's on my mind is the taste of your skin."

"Gee, I don't know. I don't really like those parent-teacher things, you know? Sit there listening to nothing at all. I'd rather stay home and watch TV with the kids."

"Feel you all wet and slippery against my leg," he crooned softly, "smell your perfume . . . go nuts . . . Did I ever tell you that you smell different when you're halfway to heaven and loving with every beat of your heart? For that matter, did I ever tell you that sometimes I can feel your pulse beating against me when I'm inside you?"

"Well, uh, I . . ." she couldn't talk, she couldn't think, she could only hold the phone and wish Bob was a million miles away. Or she was. No, not a million miles—six or seven hundred, where Devon was.

"Yeah. Well. I guess I better let you get back to your old man, okay?"

"Yeah. Right. Listen, I'll see you around, okay?"

She went directly from the phone to the laundry room and busied herself pulling clothes from the dryer and folding them with shaking hands. Bob never even asked who had phoned her about the parent-teacher meeting.

It's always Other People commit adultery. Other women are mistresses and kept women, other women are homewreckers. Nobody ever believes the other woman is just an ordinary person like any of the rest of us. Even Bob couldn't nurse his suspicions forever. He was the only one who had ever had them, and without someone to agree with him, his distrust withered like an unwatered plant.

Lizzie worked until her seventh month, and then her boss laid her off, saying it was shortage of work so she could get unemployment insurance, and told her she could have her job back when she was ready. She wanted Devon to be with her, but she didn't know where he was. Anyway, he didn't know it was his baby, or even that she was pregnant.

It was an easy birth, so easy she hardly believed she was in labour. Then she was holding her daughter, tears of joy pouring freely down her face.

"Oh, she is beautiful!" she thrilled. "So very very beautiful."

"What are you going to call her?" the nurse asked, happy to see a welcomed and loved baby.

"Chantal," Lizzie said firmly.

"What second name?"

"No second name. Just Chantal."

Lizzie wasn't the only person thought Chantal was beautiful. Her parents gazed at the baby, then smiled widely and began to find features exactly like some other member of the family: Aunt Marie's eyebrows, cousin Alice's fingers, and didn't Bob's own mother have the most incredible cheekbones you ever saw in your life? In Lizzie's opinion, which she kept to herself, Chantal looked so much like Devon there was no other term for it but two peas in a pod. Thank God nobody in her family had ever heard of Devon Williams.

But before Chantal was two, the civilized world knew Devon's name, the sound of his voice, the grin, the incredible head of hair. You couldn't turn on the radio without hearing either his voice or the voice of his sister Jessie. And then you could hear them both at the same time, singing together, their album going gold, then platinum. Not just one song, not even two songs, but every song on both sides of the album was a hit. You couldn't walk down the street without hearing Devon singing about love, or the sky, or how it felt to be out in a boat on a misty morning, or how lonely it was to sit in the dome car of the transcontinental watching the moonlight shining on a land that could never be your own.

The postie delivered a parcel to the door, and she knew before she opened it he had sent her a copy of the album. There were others after that one, and it never occurred to her she was just a name and address on a list in a computer, with a secretary mailing out promotional freebies. Lizzie believed Devon had sent them to her. She lay in her bed at night listening to him sing, sometimes alone, sometimes with his sister, and she dreamed of how he would do a concert close by, and she would go. She'd send him a note backstage, and someone would come to get her. After the concert they'd go to his hotel room and this time, when he asked her, she'd say yes, and she'd go with him.

She heard about Devon's death on television. She was ironing, with the board set up in the living room so they could all watch the movie when it came on, and before the film started, the announcer's face came on to give a news round-up. Lizzie didn't believe Devon was dead, so she didn't cry, or take hysterics, or fling herself on the floor and roll in agony. She just kept on ironing, because of course it was a lie, of course it was a mistake, of course it was just another vicious rumour. Devon didn't do drugs. Devon didn't sniff cocaine or shoot junk or smoke marijuana so why would he mess with this stuff they called "crack"? How could people tell those lies? Why didn't somebody just sue them all to a fare-thee-well, make them apologize for the awful things they said, apologize for the lies about the party and the underage girls and why didn't someone speak up for Devon and tell everyone that he wouldn't do dirty stuff like that?

It was on the late news, too, and in the papers the next day, the same lies, the same terrible lies. They said Devon had been drinking heavily for months, and doing drugs for two years or longer. They said that he had finished his concert and gone back to the hotel suite with half a dozen little girls, some of them barely into their teens, and they said he gave them alcohol, gave them drugs, engaged in sexual acts and even had someone videotape what went on. They said Devon went into a bedroom with two girls, two children, really, and that one of them had come out crying, almost hysterical, but had been calmed down and sent back to the room. They said the party got louder and louder until the hotel had to ask them to tone it down, but they didn't tone it down. The suite had been damaged. Some of the girls left, drunk, drugged, and weeping, then the girls came out of Devon's bedroom and had to be calmed down, had to be helped to tidy themselves up before they left. Devon came out of the bedroom, lurching and laughing, and they said he chug-a-lugged some Jack Daniels, then went back to his bedroom with several big pieces of this stuff they called "crack." They showed part of the video. They showed Devon with his shirt undone and his hair in disarray, leaning against a door frame, laughing like a fool, looking beautiful, looking like Satan must have looked when he was still Lucifer, the star of the morning, most beautiful of God's creations. Laughing and drinking from a bottle.

They called themselves his friends and they told awful lies. When the police arrived it was because of what the teenagers had told their distraught parents. But Devon was on his bed, lying on his back, dead on the blood-stained sheets. Whose blood?

She took the day of his funeral off work and sat in the living room watching television, going from channel to channel, from news broadcast to news broadcast, watching time and time and time again as his coffin was unloaded from the private jet a few miles from his birthplace. She watched in numb disbelief as the cameras showed his parents standing beside the big black Cadillac, as dazed and dry-eyed as she was herself, watching Devon being loaded like a parcel or a side of beef, watching the circus they called a funeral.

She didn't cry until the eleven o'clock news special when they showed the film they had been allowed to shoot inside the little church. None of the crazies were in there trying to be part of Devon Williams' last show. Only the family and the relatives and friends who had known him before he was a big star. There were flowers, and there was a heartfelt eulogy, and the camera turned away politely when Devon's mother began to weep, turned to her husband and sobbed against his chest. When Devon's sister Jessie moved to the front to sing, the camera held on her as she stood in white pants, white shirt, white boots, holding the most beautiful guitar in the world. She sang "Peace in the Valley" until you thought your heart would break right along with hers. If you hadn't loved Devon, if you'd never even heard of him, if you'd only stepped into that church to get out of the rain while waiting for a bus, the sound of Jessie Williams singing that song would have cracked your heart for all time.

Lizzie wanted to howl and roar, scream and throw herself on the carpet, pound her fists and thrash until there was no feeling left in her body, but she could only sit, tears streaming, watching the television and listening to Jessie Williams. She sobbed through the part where they showed the lines of cars moving along the Island Highway to the cemetery. At graveside, Jessie sang again, not just once, not just twice, Jessie Williams sang until it seemed there couldn't be a song left in her heart or in her throat. She sang "Amazing Grace" and she sang "Old Rugged Cross." She sang "How

Great Thou Art" and she sang "When the Roll Is Called Up Yonder I'll Be There." She sang "Jewels in My Crown" and she sang "Jesus Wants Me for a Sunbeam." She even sang "You in Your Small Corner And I in Mine." At first she sang alone, but then someone else started to sing with her, and then someone else, and then several men with lined, tanned faces, dressed in dark suits with white shirts and dark ties, joined in, helping her. When Jessie sang "It Is Better to Light Just One Little Candle than to Stumble in the Dark," Devon's mother wiped her eyes and nodded.

Then Jessie Williams did the most unbelievable, ungodly, un-christian and unreligious thing you could imagine. She stopped singing hymns. She started singing a song with a strong rhythm, a song everybody knew, and she patted the beat on her guitar, and even Devon's own mother began to clap her hands, weeping and smiling at the same time, until Lizzie wondered if everyone in Devon's family was six bricks short of a full load, because they were all singing and swaying and keeping time, and it was wrong, all wrong, except it felt so good, and so right, and dissolved the lump of horror in her throat.

They started coming out of the woodwork right away, crawling out from the baseboards and slithering from the wall mouldings, leaping for telephones, calling reporters, and there were more pictures of Devon staring from more covers of more tabloids in more supermarkets than you would have thought existed. "Teenaged Mother Claims Devon Williams the Father of Her Son," "Everyone Says He Looks Like His Father," "He Even Sings," "Divorced Wife Says Devon's Child Is Mine," "Count Six in Devon Paternity Race." Women from towns nobody had heard of claimed to have spent torrid and fertile nights with the dead millionaire. Women in every town Devon had ever played produced children they claimed were the love-children of the departed singer. Husbands and ex-hus-bands, lovers and ex-lovers, boyfriends and ex-boyfriends of the women spilled their guts for money and told the world how their hearts had been broken and their lives altered because Devon Williams had trespassed on their private preserves.

The Williams family ignored it all. Each claim was handled by the lawyers and the courts. It was amazing how many stories of undying love stopped being told as soon as it was known the police and courts would be the ones investigating the claims against

Devon's estate. "I Don't Want Money Young Mother Declares." "They Can't Buy My Son Divorced Mom Says."

And Lizzie was glad she had never said a word to anyone. It almost seemed as if Chantal was the only child under the age of six who wasn't publicly purported to be Devon's woods colt.

Bob came back from camp and moved in full-time, saying he would take over the reins and run the family the way it ought to be run. He was angry, and she knew it was because he had been told he was too old to continue working for the company, told he could either take early retirement or be laid off. He started taking his anger out on the kids, whipping off his belt and whaling on their bare butts as if it was the only thing in the world that he could still enjoy. Lizzie knew if he touched her she would scream. And she knew if she didn't let him touch her, he'd take it out on the kids. So she went into town, taking Chantal with her, and went to see a lawyer.

That night, in the bathroom, before they stepped into the tub, she took colour photographs of their poor little bums, criss-crossed with purple welts, some of the welts going up over their waists, to their backs. She gave the pictures to the lawyer. She had no plans to stay where Bob could get hold of her. Even if her parents had lived there all their lives, even if she had been born there, her children born there, she wasn't going to die there or have her children sent crazy there. She left it up to the lawyer to wrench her fair share from Bob. All Lizzie did was deliver the pictures, tell the lawyer what she wanted, then go back home again and, while Bob was off with his fishing rods and herring strip, pack. It cost extra to get the movers to come on short notice, but she didn't care. When the truck drove off, Lizzie put Chantal in her car seat, then drove to the school and pulled the boys out of class.

"Where are we going?" Brian asked nervously.

"Away," she said easily.

"Where?"

"You'll see." She smiled at him, and stroked the curve of his chin, where the bruise was light blue and still swollen and sore. "No more back-handers, no more belts. . ." He blinked rapidly, his eyes flooding with tears of relief, and in the back seat, Tony started crying softly. "It's going to be okay," she told them.

"Don't cry," Kenny told Tony. "You'll get the baby cryin', too, and then you'll be sorry."

Lizzie had never been to Bright's Crossing, but she knew it from the things Devon had told her. She knew how to get to the creek, she know how to get to the swimming hole, she knew where in the river the big fishing hole was, and she knew more about some of the families than they would ever know.

The house backed onto a grassy slope down to the bank of the creek, and there were fruit trees flanking the driveway from the side road up to the front steps. A grapevine sprawled up the ply-and-slat side of the carport, and crawled over the lip and along the slope of the shake roof that kept the worst of the alder pollen and bird dirt from the roof of the car.

Each morning, after the boys had ridden off to school on their bikes, Lizzie cleaned house, did the laundry, then went outside with Chantal to work on the garden she was determined to have. Nobody else in her family had ever lived on welfare. She supposed she ought to be ashamed of herself for not supporting the kids without charity. But Lizzie didn't care a damn! She'd made more mistakes in twelve years than most people make in a lifetime, and if going on welfare was one more mistake, fine, it was in good company with all the other mistakes. It felt like something she had to do, time she had to take to try to figure out some things that badly needed figuring out, because now her mistakes were affecting the kids and that's different from making mistakes and paying for them yourself.

She dug out and lifted away the sod, then dug up and hauled away rocks. She didn't work any harder than she had worked at the X-L, but it gave her things she had forgotten a person could get from working. When the ground was ready and the soil warm, she planted her vegetables, then planted nasturtiums around the perimeter of the garden and along the rows of beets, lettuce, corn, and chard. Once a week, on Saturday afternoon, they got in the car and drove to the Mini-Mart to do their shopping, and welfare or not, there was always money for butter for the popcorn the boys made at night, always money for vitamin pills and for the seven o'clock show at the movie house on Friday nights.

She could have got a job at the nursery, and she would have liked it, looking after the greenhouses, tending the seedlings and plants. But when she sat down and figured out how much they were willing to pay her, how much it would cost for daycare for Chantal, how much she would have left over after buying gas and oil and work clothes, and how much her insurance would go up if she used the car for driving to work instead of just for grocery shopping, it was obvious that going to work would be a mistake. A stupid mistake. At least welfare guaranteed medical coverage, glasses if the kids needed them, and dental work when it was time.

Bob showed up trying to persuade her to go back where he said she belonged. The boys sidled away from him, Brian picking up Chantal and taking her with him, watching his father distrustfully. Lizzie almost felt sorry for Bob, but only almost. He blustered and cursed, he told her she'd be sorry, and he tried to talk the boys into going with him.

"Come on," he said to them.

"No, sir," Brian said, sitting Chantal on his hip.

"You've got a nice house at home," he bargained, "and I'll get you your own radio and record player."

"No, sir," Brian repeated.

"Any time you change your mind you just phone and I'll send you the money to come home."

"I am home," Brian said firmly.

Brian went out for softball tryouts and was accepted on the Bright's Crossing Junior Boys Team.

"We got sponsors," he said proudly. "And we're gonna have team shirts, too! We get to keep 'em for the whole season, then we hand 'em in again until next year."

"Who's the sponsor?" Lizzie asked.

"All kindsa different ones," he said easily. "Different companies or people sponsor a player."

"Who's your sponsor?"

"Don't know yet. Don't got my shirt yet. Red and white, that's our colours, red and white. We get red shirts with white writing on 'em, and red pants with white stripes down the side, and red socks-with-no-feet, just like on a real team." He laughed then, eyes bright with excitement. "We *are* a real team!"

They all went down to the school playground to watch Brian's first game and Lizzie used up an entire roll of film getting shots of her oldest son in his "Pederson's Dairy" shirt. He looked like a kid who would be sponsored by a dairy, she thought. Tall, wide-shouldered for his age, pleasant looking but not handsome, with a shy smile and eyes that sometimes clouded if someone shouted and brought back memories of how it felt to have a belt wrap around your bare body.

Lizzie was enthralled by the game. She didn't really care which team won, although she supposed she should be loyal and cheer only for the Salmonbellies, where Brian filled the hole in centre field. But she didn't always remember which side she was supposed to be on, it was like watching a cross between a chess game and a dance presentation. Legs stretching, feet pounding, arms slicing as they strained for the base, flinging themselves unafraid of the consequences, as if convinced there really was a heaven with God sitting in it, his eye on them as well as on the sparrow.

She held Chantal on her knee and the little girl laughed and shouted each time her big brother moved, even if all he was doing was taking off his team cap to scratch his sweaty head. Chantal screeched joyously when Brian actually managed to hit the ball and make it to first base, and when he was put out at second, Chantal cheered as if he had done something uniquely marvelous. When she got tired of sitting on Lizzie's knee, Tony took her behind the backstop, where she could putter around piling stones in heaps and kicking them over again.

"What's your daughter's name?" a voice asked.

"Chantal," Lizzie answered, smiling. She turned, still smiling, then froze, her face paling to cottage cheese white, then flaming crimson. The other woman froze, too, her eyes widening slightly. Then, with an obvious effort, she nodded and said something friendly, something about Chantal being a lovely name and then something else about what a lovely, happy child she seemed to be.

More than half an hour of Lizzie's life vanished in a tight-muscled dry-mouthed nervous uncertainty. She knew who the woman was. She had seen her on TV, turning blindly to her husband, sobbing helplessly. And what do you say, what do you do, what kind of a fool do you look like whether you say something or don't? Lizzie decided it was ridiculous to ignore the obvious, ridiculous to try to pretend she didn't know who Esther was, who Devon had been. She decided it wouldn't be pushy, or bad manners, or out of line to at least tell Devon's mother that she was very sorry her son was dead. She turned, intending to say she hoped the pain was passing and life starting to assume normal proportions. The words stuck in her throat. Esther was beaming happily, holding Chantal on her lap, brushing the thick mop of half-curly hair back from the brow that was so like Devon's. Lizzie almost spoke then, but couldn't. Chantal had Devon's hairline, his thick hair, the large, deep-set, bright blue eyes. It was so obvious to Lizzie that she knew it was obvious to Esther, too.

"It's a lovely name." Esther was looking at the little girl, but speaking to Lizzie.

"Yes," Lizzie smiled, relaxing, even managing to breathe again.

"Is she a good baby? A happy baby?"

"She's the best thing ever happened to me," Lizzie said honestly.

"She doesn't look like you." Esther turned then and looked at Lizzie. "She must look like her father."

Lizzie couldn't answer. And she couldn't look away. Esther's eyes were exactly like Devon's eyes, exactly like Chantal's eyes and Lizzie knew Esther knew. And knew that Esther knew she knew. But Esther never asked, and Lizzie never offered. Esther stroked the soft curls back from Chantal's forehead, then kissed the soft tanned skin.

"Her brothers seem crazy about her," she said.

"We all are," Lizzie smiled. "She is a gift."

Months later, as she was trying to shovel the snow off the driveway so she could coax the car to the side road, a heavy truck with chains clattering on the back wheels came down the road and turned into the yard, pushing easily through the ridge of snow left by the plough. Lizzie stepped aside, into snow over her knees, then dug in her pocket for a tissue to wipe her numb and dripping nose.

"Missus thought you might need a hand," Blackie Williams smiled. Lizzie didn't know whether she'd been punched, stapled, or folded. She looked at the house, then at the big truck with "Williams Well Digging" written on the side.

"Thank you."

"Tell you what." He opened the truck door and jumped out easily. "Whyn't you give me the shovel while you go get the kids into their jackets." He took the shovel and started moving the snow easily. "You oughta get that damn grapevine pruned," he warned, "or it's gonna rip the shakes right offa the carport roof. Get more grapes if you cut 'er back some, too."

It was only neighbourly to invite him in for coffee when they got home and only neighbourly of him to accept. She put away the groceries and nodded permission for the boys to go sledding behind the community hall. Blackie sat with Chantal on his knee, helping her dip a cinnamon bun into his coffee, accepting bites she shoved at his mouth, wiping her chin when she dribbled.

"How you making it for money?" he asked.

"Fine," she answered shortly.

"No need to get proddy," he said gently. He looked at her, the slope of his cheek so like Devon's. "If you don't want to talk about it, that's your business and I respect that. What I don't respect, what I'll get right ugly about, is if any of these kids ever have to do without something they need."

"I didn't come here to . . . sponge off you." Lizzie felt as if she were about to weep. "It was just . . . he always talked about it as if it was heaven on earth . . . said you'd caught a huge trout one time . . . I wanted . . . I wanted my kids to have . . . something better'n they'd ever had or would have if I stayed where their dad could whale away on them . . . And . . ."

"Tasted like mud, that fish," Blackie grinned wryly. "Prob'ly some kinda message in that."

She refilled his coffee cup. He added cream, then allowed Chantal to stir it for him.

"There's not much use askin' why," he mused. He pulled out his tobacco pouch and papers and rolled himself a smoke. He lit it with a paper match and held the match for the little girl to blow out. "No use at all," he continued slowly. "No use askin' why we do this or why we don't do that or why we think or don't think one thing or the other."

"They were just little girls," Lizzie mourned. "And what they said . . ."

"Oh, covering their own asses most likely," Blackie soothed. "But he was a devil was Devon, no doubt about it. Never any halfways with him. When he wasn't sweet as sugar, he was shit."

"Devon?" She stared. "No, not Devon!"

"I'm glad," Blackie smiled, "you never got to see the shitty side of him. Glad he didn't feel he had to show it to you. It's strange how things happen, you ever notice? Some people, they say their well is half full; others say it's half empty. Had a brother like that. Don't know where he got it any more'n I could ever figure out where Dev got it, but whatever it was, it ran in both of 'em. Just a streak of mean, I guess." He finished his cigarette, stubbed out the butt, and stroked Chantal's face with his big work-calloused hand. "Sure is a nice little girl." He held her gently against his chest. "I got a snapshot of Dev at the same age. You might like to have it. Honest to God, a body'd have to be blind and stupid both not to know at a glance. And I'm glad."

Now she could bring out the tapes and records again, and play them once more, capturing for a few hours some of what she had once dreamed. The snow turned to rain, the world became slush, everything dripped, the back porch was thick with mud. The gumboots never quite dried inside and everyone's socks went a kind of detergent-laundromat grey. Lizzie didn't care. There was something to look forward to now. Something to think about and to wonder how it would turn out. The holes in her life began to fill in, she began to think that maybe mistakes weren't really mistakes, after all, just something that happened, neither good nor bad, and not at all indifferent, just how it was and how it would be before it got better. She knew it would get better.   🍎

Louella

❦

The cat had vanished in the furor of unpacking and settling in, and Louella almost hoped the damn thing would stay lost out in the green that blocked the horizon in every direction. The girls moped and blamed each other, Dave joined Louella in ignoring their pouting and the reason for it. At times Louella almost wished the girls would go in search of the goddamn cat and get themselves lost out there, too. How much help was she getting from them? And even when she did, was it worth the tooth-gnashing, hair-pulling, and TV-soap theatrics of it all?

The more Louella ignored the girls, the harder they tried not to be ignored. The more they demanded her attention, the more obnoxious they got and the harder Louella worked at ignoring them. "Dear God," she wrote, composing a letter in her head. "Please forgive me for ever having doubted your wisdom. Thank you for making me a barren woman and please forgive me for getting tangled up in a mess that brought someone else's kids into my life. You were right. I shouldn't have any kids. If you will only please make these ones disappear I will never again in any way whatsoever do anything which might interfere with your scheme of things. Yours sincerely, U-No-Hoo."

But God wasn't letting her off that easy. The girls didn't vanish in a puff of smoke, they didn't turn into pillars of salt, they didn't climb up the ladder after Father Jacob. And then the cat came back.

It was a teen-age stiltman named Kevin brought her back, holding her gently, rubbing her ears, talking softly to her. "She's too tame to be a wild one," he grinned, "and since she doesn't know her way around, she has to be new in town, and you're the only ones new, so . . . elementary, my dear Watson."

"Thank you." Louella made herself smile and reached for the cat. She wasn't sure if it was Gillian or Patsy standing behind her, but whoever it was, her breath was warm on the back of Louella's neck. "I'll put her in her travel cage for a while," Louella decided. "Maybe put butter on her paws to persuade her to stay." She held the cat firmly, took the cage from the hall closet and set it up, put the cat inside, got the butter dish and a bread knife, took a decent-sized dollop of butter and spread it on all four soft black pads.

She wanted to open her mouth and yell a paragraph or two about the goddamn cat and whose goddamn idea had it been to bring the goddamn thing home. Instead, she just sighed and went back to the endless job of putting laundry through the twin machines in what the mobile home brochure described as a utility area. It was about as utilitarian as a ruffled parasol. She lifted a load of washed bedding from the machine and stuffed it into the front-loading dryer, closed the door, turned the knob, pressed the button, and the sheets and pillow slips started turning. Another load of sheets and pillow cases into the washer, add half a cup of detergent and a generous handful of powdered bleach, and start the machine. Louella grabbed the load of dry sheets and took them into the living room, dumped them on the sofa, and began to fold them, deliberately ignoring Kevin and the girls who still stood in the open doorway. The dry load was folded, the sound of running water stopped, and the washer started to rumble comfortably, swishing the load of sheets through the hot water. Louella moved to the kitchen and started scrubbing vegetables for supper.

There wasn't a piano in town, and the only places the least bit oriented towards recreation were the leaking movie theatre, the chlorine-reeking community swimming pool, and the bar, with its constantly playing and re-playing tape of the top twenty middle-of-the-road mouldies. Somehow, with such an overwhelming choice of entertainment beckoning beyond the thin metal walls of the trailer, it didn't bother Louella that she was too tired in the evening to want to go anywhere. She supervised the dishes, helped clean up the kitchen and was part of the assembly line making sandwiches and packing the lunch kits. A bath, a drop of something to help her unwind, and all she wanted was her bed.

Dave didn't usually last as long of an evening as she did. He came home, stripped off his wet and muddy clothes in the utility area, pulled on the dark brown robe that came only to his knees, and padded barefoot to the bathroom, where he soaked in a hot tub, his face lined, his eyes dark-shadowed. Louella always made sure she had the time to take him a bottle of cold beer, which he accepted gratefully. Some evenings she had a minute or two to sit on the lowered toilet seat lid and talk quietly, but most of the time she just handed him his beer, kissed him, and hurried back to supper.

When he had eaten, Dave went to what the mobile home brochure called the master bedroom. There he spent an hour or two transcribing scribbled notations from the mud-stained little book he kept in a sandwich baggie in his flannel shirt pocket, to a large hard-backed account book kept in a drawer under the arborite-topped counter described as a decorative feature. Louella had no idea what these notations were, and Dave seemed to have no need to discuss them.

When he had finished his book work, he went to bed. By the time Louella joined him, he was sprawled, asleep, breathing heavily, his skin sometimes sheened lightly with sweat. Often his legs jerked, shaking the entire bed, disturbing her rest, startling her briefly awake.

Sometimes they had time for a precious bit of time together in the morning, over a mug of delicious coffee, before the rest of the crew came in for breakfast.

"It's a fuckin' mess," Dave sighed. "There's been a-holes and gomers, lugans and know-nothings all over the place. Someone went in and primed 'er some ten years back, and of course forestry, buncha useless twits, they know nothing about it but the best timbers gone and there's no money in stumps. There's part of a skid road up behind the bluff and there's what was probably someone's cook camp down by the beach, and forestry don't know dick-all about that either. There's been shake-bolt cuttin' and there's been . . . ahhh, hell," he sighed. "I wouldn't be surprised if someone wasn't exportin' itty-bitty Christless trees out of there, too."

"Bah humbug," she smiled.

"For sure bah humbug. But," he shrugged, "long's I keep track of it all and make damn sure there's lots of reports go in to those witless cocksuckers, I can squeeze 'em a bit and maybe get another hunk to make up for the mess I inherited here." His eyes lit up and he smiled. "Maybe even get me a piece of prime. On which," he added darkly, "no tribe has laid land claim!"

She might have learned to like the place in spite of the isolation, the scarcity of fresh or even half-fresh vegetables, the astronomical prices of food, the yogurt only two days away from expiry date, the milk usually two days over. She might have adapted to the hard work and the long hours, she might have found the energy to start enjoying life. Except for the accident.

One gallon of gasoline does the work of 120 sticks of dynamite, and it was a twenty-five gallon tank that blew. They found fragments of the oil drum, but no fragments of Dave Riley or the two other men who went with him. When all the investigating was finished, someone decided that the drum was left over from whatever had gone on there before, that it had been left behind, forgotten against a log. The track machine had gone over it and crushed the half-rusted barrel, then the metal track had knocked a spark from a rock or maybe from the barrel itself, and that was all she wrote.

"They don't rightly know," Louella realized.

"No. They don't know fuck-all," a man agreed. "They never knew nothin' about nothin' and then they were on their way to glory."

"Jesus, Jesus, Jesus," Louella kept repeating to herself, "Jesus, Jesus, even if they'd'a found him, this pissin' place don't have so much as a cemetery. You can die here, but you can't be buried here. Mind you," and she took the big glass of whiskey Gillian handed her and gulped some of it down desperately, "I myself wouldn't be caught dead in this goddamn hole!"

Neighbours she didn't know came to the trailer bringing food. They tried to talk to her, quickly realized she wasn't clued in to the real world, and so, instead of annoying her or bothering her or stupidly trying to snap her out of it, they vacuumed carpets, scrubbed walls, and warmed the food they had brought, even spooned and forked it into her mouth and waited for her to chew and swallow. She sat, staring at the cat with her litter of motley-coloured kittens, and listening to the girls sobbing bitterly in their room. She supposed a real mother would go to them, try to console them. But she sat in her chair and tried to deal, as best she could, with the realization it had come late in life and she hadn't had it for long enough, not anywhere near long enough, and now it was gone, ker-thunderin-pow, it was gone and Dave was gone and it was all over, but by God, she'd had it for a while.

"Jesus, Jesus," she intoned until she was sick and tired of the sound of her own voice. Then she got up out of the recliner and started to pack her stuff.

"What should we do?" the girls asked, staring at her as if the answer to everything were written on her forehead.

"Where are we going to go?" Gillian asked.

"What are we going to do?" Patsy asked.

Take a hike, Louella wanted to say. She wanted to say, Hey, I was shacked up with your father, not with you. She wanted to say, Phone your aunts and uncles. She wanted to remind them she was not their mother, they were not her responsibility, none of it had anything to do with her.

"Stay off back roads," she said firmly, "and for godsake don't ever move to any place as what shows up on a map smaller'n a pellet of mouse shit!"

Louella had never sat down and thought about life, death, and the meaning of it all, so she hadn't thought about what would happen if Dave died. As it turned out, there was virtually no mess or confusion. Dave had papers with a lawyer, he had instructions with his sister, he had insurance policies. He had it aced, and he had the beneficiary down as Louella.

"I didn't know," she mumbled stupidly.

"Only to be expected," someone said. "After all, there's a logger killed every day of the year. A cop gets shot, your TV is full of it, you get all the propaganda about how they died protecting you, personally, but you never hear how every board in your house is stained with some poor fucker's blood."

Louella contacted her booking agent and for a few months she and the girls lived in a motel in Nanaimo while she played six nights a week in a medium-sized, half-decent lounge. On her own, with no help at all from the leech who was supposed to be busy finding work for her.

Then she found out about an inn a few miles out of town, and she drove out on a Wednesday to see if what she had heard was even half true.

"It's my back," the man insisted, and Louella knew it was nothing of the sort. "I just can't do any of the heavy work with my back the way it is."

"The kids quit school and moved away," the wife said quietly, "and we've been shut down half the time ever since."

"Can't get good help," he sighed. "And with my back like it is, I can't do it all."

Louella asked to see the books, read the message clearly written there, then left, promising she would be in touch within a few days. Instead of driving directly to the city, she took a tour of the area. There were no streets, no avenues, no drives or crescents. Just roads. Some of them paved, most of them gravel. Old farmhouses sat on one- and two-acre lots with new houses on half-acre lots on either side of them, even behind them. The history of the loss of dairy farming was there for the world to see and few to mourn. Fruit trees flanked the fence parallel to the road, and behind the huge apple, pear, and cherry trees, the newer ornamentals looked alien and unreal. The old farmhouses had duck ponds, the newer ex-urban palaces had goldfish ponds, with herring net strung over top to keep the glorified carp safe from eagles and kingfishers. Station wagons, tricycles, and two-wheelers with extra sets of training wheels rested in gravel driveways while shaggy big dogs lay on the back steps or sprawled in the shade. None of it pulled any heartstrings or struck any chords of memory, and yet, back in the motel unit, getting ready to go to the lounge, Louella heard herself describing it all to the girls.

"Buy it?" Patsy gaped. "Us?"

"If they're going broke on the place, how do we know we won't go broke, too?"

"It's something to think about," Louella smiled. "After all, neither of you is the least bit interested in getting yourself enrolled in school, or you'd have done it before now; and neither of you seems able to find anything remotely resembling a job, or you'd have started in on that, at least. So, if the insurance money got put into the inn, you'd at least be working instead of sitting on your ass growing zits on your face."

"Zits!" Patsy screeched.

"No need to get nasty," Gillian sulked.

"No need to sit on your arse and let me feed you like you were a baby bird, either," Louella smiled. "After all, you're stronger than I am, you're younger than I am, you've got hell's own energy more than I have and there's no reason for you to loll around all day as if you were the children of the crowned heads of Europe."

"Everybody knows," Patsy argued, "that there's a recession going on. No jobs. More than twelve per cent unemployment!"

"And higher in the under twenty-five age group," Gillian added.

"Ah," Louella smiled, "but there is always school, isn't there?" And she left to sit in a smoke-filled bar and play other people's requests until after midnight.

She thought about the inn often during the next few days, but thinking isn't doing, and the next time she drove out to have a look at it there was a big sign in the window reading "Under New Management."

"Well, "she thought, "that's that, isn't it," but got out of the car anyway and walked to the office. She had a very pleasant conversation with the new owners, everybody shook hands with everybody else, and Louella drove her car back to the motel unit. There she had a long bath and a brief nap, then got ready to go to the lounge.

"A permanent job?" Patsy gawked.

"How is it you can find jobs when nobody else can?" Gillian stared at her.

"For a start," Louella said, "I've got something I can do that not everybody in the world can do, and I do it well. Not the best, but good enough. And," she smiled her coolest smile, "I go looking for them."

"How long are we going to live in this motel?"

"I don't know about you," Louella said, "but I myself am moving at the end of next week."

"What does that mean?" Patsy asked.

"It means you've got a week and a half to shit or get off the pot. Either you're in school, or you're actively looking for a job, or you're on your own. Welfare pays just about enough for you to live in a roach palace and eat one meal a day."

"What about the insurance money?" Gillian flared.

"What about it?"

"Well, after all, he was our dad for years and years and he only knew you for a little while!"

"He left it to me," Louella said firmly, "because he knew I wouldn't let you two bimbos live like grasshoppers, fiddling away that blood money. He knew it would get used for something if I had hold of it. And believe me, if you want any of it, you'd better stop sitting on your ever-widening butts convincing yourselves the world owes you a living."

It was like a re-run of something she didn't want to go through again, only this time she didn't have Dave there to put down his big size thirteen and roar, and this time she didn't think she'd get away with it if she hauled off and slapped one of the two enraged faces. They were big enough to haul off and hit her back.

Four and a half days of total hell. Four and a half days of muttered insults and accusing how-can-you's. Wailing "I wish my dad was still alive." Bawling "Oh, why did my grandma have to die." Sobbing "If only my mom was here." Finally Louella sat them down and put it on the line.

"Listen," she said firmly, "I know it's a brick of shit. I know not many kids your age have to lose first their mom, then their grandma, and then their dad, all in a few years. I know it's scary; hell, you must look at people on the street and wonder which one is going to drop next. But I didn't make it happen, and it isn't going to go away just because you don't like it. I figure right about now you've got a choice. You can either pull up your socks and get tough, or you can sit and woe-is-me until you're two more of those sad-assed go-nowhere jamtarts who go from one therapy group to the other, looking outside of themselves for help, waiting for someone else to make things better. Nobody will. And you probably won't believe this," she said flatly, "but the world is full of people worse off than you."

They stared at her, then stared past her, and then Gillian started to grin. "If you fuckin' dare," she said softly, "say that thing about how I felt sorry for myself because I had no shoes until I met someone who had no feet, I think I will puke."

"That's better," Louella grinned.

"So what," Gillian challenged, "do you think I should do?"

"What do you want to do?"

"I want to go to sleep and wake up tomorrow rich, beautiful, educated, employed, and talented. Failing that," her eyes flooded but she blinked back the tears, "I want someone to help me figure out what there is to choose from because I can't think of anything at all! I really can't. I know it looks like I'm just being a big Saddo, but every time I think I might have some clue, something I thought was a good idea looks like a dumb idea. I'm scared."

"School," Louella said quietly. "Tomorrow. First thing. In you go and register."

"Okay." Gillian agreed so fast Louella wondered if people could really fall off their chairs in shock.

"Me, too," Patsy added, openly relieved.

"My ass," Louella sighed. "Now will someone tell *me* what to do because I get scared, too, you know. I've been scared for longer than you've been alive."

"I guess," one of them suggested, "you just kind of put on your face and head off to work, right?"

"Right." She stood up and smiled at them. "Any suggestions what face I should wear tonight? Cleopatra? Joan of Arc? Madame Curie?"

"Any or all of the above." Gillian was weeping suddenly, but smiling too. "Boy, it sure doesn't get any easier, does it?" 🍎

Betty

Betty Campbell made her living by setting crab traps, waiting for crabs to walk into them, then hauling up the traps and keeping only those crabs bigger than the minimum legal size. Some days she made good, some days she made poorly, and some days it wasn't worth getting out of bed.

It had been like that for over three weeks, not a goddamn crab to be caught, regardless of size. Not just her, everybody was burning gas and getting skunked. Most of them shrugged and stayed home, saving their gas money, sitting with their feet up drinking tea and watching TV game shows, cursing the government and the goddamn spawn of men in suits who opened pulp mills and then broke every law known to God and man and dumped crap into the chuck, chasing away other people's livelihoods and may they all rot in hell for eternity and a day. But Betty went out, even though she knew she wasn't going to catch crabs. She went out because when she didn't, she felt discombooberated, like a smoker who can't find her cigarettes.

She threw in a crab trap or two, then stopped pretending and sat on a yellow plastic milk crate, baiting the enormous hooks she used to jig cod. No money in jigging cod, but you could at least trade it for something, and, barring that, eat it yourself. She tossed the hook over the side, lit a smoke, jigged the line, puffed a couple of times, watched the shithawks slicing the air, jigged, felt something tug, and reefed on the bugger, hauling as hard as she could.

Something tugged all right. Something damn near dragged her over the side of the boat. Betty wasn't pissing around like some sports fisherman, nor was she playing with a thin leader or a short deck. She was using good strong never-bust line with leader made of tempered wire. She fastened the bugger onto the come-along and hit the switch. The come-along set itself to the task and the heavy line started up over the side of the boat. Whatever in the name of Jesus was on the other end, it fought back to beat the very devil.

And yelled. Betty had never heard a sea creature yell. She'd had them snap, she'd heard teeth gnash, she'd even heard them hiss, but she'd never heard anything yell. Mind you, she'd never seen a sea creature with long hair hanging down almost to its green-barnacled tail, either.

It was female, no doubt about that. It had the same kind of pouty slit a young orca female has, but more to the proof, it had two breasts, lovely breasts, with pink nipples set in rosy circles. The face was lovely, too, or it would have been if it hadn't been bright with rage, mouth open, cursing in what Betty figured was two or three languages at the same time. The cod hook was caught right below where the waist ended and the hips swelled into the long, scaled tail.

"Son a *bitch*," it yelled.

"Shut up," Betty said bravely, lifting the fish club, "or I'll brain ya."

"In a pig's eye!"

"What would a first cousin to a cod like you know about pigs?"

"Cod? First cousin to a . . . you slut!"

They went back and forth like that a few more times, the critter trying unsuccessfully to get the cod hook out of her butt, and Betty brandishing the lead-weighted club. Then the seawoman gave up and lay on her belly on the deck, gritting her teeth—her sharp, pointy, back-curved teeth, very much like the ones in the jaws of a dogfish, which is a small version of the shark.

"Lemme go," she said quietly, "and I'll make it worth your while."

"You'd have to work overtime to do that," Betty countered. "I could get me a cool million from the Aquarium. Get another million from CBC Television. Get who knows how much from the Pacific Biological Station over in Departure Bay. Christ knows how much the Trollers Association would chip in. You're the reason there's no crabs around here, I bet. Nor much in the way of chinook, either."

"Blame me!" the seawoman snapped. "I been eating the same amount I been eating for two thousand years. If you're short of chinook, you might look closer to home for the cause of it."

"You're probably right." Betty reached for the snippers. "So, how worth it are you going to make it for me?"

"You set me loose and I promise you'll never go short of whatever it is you're fishing for. Crab, salmon, I don't give a damn, you'll have a hold full every day. And," she smiled, showing those sharp shark teeth again, "I'll give you these." She held out some seeds. Looked exactly like the seeds you'd find in any apple. A full dozen of them.

"What do I do with them?" Betty asked.

"You give one to your dog and one to your horse. One you plant in the back yard, and one you take yourself. Save the others, you'll know what to do with them when it's time."

"And what'll happen?"

"Why don't you wait and find out? What's the use of magic if you know ahead of time what it's going to be? No smoke and mirrors, I promise you."

"And a good catch every time?"

"Yes," the seawoman said, "a good catch every time." She clenched her pale hands into fists and squinched her eyes shut. "Now get it out of my butt."

One snip and one tug and the cod hook was out. The seawoman grabbed the rail, hoisted herself over, and flopped down into the sea. Betty watched her splash in the water, wiggle her big tail a few times, then dive deep. The bubbles frothed, the water swirled, and the seawoman stuck her head up out of the waves, laughing mockingly.

"I'll be back," she promised. "I want your son when he's three years old!"

"Fuck you," Betty laughed. "I'm not even married, let alone the mother of a son!"

She went into the galley and made herself a cup of coffee, trying to convince herself none of it had happened. It didn't work. But she knew she wasn't going to tell anybody about it, either. They had their ways. Next thing you knew you were across the pond in Riverview in a rubber room, with your relatives fighting like weasels over your last few possessions.

She hauled in her crab traps and somehow wasn't at all surprised to find both of them jammed full of the biggest Dungeness she'd seen in years.

There'd been such a dearth of crabs she got top price for them and by the time the evening news came on TV half the town knew she'd caught some real ones off Protection Island. When she headed out in the morning half the fleet followed her. She tossed her traps overboard and sat on deck reading a book for an hour or two, then hauled in her traps, all of them stuffed. She felt edgy, uneasy, and more than a bit scared. Ghostbusters, my ass, she growled. There's things too weird for anyone to talk about, and if you can't talk about it you should keep away from it.

She sold her crabs and went home with her money. Sitting in her little living room watching a rented video, she remembered the apple seeds or whatever they were. She took them from her pocket, looked at them a minute, then, almost as if she had no control over it, she gave one to the dog; then she took one out to the back yard, poked a hole in the mud, dropped in the seed, and squished earth around it. She didn't have a horse to give a seed to, so she ate the third seed herself as she walked back to the house. It tasted exactly like the little nuts you find in apricot pits, the ones your mother told you not to eat or you'd die, the ones you ate anyway and didn't die.

Nothing happened. She put the other seeds in an envelope and put the envelope in her top drawer with her socks and underpants. The dog didn't seem any different, either.

She went out every day of crab season and harvested impossible numbers of crabs. Nobody else got enough to write home about. After a while they stopped making jokes about it and started giving her the evil eye, cursing her under their breath, and refusing to sit next to her in the beer parlour.

And then she realized her period was overdue. "Goddamn," she cursed. "Goddamn, it's impossible!" She hadn't been near a man in three and a half years, and for all the fun she'd got out of that she might as well not have bothered.

She went to the doctor, expecting to be told she had cancer or something even worse, but the doctor took this test, that test and the next test, then phoned to congratulate her.

"I gotta go," she said rudely. "I gotta go watch out my living room window. The last time this happened three smartie pants on camels rode halfway around the world looking for a star. I missed that one, but I'll see 'er this time so help me God!" and she slammed down the phone.

She didn't stand at the window. She picked up the phone and dialled a number she had never thought she would use. It was easy. The next week she went to the mainland and went to the clinic and lay on a table and they spoke to her and put something in her arm and she got dozey and when she woke up they told her the suction abortion was finished, and she was to lie still for a few hours, but she could go home that evening.

She went home. She stayed home a few days, then, feeling healthier than she'd felt in her life, she went out on her boat, set her traps, caught a shitload, sold them, and went back to the house. She felt great.

She didn't get her period that month. Nor the next month. And her jeans didn't fit so good, either. This time she didn't phone the doctor or the clinic. She knew, with that dumb, numb certainty you have when you lose your wallet with all your identification in it, she knew it was all beyond her control.

People started saying they didn't know why Betty even bothered to go out on her boat, she could drop her traps in at the end of the wharf and the crabs would walk from Alaska just to crawl into them.

Her jeans got tighter and tighter, and finally she had to trade them in for a pair of those godawful things with the elastic panel in the front. Her mother kept asking her who the father was. Men who hadn't spoken to her in months began to smile, as if hoping to get on the good side of her before the kid came so they'd be on the good side of her when she was ready for more action.

She had never felt better in her life. Except that she knew she looked like the ass end of a southbound bus. No varicose veins, no morning sickness, no sore back—and, when the time came, almost no warning. She went to the hospital because her water broke, and an hour later her son was born. Beautiful. No doubt about it, beautiful. Curly blond hair, huge blue eyes, perfect hands, feet, arms, legs, totally human to all appearances and smiling happily.

She breastfed him until his teeth came in, straight, even, and perfect, and then she switched him to cow's milk from a cup. He smiled, he drank, he gooed, he gurgled, he ate everything she gave him, and he got lovelier every day. He sat up when he was supposed to, he crawled when he was supposed to, and when it was time, he learned to walk. That was when the dog, who had been spayed when she was five months old, gave birth to one coal black bitch pup with the most unusual red eyes anybody had ever seen. It was also the time a tree sprouted in the back yard.

Betty knew things had been set in motion and nothing, least of all herself, was going to stop that motion. It all had to do with the law of inertia, and how, once overcome, it took more to stop the forward motion than it had taken to start it all up. And what had started it up was hooking the ass of the seawoman.

She wasn't surprised when the time came that the seawoman appeared beside the crab boat and asked Betty where her son was.

"He's at home," Betty said, reaching for the fish club, "and you're not getting him! I'll kill you if you make a move towards him."

"Won't do you any good," the seawoman warned. "A bargain has been struck."

"Bugger that," Betty answered. "You tricked me! I let you go in return for full crab traps, that's the only bargain we made."

"You put a cod hook through my butt and you'll make reparation!"

"I let you go!"

"And your traps are full!"

"Keep your goddamn crabs and stay away from my kid!"

"In a pig's eye," the seawoman laughed. But she vanished under the waves.

Afterwards, Betty could never remember how it was instead of nine seeds in the envelope there were suddenly only six. She didn't remember planting any. She didn't remember giving any to the dog. She didn't remember eating any. But there she was, looking like she'd swallowed a pumpkin seed. Her mother wailed and moaned about the disgrace of it all, one illegitimate child was bad enough, but two, oh my God what will the neighbours think.

"My neighbours aren't capable of thought," Betty said, "and neither are yours. Besides, half the judges and lawyers in this town are provable bastards."

Her second son was born as easily as the first. And he was just as beautiful. Curly brown hair, big brown eyes, gorgeous smile, and the second most pleasant disposition on the face of the planet. She breastfed him, and when his teeth came in she weaned him onto a cup. He did all the right things at all the right times, and when he started to walk, the spayed bitch gave birth to one black bitch puppy with glowing red eyes, and a second tree began to sprout in the yard.

When the second son was three and a half, his older brother was seven years old, and the seawoman came back wanting one of the kids. Betty was ready for her. She heaved lead sinkers at the seawoman and had the satisfaction of seeing one of them bounce off the critter's head.

"Now piss off!" she shouted, "or I'll cut loose with the three-oh-three."

"You can't change destiny!" the seawoman raged.

"Go tell someone who cares!"

And now Betty was again pregnant, her mother was again in a panic, and the people in town were wondering aloud who the guy was. Nobody ever saw Betty with anyone. Nobody ever saw anyone coming out of her house before dawn, or after it for that matter. You could go around any hour of the day or night and you would never find some man in his sock feet watching TV and drinking beer, so what was the answer? Someone decided Betty was going to Vancouver, to the sperm bank, and making withdrawals. The men growled about it. The women looked interested: here was a way you could have a kid and not do the other things, like wash stinking socks you'd rather toss into the incinerator.

The third child was a boy with curly black hair, dark eyes, long thick dark eyelashes, and a smile guaranteed to melt the heart of a principal. As with the other two, so with him. When he was three and a half his brother was seven and his oldest brother was ten and a half and the seawoman came back looking for one of the kids. This time Betty fired a load of salt from a shotgun, and the seawoman ducked under the water just before the stinging bits of salt crystal reached her face. Whatever it was she yelled got lost in a column of bubbles which rose up beside the crab boat and broke, splashing rainbow droplets onto the deck.

Then the last three seeds disappeared. Betty searched high and Betty searched low, but there was not a sign of them anywhere. She had one old spayed black bitch in the house and three young jet black bitches with red eyes in the back yard, she had three trees like no tree she had ever seen before, she had three gorgeous sons, and she had another pot belly growing under the waistband of her jeans. She suspected if she'd had a horse, she would be up to her eyebrows in pony harness.

The fourth child was born and it was a girl. Betty was so amazed she almost blurted out the whole story, but she was only amazed, not stupid, so she just stared in what the others thought was wonder at the little girl staring back up at her. "Looks just like her mother," they said. Betty waited until they were out of the room, then she unwrapped her daughter and checked to make sure she had legs instead of a fishtail.

When the little girl was three and a half years old her next older brother was seven, the one up from that was ten and a half and the oldest was fourteen. This time the seawoman did not appear demanding one of the kids. It wasn't until the oldest boy was sixteen and Betty had started to relax, that the seawoman leaped from the water and landed on the deck of the crab boat, with what Betty knew damn well was Neptune's triton held threateningly in her hands.

"Don't move," she said, "or I'll spear you through the belly."

"You're not getting my kids," Betty vowed.

"I'll get the whole shiterooni one way or the other. You'll see!" And the seawoman garbled some nonsense in a language Betty didn't understand, spit on the deck, and sailed back over the side into the chuck.

The next day the first-born son told Betty he was going out into the world to seek his fortune. "I'm sick of school," he said, "and I've quit."

"Don't do that," she begged. "You don't know what's waiting for you out there."

But nobody ever talked sense to a sixteen-year-old. The next morning off he went with his black bitch with the red eyes. He got as far as Nanoose when fate caught up with him. Fate in the shape of a sweet-faced young girl in blue jeans, a cotton knit sweater with the sleeves pushed halfway up her arms, and a pair of sneakers on her feet.

"Hi," said the first-born son.

The young girl did not smile at him. She just nodded hello and a big tear slipped down her face.

"Why are you crying?" he asked.

"Because," she said, "there's this awful evil old ugly lives in the bay and my father has said I'm to marry the man who can get rid of it. And the only men who have showed up to try are old, fat, bald, ugly, and half of them chew snoose. If they don't kill the evil old ugly it'll take me off and I suppose gobble me up, and if they do kill it I'll wish they hadn't because being eaten up would be great compared to marrying to one of them!"

"Ah, hey," he said, "it won't be that bad."

He went down to the beach at Nanoose Bay and sat in the shade of an arbutus tree.

"What are you doing?" the girl asked.

"I think I'll catch me some rays," he said. "If the evil ugly awful wotzit shows up you can wake me up by putting your earring in my ear." He went to sleep.

"Some help you are," she sniffed.

The evil ugly awful old wotzit came swishing and slithering through the water. Six fat, old, bald, ugly, snoose-chewing losers leaped from the bushes to do battle with it, and they all lost. Just before the evil ugly awful old wotzit grabbed the pretty young girl, she took her earring from her ear and pushed it through the lobe of the first-born son's ear. He got to his feet, picked up a stick in one hand and a stone in the other, and went at the beast with a vengeful fury. "Sic 'er," he yelled, and the black bitch with the red eyes got into the act. The beastie decided enough was enough and off she or he or it went, roaring bloody murder.

The father of the lovely young girl had no choice but to give permission for her to marry Betty's first-born son. The wedding party lasted a year and a day and everyone showed up to dance, sing, eat, and celebrate, including Betty, her other two sons, and her young daughter.

When the wedding party was finished, the oldest son set about being a mature and responsible married man. He went out every day with his black bitch with the red eyes, and he looked for work. Or something.

Not far from Nanoose is a high sandstone bluff on which is painted Jesus Saves. Nobody has ever said what it is gets saved, and nobody knows who the tinderwit is who went up there to paint the message. But half a mile in back of that bluff, hidden in the green forest, is the castle of a giant with one eye in the middle of his forehead. The oldest son, out in search of a job, with all the intelligence of any seventeen-year-old, climbed up the bluff and entered the bush looking for work.

Instead of work he ran into the one-eyed Fomor, who immediately tried to rip his head off and push it down his throat. The black bitch with the red eyes leaped forward and fastened her teeth into the shoelace of the giant. He tripped over her, fell down, hit his head on a rock, and was knocked unconscious. The oldest son quickly pulled the giant's sword from its scabbard, lopped off the giant's head, then, because he might have been stupid and he might have been a fool but he wasn't without some basic survival skills, he took the giant's armor, which was studded with jewels and gems inlaid in silver and gold. He then beat a hasty retreat, as they say, leaving the body to the crows and coons, and arrived back at his father-in-law's place with the giant's goodies.

"Not bad," the avaricious old man said, "not bad at all," and he took it all as payment for room and board. Which left the oldest son with nothing for himself except the earring his wife had given him before he had scooched off the evil, ugly thing. But he had his room and board and he didn't feel so pressed to find work, which gave him time to learn to play the guitar.

The evil ugly he'd chased off heard the sound of the music and came back to investigate. "Hey, you," said the father-in-law, "get out there and get rid of that thing or I'll. . ." He never did say what. The eldest son went out to do battle with the evil ugly. He took the Fomor's sword with him and swung it and swang it and flailed with it. He cut, he jabbed, he parried, he hacked a big hunk off one of the heads of the awful thing. The head landed on the sand, wailing and howling horribly, and while the eldest son kicked at it to shut it up, the rest of the beast heaved itself up and grabbed for the young wife. And got her.

"No!" the boy yelled. "No, not her! I'll give you everything I've got but not her."

"You don't have anything," the evil ugly awful said.

"Me! Take me!" he pleaded. So the evil ugly awful put the young wife back on the sand and reached for the oldest son.

"Gotcha!" he yelled triumphantly, slicing off another head.

"*Liar!*" the evil ugly awful thing screeched, retreating.

Everyone figured that the loss of two heads would be enough to keep the thing out of the area for years to come. Even the father-in-law was impressed. Everything seemed fine and dandy. But, walking with his wife along the beach, just across the island highway from the Jesus Saves sign, the young husband saw a hoochie built up against a bank.

"Who lives in that mess?" he asked.

"Don't you go anywhere near it," his wife told him. "It's an awful place. Nobody who goes there ever comes back."

Betty's oldest son was all of eighteen by now, and what good did it ever do to tell any eighteen-year-old to stay away from dance halls, pool halls, beer parlours, or whorehouses? Bold as a jay he walked up to the hoochie and knocked on the door. An old old old old old *old* woman, who was really the seawoman in disguise, came to the door and smiled from ear to ear.

"Welcome, young sir," she said. "I have seen your deeds of derring-do on the beach. Come in, come in and let your granny make you a cup of tea and fill you full of chocolate chip cookies."

"You come back from there," his wife hollered. So, of course, he stepped through the door of the hoochie and *kerpow*, the old old old old old woman who was the seawoman in disguise hit him a lick on the back of the head with a hunk of wood and he fell down on the floor as stiff as a corpse and he lay there. Finished.

One of the trees in Betty's back yard died. Immediately. The leaves fell off with a clitter and a clatter and the sap drained from the wood. What had been a living tree at three in the afternoon was a bunch of dead dry sticks at three-oh-five.

"Something," said the second son, "has happened to my older brother." He called his dog with the red eyes and headed off up the highway, thumb out, and not two seconds did he waste listening to what his mother thought about it.

As with the first, so with the second. Everything. Right up to the time he was walking along the beach with his wife and he saw the little hoochie and asked who lived there. "Oh, stay away, please," the young wife pleaded, "my last husband went there and . . ."

And up he marched and banged on the door. An old old old old woman opened the door, invited him in, and promised him tea and cookies, and he said, "Oh, I don't think so. My brother went in there and hasn't been seen since."

"Hasn't been seen since," the old old old old woman laughed. "*I've* seen him every day since. Look, there he is, sitting at the table, eating cookies."

The second son poked his head inside to see his brother and *whack*, the seawoman in disguise let him have it on the back of the neck with a big stick and he fell inside the house, landed on his face on the floor and then lay there, deep-sixed.

The second tree died in the back yard. And you know what happened next. The youngest son set off with his black dog and as with the first two, so with him, right up to and including the time he got biffed on the back of the head and laid out on the floor like another piece of petrified cordwood.

The third tree died. Betty looked at her little daughter and sighed. Thank God. This one was too young to go trudging up the island highway yammering on about adventure and seeking a fortune. Everyone knew crap like that was gender stereotyped. Besides, the kid was too young.

So the three brothers lay stretched out on the floor of the hoochie and the evil awful ugly horrid beastie rambled around doing awful things to unsuspecting people. The father-in-law kept pawning jewels he pried from the armour of the Fomor. The thrice-widowed young woman sat in her window sewing fine seams until even she began to think it a thankless task. Betty went out every day and caught crabs, sold them, put the money in the bank, and watched her daughter grow to puberty.

Puberty brings change. And those changes turn a little girl riding a tricycle into a young woman dancing holes in her shoes at the Black Cat Bar and Grill. And one night while sipping a beer she heard a story about three brothers who fell afoul of the old old old old witch at Nanoose. "My brothers!" she cried.

She went home, told her mother to stop sniffling and weeping, called her black bitch with the red eyes, and headed north, towards Nanoose. As with the first three . . . not on your life!

The first thing she did was go to the father-in-law and, cool as a cucumber, take the sword off the wall. "This isn't yours," she said quietly. "It belonged to the Fomor and then to my brother and so now it's mine. And you, you old hooligan," and she held the tip of the sword against the old man's bulbous nose, "had better stop pawning those jewels or you are going to be in serious trouble and there will be another kind of jewels on the chopping block, you dig?"

Then she went out on the beach and played her oldest brother's guitar. The evil awful ugly horribilis heard the music and came to see who was so stupid as to invite her to visit.

"Hey," the young woman hollered, "how come you're so hard to get along with, anyway?"

"I don't know," the beast replied.

"Think about it."

"How do you do that?"

"Dummy, you put your heads together!" So the horribilis did and when all the heads were together, the girl lopped them off in one swish.

"Are we supposed to get married or something?" the young wife asked.

"Not likely," the girl replied. "You've already got husbands stacked up like cordwood in that hoochie up the beach." And she headed up to the hoochie, dragging the sword behind her. She knocked on the door and the old old old old woman who was really the seawoman in disguise opened the door. She stared, puzzled as all get-out to see the young girl.

"Who are you, dearie?" she asked.

"Why have you got my brothers stacked up like cordwood in that hoochie?"

"Your brothers?" the old old old old woman laughed. "No, I think not, my dear."

"So why are they in there?" the girl insisted.

The old old old old woman told her the story about the cod hook, and the price to be paid for insulting her. "And so, since their mother wouldn't give me one of them, I took all three of them, and I'm going to keep them!" she cackled.

"What an asshole you are," the girl yawned. "You've got three unconscious men in a rathole of a hoochie, and you've got three black bitches with red eyes howling around on the beach so you can't even come out and go into the water for a swim, you're a prisoner in your own lean-to shack, and you think you *won* something? My mother lives in a nice warm insulated house, she's got TV and hot running water and a microwave and a new car and she eats three squares a day and drinks beer if she wants and *you* think you've *won* something." And she laughed. And laughed.

"You shut up," the seawoman bellowed, and she charged through the door, intending to rip off some skin and pull out some hair. There were at that point four black bitches with bright red eyes howling around in the dried seaweed and assorted flotsam and jetsam and they went for the old old old old woman who was the seawoman in disguise and that was the sum total of that.

The young woman went into the hoochie, leaving the dogs to do their bit in the story, and with the sword she tapped each of her brothers lovingly on the top of the head. "Rise, oh idiot," she laughed, and each of them rose, the third one first, the second one second, and the first one last.

All three were overjoyed at finding themselves resurrected, and all three kissed their baby sister on the cheek. Then all three headed off down the beach to have a heart-to-heart with their mutual father-in-law about jewels, gems, and debts owing. What they ever decided about the pretty young wife is really nobody's business but their own.

The young girl whistled for her dog, and, trailing the sword behind her, followed the brothers down the beach. She traded the sword for the guitar, and went back to her mother's house knowing even before she got there that she would find all the trees growing happily in the back yard, healthier and stranger than ever.

"It's over, then," Betty sighed happily.

"It's over," the daughter agreed.

And it was. The next morning when Betty and her daughter went down to the pier to take the boat out, they were stopped by the fisheries inspector who told them that all crab, shrimp, and prawn fishing on the coast had been suspended indefinitely.

"Why?" they asked.

"Dioxins," he said, pointing to the putrid mess pouring from the pulp mill.

The daughter shook her head, anger beginning to boil deep inside her. "Just goes to show," she sighed. "Not all the evil, awful, dirty, rotten, ugly, scumsuckers are gone, after all!" And she sat down on the pier to plan her next move against those who would ruin life for the rest of us. "There's gotta be," she mused, "some way to get those bastards to put their heads together!" 🍎

Peg

. . . and whatsoever Adam called every living creature,
that was the name thereof. . .

Genesis 2:19

This story is for Nancy Mitchell, who actually DID!

The first time Peg Brady heard
her English teacher read out the line "What's in a name? That which
we call a rose / By any other name would smell as sweet," something
inside her relaxed. Why, of course! Even if you called it a cabbage,
a toad, or a waste paper receptacle, it would be a rose and smell as
nice, have thorns to rip your skin and come in any number of
varieties and colour combinations. People would still plant them
along fences and in front of picture windows. Even if you called
them stinking bait cans you'd want them rambling up a trellis
alongside the back steps so you could sit of an evening in the dappled
shade and listen to the contented hum of the bumbly-bees or the
zinging zip of the ruby-throated hummingbirds.

And not just roses; angels would still be angels, even if you called them chicken pox. They would still fly around heaven and play harps and watch over you at night and be there to whisper in your ear if you were in danger of being tempted. You could change the name of Haslam Pond, you could call it anything you wanted to call it, the silliest name you could come up with, and it would still be what it was, and the dragonflies would still zip back and forth, stitching each minute into the fabric of the day, each day into the tapestry of time. Frogs would plop into the water, ripples would tremble wider, wider, until they were lost from sight out near the deep part where the big kids dove from the rock in the summertime. Whether you called them night hawks or skeeter hawks or soapsuds, they would still swoop and dive against the pastel evening sky, and their call would still make your throat tighten up until it felt like getting ready to cry, only happy.

That one line solved a lot of problems for Peg Brady, and helped form her entire personality. She never did understand the big deal people made out of names. When Rupert Van Horne publicly stated he hoped his pregnant wife would give birth to a boy "to carry on the family name," Peg looked at him with open puzzlement and didn't say a word. Rupert misunderstood both the look and the silence, interpreting them as being some kind of radical feminist statement.

"Of course," he hurried to add, blundering in ever deeper, managing without half trying to trap his own foot in his own mouth, "of course, if it's a girl she'll be welcome; after all, more and more girls are choosing to keep their own names when they get married."

Peg continued to stare. The poor kid wasn't even out yet, and Rupert had her married off, he'd be a grandfather in five minutes at this rate.

"Oh, now, Peg." Rupert acted and sounded as if Peg had said something incendiary." You know what I mean."

"Rupert," Peg confided gently, "half the time I don't even understand what you *say,* how could I even begin to understand what you *mean?*"

"Ha ha," said Rupert, preferring to pretend it was all a big joke. Better to pretend to joke than to run the risk; you never knew with Peg Brady. She might look at you with wide brown eyes and then burst into laughter, or she might lift you one alongside the ear and send you arse over appetite.

Peg did not, as did her many brothers and sisters, drop out of high school and take a job. She stuck it out, the first of the family to stay long enough to graduate. So everyone got into the act. Never mind the notes and letters mimeographed on pink, green, yellow, and buff paper, explaining that the school hall was small, space was at a premium, and please invite only your parents to the big do. All of the Bradys scrubbed themselves shiny clean, pulled on their best outfits, shined their boots and shoes, and trooped off to see Peg get her paper. No sooner was it in her hand than they were on their feet cheering and clapping, whistling as loudly as if they were at a soccer game with the home team sliding the tie-breaker past the goalie seconds before the whistle blew. "As if," sniffed the assistant vice-principal, "any of them had cared a whit for education at any other time in their lives."

Peg toyed with the idea of university and rejected it. There wasn't anything she wanted to do or be enough to spend all that money, and she believed she'd go weird sitting around in school day after day listening to adenoidal explanations of things she hadn't really wanted to know about anyway. So she went to work on her Uncle Gus's fishboat, cooking and deckhanding, making good money during fishing season and sitting around on pogey when the season was over and the fleet was on the beach. She learned to drink draft beer, play pool, and sock her money away when it was coming in so she'd have some when there was only pogey between her and the cold winds of winter.

Then the bottom fell out of fishing and Uncle Gus lost his boat to the bank. The government responded to the economic disaster which, in the opinion of the coast people, was the result of the government's own stupid policies. Seventy-thousand-dollar-a-year bureaucrats arrived to study the situation, and they met with sixty-thousand-dollar-a-year experts in marine resources, and they all sat around in board rooms and studied charts and statistics, graphs and analyses, and never so much as looked at the ocean or the spawning streams, or the shameful logging practices which had turned the spawning streams into disaster zones. The logging companies denied any responsibility. The bigger the company, the louder the denial, until the corporations were screaming and yelling, hiring academics to proclaim and yell along with and for them.

Now any bushbunny or ridgerunner knows that it takes four to six years for the roots of a downed tree to start to rot, and that once the roots start to go, there's nothing left to hold the earth in place.

Enough wells have caved in, enough outhouses have suddenly dropped into their own holes, for even the most slack-jawed and vacant-eyed to make the connection between falling a tree and having the earth cave in. But when a steep slope in the Queen Charlotte Islands, logged bare and left naked under the constant rain and mist, suddenly shifted, and a mile-wide slide went downhill, erasing forever a spawning stream, an academic with a degree in forestry said publicly the clearcut logging and subsequent erosion had nothing at all to do with the mud slide. "It's rain," he said seriously, "causes mud slides." Which ought to be expected in a place known as a rain forest. Six other slides in six other places that year caused six other spawning streams to vanish, and it was the same all up and down the coast, and had been for years. But cast not too many aspersions on the forestry expert; there was once a president of an enormous navel-gazing country who believed acid rain was caused by trees, and water pollution caused by duck droppings.

"What you going to do, Uncle Gus?" Peg asked.

"Me?" he laughed. "Hell fire and damnation, girl, I'm gonna get pissy-eyed drunk. Then I'm gonna go tell the man at the bank that if his parents ever decide to get married I'll donate a coupla bucks to the party. And then," he almost managed to grin, "I guess I'll put in for pogey and when that's finished, I guess get myself into that there whoofare line."

Peg talked to Raspberry about it and he agreed with Gus. Raspberry's real name was LaFramboise, and if he had a first name, nobody knew what it was. He cursed in two languages and vowed to God he'd kill someone sooner or later, but other than that everything he had to say fit hand-in-glove with what Uncle Gus had said. "Fuck 'em all."

"What you gonna do?"

"Me?" Raspberry put a bit of snuff under his bottom lip and sucked on it idly. "Ah hell, I don't know. Prawns, maybe, if the dioxins from the pulp mill have left any of 'em fit to eat. If not, well, I guess I could run dope the way they used to run booze. Be better'n doin' charter for those goddamn gringo tourists."

Peg collected Unemployment Insurance for five months, then got a job driving a five-ton stake truck, delivering alder firewood, sixty dollars a measured cord. She didn't have to fall the trees, she didn't have to buck off the branches, she didn't have to cut it into stove-length rounds, she didn't have to split those rounds into pieces. All she had to do was load and unload the truck. All she had to do was back up the truck to a mountain of stove wood, heave it one piece at a time onto the back of the truck, climb up onto the truck bed and stack the wood, load the truck from front to back, secure the stake sides, be sure her red plastic was flapping so the cops wouldn't have anything to bitch about, drive the load to the address, and unload it. Unloading was easy. All she had to do was find out where the householder wanted the wood, then start dropping it off the truck.

Load after load, day after day, five, sometimes six days a week, and the pay stank like old camel shit. Sixty dollars a cord and out of it came the wood lot permit, gas for the truck, gas and chain oil for the saws, new tires and repairs to the truck when needed, new chain and repairs to the saws when needed, the wages of the guys sweating their guts out in blistering sun or bone-chilling rain, and her own wages. Peg figured that all in all, the gas and oil companies profited more from her calluses and her aching back than she did.

"I figure," the exhausted little man sighed, sharpening his chain saw with practised strokes, "the fuckin' stuff costs us forty dollars a cord before we start payin' wages."

"You'd be better off on welfare," Peg suggested carefully.

"Hell, honey," he laughed, "I *am* on welfare. And the fuckers subtract what I make doin' this from the monthly cheque. So," he shrugged and spat something more than tobacco juice into the fine sawdust, "So, official-like, my wife and me's split up. That way she gets better whoofare."

"Holy shit," Peg breathed.

"Oh well." He packed away his saw file. "Adds some spice to it all. Been together eighteen years and here I am, sneaking away before dawn, just like when we was goin' together. That way, her'n the kids is better off, and I can fuckinwell prove to the income tax that I don't make enough at this bullshit job for them to get too excited." He rose slowly and crinked his back to get the ache out of it. "Read in the paper where the Prime Minister just spent hisself a hundred and fifty thousand tax dollars to get his official residence redecorated. Hundred and fifty thousand goddamn dollars! To redecorate. Hell, my entire life ain't worth a hundred and fifty thousand dollars. Ain't a house in the whole town worth that. You can just bet it'll be a cold day in hell before I pay any more income tax, I tell you."

Peg nodded, pulled on her heavy leather gloves, and began heaving pieces of wood into the truck. She figured she was making about a dollar an hour less than the legislated minimum wage. The only good thing about it all was she had listened to every word of advice from Uncle Gus, Raspberry, and Howie the faller. The job was under the table, free and clear, and she didn't declare it.

Hung by the petard of widely advertised election promises, the federals were finally forced to stop talking and do something. Their solution was re-education for the unemployed.

Peg didn't really want to go to college for a year or so to become a hairdresser and go on welfare with all the other unemployed hairdressers. Nor did she want to go to college to become a practical nurse, to join all the unemployed practical nurses.

She didn't want to go back to school anyway. All she wanted to do was get a job that paid a living wage without killing or crippling her. But Trades Training for Women paid you at least as much as she was getting doing firewood, and maybe she'd get something out of it. Maybe an apprenticeship and a chance to work towards journeyman's papers. Although how a woman could become a journeyman puzzled her, and she wasn't sure what good it would do to become a tradesman in a place where fifteen thousand master journeymen were already unemployed. But what the hell, firewood season was winding down and her back ached like fire.

There has always been doubt on the coast about whether or not the governments, municipal, provincial, or federal, know what in hell they want or what in hell they are doing. But in this case, every level of government knew what they did *not* want. They did not want any hard-headed ham-fisted red-necked instructors asking why in hell they should teach the wife how to be a pipefitter, Chrissakes, I been fittin' pipe for sixteen years and I got my ticket and I'm still outta work. They did not want any gravel-voiced old bozo squinty-eyeing them and asking what use could come of teaching a twenty-four-year-old five foot two and a half inches tall one hundred and twelve pound person how to be a diesel mechanic when eight per cent of the qualified diesel mechanics in the province were standing in line for a chance to be retrained so they could step into the electronic age. They did not want any snoose-lipped second genera-tion Swede who had gone from grade eight to the bunkhouse, from whistle punk to second loader asking what christly good it was going to do to teach women how to drive truck when there wasn't a logging operation in the whole province with a full crew working full time. Above all, they did not want some smart-ass advisor like Uncle Gus telling the women to forget about fishing or marine mechanics and get into electronic technology. So they bypassed those steely-eyed losers and turned instead to a group of people who would never be a threat to any part of the system.

Few if any had their tickets. Fewer still had actually worked at what they were going to teach, and those who had worked, hadn't worked full time or seriously, and certainly not soberly. But they could all talk like hell and before you had a chance to ask them, they would jump up, smiling widely, to tell you, whether it interested you or not, that they, in fact, thought, and practice, were feminist men.

Nobody stopped to consider that the term feminist man makes as much sense as the term peaceful weapon or the term military intelligence, nobody stopped to consider that hiring counterculture people to supervise, organize, and teach trades training courses makes as much sense as expecting the academics to understand education from the point of view of the long-suffering kids. These were gentle, sensitive, non-threatening men with highly developed communication and comprehension skills. Most of them had skipped over the forty-ninth at about the time Vietnam was dying on colour TV in the living room. That noble and worthy act of conscience was, for many, the last move that got made for years. They brought with them some of the most highly advanced educations ever seen on the coast and took those educations into the toolies where they grew beards, ate granola, contemplated their karma, refused to use birth control because it was not bio-degradable, refused to send their kids to any kind of school, and designed and built houses with materials they scrounged and salvaged from the beaches. These examples of playschool art and tree house construction were patterned on the principles of cosmic carpentry, which hold that what comes around goes around and what is held in place with a mortar of honey and bulgur wheat will never succumb to gravity. Electronic engineers smoked dope, kept goats, and had open-ended meaningful relationships with as many others as they could find time and energy to accommodate. Some sat for hours chanting Om mane padme hum and others stood twitching and humming hari hari until even the goats began to complain. They might all still be up in the ferns, salal, and weeds except for two overwhelming influences: the word of Werner hit the west coast, and feminism made it from the radical ranks to the India cotton crowd.

The word of Werner was heard and suddenly, incredibly, overwhelmingly, they all had elitist peer group approval to shave their beards, throw off their Pied Piper rags and tatters, pull on polyester suits, and become exactly the kind of people their New York, Los Angeles, and Detroit parents had wanted them to be. They sold their pickup trucks, phoned Daddy and Mommy, floated what were called loans but known to be gifts of money, bought silver Malibus, and headed out into the world, only some twenty years late, to sell real estate to each other and re-enter the system with a mature view towards altering it in humanistic patterns. There they ran headlong into the changes which had taken place while the gentle sensitive non-threatening guitar playing men had been out in the ozone.

They ran into women who were no longer ready, willing, able, and eager to leap into long cotton skirts and wander barefoot and passive, having endless numbers of snot-nosed and runny-eared kids named Comfrey, Raven, Sturgeon, or Evening Star. Nor were the women any longer willing to accept it was their purpose in life to do all the work while the men sat around discussing meaningful things like How I Coped With Primal. Instead of digging, hoeing, raking, planting, watering, weeding, harvesting, and cooking the produce of the gardens while clearing land, milking all those goddamn goats, fixing the roof, digging the wells and outhouses, and organizing playschool, primary school, and correspondence courses, the women were looking to their own ideas. Instead of listening to the men's analysis of birth control and abortion, the women were belatedly realizing who it was had cared for and worried over and brought up the toddling paragons of virility and ego. Better late than never they said, and handed the kids over to the men.

Stuck with the kids, up to their ears in goat shit, and facing the horror of having to make some meals themselves, the men looked around wildly for an escape. And found it where they had always found it. In the system they had pretended to reject. They ran home to Big Daddy and he, in the form of government, rewarded them by making them the instructors in the Introduction to Trades Training for Women program.

None of the patrists cared that in a region where women have always learned to drive logging trucks and city busses, own and deckhand fishboats, apply shakes and shingles to their own roofs, chop and stack wood, and generally do whatever needs done, there might be some women who could teach trades. The patrists managed to overlook entirely the island's considerable population of women carpenters and welders. They looked on hippie men the way the father of the prodigal son looked on him, and if they didn't quite kill the fatted calf, they did add to the ranks of fat cats.

The gentle sensitive non-threatening men learned the few words of formula-speak required, and made their moves. Gotta go to work, honey, they said, handing back the kids they had never wanted to look after. The counterculture women gaped. What was this? Work? He is actually going to go to work? All their mothers' conditioning snapped into place. They left the consciousness-raising groups and began to lay out the work clothes, pack the lunches, set the alarm clock, get up first, start the woodstove, make the coffee, waken the working man, feed him his breakfast, stuff him into his clothes, wind up his key, and head him off in the right direction.

And Peg Brady ran headlong into them when she started back to school. Peg did not need to learn how to handle a chain saw. There was nothing could go wrong with her car that she couldn't fix with her automotive repair manual. She did not yearn to be a plumber and clean shit-encrusted plastic toys out of the gooseneck. But times were tough and they were willing to pay her to go to school.

She had expected almost anything. She had not expected what she ran into when she ran into the gentle sensitive non-threatening pacifist anarchist former longhairs. Most of what they said made no sense to her. Half of what they said contradicted the other half of what they said. They talked of the need for environmental awareness while insulating their vans with styrofoam, they talked of non-oppressive non-colonialist non-imperialist principles while vacationing in countries where people were so poor they sold their children to the male tourist industry, they talked of not being part of the consumer society while buying the most expensive and trendy camping gear and photography equipment.

The conversation of the women she understood. "After all," one said, "if I have to have some kind of shit job, it might as well pay twelve bucks an hour as three-fifty."

"After waitressing," another agreed, "anything will seem easy."

"After marriage and three kids," a third laughed, "even waitressing seemed easy!"

"Yeah," agreed the gentle, sensitive, non-threatening instructor, "you could take the mechanics course and then you'd be sure of an oil change every day. Ha ha."

"Oh God," the women groaned, "here come the barefoot-and-pregnant jokes."

"Get to play around with a dipstick whenever you want, ha ha," he laughed.

"Give it a rest, will you?" they asked.

"Or maybe you could be an electrician, get to pull a wire all day," he teased, and when nobody laughed, smiled, or grinned, he shook his head the way you do at a child. "The trouble with you women," he said, "is you don't have any sense of humour."

"Sure we do," Peg countered, "we're laughin' at you all the time," and the women guffawed, hoo-rahed, laughed, and chortled.

Gentle sensitive non-threatening counterculture men do not like to be taken lightly. They expect nothing but the fullest and most gentle of consideration. They insist at all times on being treated as something extremely precious and wise. It's their reward for pretending to be gentle sensitive and non-threatening. Otherwise they might just as well drink beer, eat pickled eggs, and fart all night like the others.

But it all had to come down in the guise of jokes. Anything else would expose how thin the veneer of supposed non-sexist awareness really was. Tradition, rumour, and mythos insist women have no sense of humour, and everyone has heard all that so often even some women believe it and laugh without humour just to avoid being told how humourless they are. Jokes about rape. Jokes about incest. Jokes about the guy who beat his wife over the head with a fifteen-pound rooster, then charged her twenty dollars so he could buy a new one because the rooster had died and it was her fault for being so hard-headed ha ha ha. Jokes about how a woman is like a rug and needs to be beaten every day to keep her in shape ha ha ha. Jokes about how a woman is like a violin and has to be played every day to keep her in tune ha ha.

Peg Brady was not amused. She'd been hearing jokes all her life, some better, some worse, and had long ago given up laughing at what she did not find funny. She wasn't the brightest woman in the world but she knew if someone keeps on telling jokes to someone who isn't laughing, then there is more than humour coming down, and she thought about that. She thought of her immigrant grandfather, with nothing more in common with the men he worked with than his biological plumbing arrangement, but those men accepted him in ways they would never accept Peg. She could talk their language, read it and write it, had known them all from birth, but even if she bothered to learn how to pee standing up there would be a barrier. And those jokes. Woman driver jokes, woman doctor jokes, did you hear about the woman who got her Delfen mixed up with her Crest toothpaste and when she woke up she had forty per cent less cavity, ha ha.

If she told her Uncle Gus, he would happily tap dance all over the instructor's face, but what would that do? Anyway, if it came to punch-out time, Peg could do the job herself. And even Uncle Gus, who loved her, made jokes about hookers and whores, about how if sex is a pain in the ass you're doing it the wrong way, ha ha. Even Uncle Gus thought it was a compliment to tell her she had a mind as good as a man's.

Peg thought about names, and the power of names. She thought about naming and the power of naming. She even spent a bit of time thinking about the Trojan horse and how they had thought it one thing and it turned out to be another, and how a joke was supposed to be harmless but could wear a hole in your soul that let your courage leak out and evaporate. A rose by any other name; an insult by any other name.

"Hey, Peg," the instructor called across the room, already grinning and laughing, "what's the difference between a fertilizer salesman and a woman?" Peg knew he had aimed it at her because she never laughed, and she knew from the faces of the other women that they knew as well as she did what was going on. What was really going on.

"Ah, for cryin' out loud," she exploded, "you still on that put-down kick of yours? Why don't you just come right out and admit you hate my guts instead of hiding behind this string of insults you call jokes?"

"What's the matter?" he teased. "Can't take a harmless little joke? What kind of person are you to get mad at a harmless little joke?" He looked around at all the women. None of them smiled, all of them refused to laugh at his jokes. "The answer," he said loudly, "is that the salesman sells his shit, the woman hands it out for free," and then he was laughing again.

Peg took a deep breath and very carefully put down the hammer she was holding. If you split the fucker's head open, she warned herself, you'll go to jail the same as if you'd assaulted a human being. Don't kill him. Don't argue. Get the power. Do the naming. In the naming of is power and control over, remember that.

And then Peg Brady had her finest hour and it only took a minute. She grinned from ear to ear, forced her voice to a companionable and friendly tone, even managed to paint the edges of her voice with appreciation and laughter.

"Hey," she said, managing not to choke on her words, "that's not bad."

He stared. The woman who never laughed was grinning.

"I've got one for you," she said easily. "Can you tell me two things every married woman does with her asshole every morning?"

He gaped.

"Why . . ." Peg started laughing even before she managed to form the words, and those women who had not heard or figured out the joke began to chortle, then laugh loudly and helplessly. "Why, she packs his lunch bucket and kisses him goodbye." 🍎

Frances

❦

You're supposed to love your children and adore your grandchildren. They tell you that after your children grow up and move away you suffer from what they call Empty Nest Syndrome. They never mention that other, worse one. The Refilled Nest Neurosis. And if they never mention it, you can't very well admit to having it or discuss it with anyone else.

Frances's son Daniel was more overbearing than ever. How could anyone manage to get more overbearing than Daniel had always been? Not easy, but he had managed. His belief in himself, his conviction he knew better than anyone what was good for everyone, was like a thick skin he wore over his body, a covering so insensitive, so calloused by use, he not only couldn't give credence to anybody else's ideas, he barely granted people the right or the room to have ideas. He came by it honestly enough: his father had never been certain anyone else had much right to an opinion. Dan had taken it one step further, though. Probably because his wife, Laura, was as convinced as Dan was that he knew everything. Ask her if she thought it was going to rain and she would say she didn't know, but would ask Dan when he came home.

The two children, however, were less convinced of their father's wonderfulness. They argued with him, and with their mother, and with each other, constantly, over the most petty things, until Frances thought she would reach out and bang their heads together.

Caroline knew Daniel better than he knew himself, and her way of dealing with her brother's overbearing bossiness was to imitate a duck in a rainstorm and just let it all slide off. Which would be fine, except it spurred Dan to greater efforts. Which Caroline blandly ignored. Which made Dan even more outrageous. Maybe when Frances was finished banging her grandchildren's heads together, she'd bang Daniel and Caroline's heads, too.

Which would leave only Caroline's daughter to deal with. Frances didn't have any idea what would work best on Tobee. A brick alongside the ear, perhaps, or an axe handle across the shoulders. Repeatedly. It wasn't hard to understand why Caroline had deliberately refused to consider marriage, it wasn't hard to understand or even approve of the stated refusal to submerge her life and plans in someone else's life and plans. It wasn't hard to understand how a woman could decide to have a child and raise it alone. What grated was that having decided all this on her own, with no consultation with her family, Caroline now seemed to feel she was entitled to something extra, something special, because, after all, she was a single mother and thus carrying the burden alone, required to be both mother and father. Frances often had to bite back uncharitable remarks. The problem was she wasn't at all sure how long she was going to be able to keep her lip buttoned now that Tobee herself had started turning the emotional screws. Manipulative, some would say. Too big for her britches, Frances thought. What mother didn't wind up as the be-all and end-all? Frances believed the statistics quoted on the afternoon news, about how the average man spent less than seven minutes per day "relating" to his children. How much did a woman lose if she opted for single parenthood? Seven minutes a day, seven days a week, less than four hours a month. Hardly enough to make a difference, certainly nowhere near enough to qualify Caroline for martyr status.

And yet there was something else in Tobee. Something admirable. Any time her manipulation didn't work, Tobee eyed Frances briefly, then smiled widely, acknowledging the secret they shared, the secret others couldn't bring themselves to admit.

"No, Miss," Frances had said quietly. "Push other people's guilt buttons to get what you want, but don't try to push mine. I don't owe you anything, you don't owe me. We're even."

"You're supposed to look out for kids," Tobee replied, and her voice was serious enough, almost preachy, but her eyes were bright with laughter.

"Oh, I do that, right enough," Frances answered. "I look out for them and when I see them I run at top speed in the opposite direction," and though Tobee didn't laugh, she did grin, and the undercurrent of tension between her and Frances was eased.

What wasn't eased was the impatience Frances felt every time Caroline said anything about how hard it was to raise a child alone. As far as Frances could see, the difference between her life and Caroline's life was minimal. But you couldn't say that to Caroline; she had early in life perfected the art of selective deafness.

And now all the fuss about the land. Some brain had decided there might be natural gas trapped under the bedrock and now the big companies were trying to buy up miles and miles and miles of fine farmland, no longer content to lease a space and put up their ugly pumps, they wanted the land itself, for condominiums, for apartment buildings, for hotels and convention centres, for supermarkets and shopping malls, and Dan right in there nudging and noodling, debating and coaxing, determined to either persuade Frances to sell by the logic of his business administration mind, or wear her down by the sheer weight of the words he poured on her head. He was running out of patience, though. Each time she said no he got a bit angrier. Each time he got angrier, Frances got more determined that whatever else she did in her lifetime, she would not sell the forty acres. Not as long as she lived!

He was talking again, his voice firm, and he had paper, pencil, and calculator, busily proving for the umpteenth time that if she sold she could invest her money and live on a very comfortable monthly allowance. She took a deep breath, determined to tell him to shut up, and then she couldn't have spoken to save her life. The pain was unbelievable. If she had been able to scream, she would have screamed. But she couldn't even gasp. Her ears filled with a roaring unlike anything she had heard before, the big fist closed around her chest and lungs, the hot wire burned into her brain. The world got smaller and smaller and smaller, like the thing that happens on the TV screen when the picture tube starts to go and the images shrink, shrink, shrink down to one pinpoint of light that finally, inevitably goes out. Dan's face got smaller and smaller, as if he were going farther and farther away. Then his face was gone, there was greyness everywhere, nothing but darkness. She thought she was dead, except she could hear the voices, hear Dan hollering for her to come back, hollering and hollering as if anything he had to say was going to make any difference. Laura was crying, Caroline was in hysterics, the kids were babbling. Babbling.

Except Tobee. Frances could hear Tobee's voice talking into the telephone.

"An ambulance, please, and be sure to send the stuff for heart attacks because I think that's what my grandma is having."

She was sure she was dying. Even the voices faded. It was like going to sleep. A feeling of tiredness that spread to her arms and legs until her hands and feet weighed a ton, and she thought, It's so nice to go to sleep. I'm so tired. I've been so tired for so long.

She wakened. And yet she didn't waken. She felt as if she were awake but she couldn't see anything. She tried to sit up and couldn't move. She tried to move her leg and it refused. She tried her arm, then her hand, finally she tried to move even so much as a finger. Nothing. She tried to talk. Nothing. She tried to scream, or cry, or holler, or whisper. Nothing. She nearly went crazy then. She thought she was dead and caught halfway between the heaven they had promised and the hell they had threatened.

When she wakened the next time she knew she was in hospital. She could tell by the smell. Alcohol and antiseptic, strong floor detergent and that other smell, from clothing and bedding boiled and sterilized. She tried to move. Nothing. She could not feel the bed under her or the covers on her. She might have been floating in mid-air. Daniel must be in the room, she could hear his voice. He was pontificating again, and Laura was agreeing with him. Caroline was sobbing softly, but saying over and over, "No, Momma said no and if that's what she wanted that's what she should have."

"Have? Look at her! You know what they said!"

"I don't care what they said. You know she wouldn't want it."

"She'll never know. She'll be like that until. . .until it's over!"

"No, Dan. She might get better."

"She isn't going to get any better, Caroline, and you know it."

"It isn't yours to decide."

"Not yet. But it won't take much to get the court to declare her incompetent, and under the terms, her own terms, of her will, that means I'll. . ."

"No, you can't."

But of course he could. He would because he could. And the forty acres of second growth would be gone, the five acres of clearing would be gone, probably the old house would go, too, and a trailer court or something equally disgusting would go in. The little pond would probably be called a "feature" and they'd build a phony Oriental bridge over the creek. The turtles and trout would vanish, someone would get the bright idea to put in goldfish. Or maybe it would be those dreadful channel catfish that go up and down the stream eating everything, growing bigger and bigger until they have to go into the lake to find food. There they breed and within ten years there isn't a trout in the lake.

Frances deliberately closed it off, forced herself back into that grey nothingness, and when she floated back up out of it again, the voices were gone.

Dear God, she thought. Dear God, please.

"Don't be frightened." The voice spoke right inside her head.

Wouldn't you know it, she thought, panicked beyond fear into some other kind of awareness. Wouldn't you know it, the one time you want to holler and screech and yell and roar and dither and blather, you can't move a muscle or make a sound.

"Please," the voice in her head said. "Please, don't be frightened."

"Who are you?" she demanded silently.

"Please. . ." The voice was thin, the words hesitant, and whoever, whatever it was, sounded as terrified as Frances herself was.

"Who?" she insisted silently. "Where?"

There were images, confused images, as if someone were shuffling a deck of cards. Frances thought of an out-of-control car she had seen once, slipping, sliding, slithering on black ice, and then she could see as plain as day something falling. The seeing became the feeling, and she was falling, falling, falling, tumbling over and over, bright flashes of light zooming past, like comets and meteors and even stars and planets.

"Oh," she managed.

"I can't do anything if you don't want me to do it," the voice pleaded. "You have to give me permission or. . ."

"Who are you?"

"I don't know what you mean."

"Are you. . . an angel?"

"What is 'angel'?"

Frances thought of angels. She thought of little chubby-faced cherubim and dignified seraphim and authoritarian archangels. "No," the little voice said, "I'm not one of those."

Frances never did come up with any kind of image that identified the little voice. Unless you considered a flickering candle flame an image. But even that wasn't right, it was just as close as the two of them could get.

"I can't make you think of something you don't know anything about," the little voice admitted.

"Do you have a name?"

"My name is Swoosh."

"Swoosh?"

"Well, that's what it sounds like. It isn't what it *is*, but it's what it sounds like."

"Does it mean anything?"

"Does Frances mean anything?"

"I suppose it does. Or did. Some names mean things. Like Peter means rock and James means . . ."

"Is Peter your name?"

"No! Frances is my name."

"And it doesn't mean rock?"

"No."

"Oh."

"What are you doing inside my head?"

"I'm not really inside your head, I'm just . . . here . . . and I don't think I can go back!"

Frances tried to console little Swoosh, and fell asleep trying. When she wakened she could open her eyes. Sunlight was coming through the window and it was so beautiful she wept.

"Oh. Oh, I can't stop it!" Swoosh almost panicked.

"It's okay," Frances said, and knew her voice was working again, too. "It's okay."

"What?" a voice cried. Then the face of the nurse came into focus, and Frances smiled. A lop-sided smile, but a smile. The nurse's eyes widened, then she smiled, too, and her smile wasn't at all lop-sided.

"Oh, how wonderful!" she thrilled. "How wonderful!"

"What," Frances managed to croak, "does a body have to do around here to get a cup of coffee?"

"You've got it," the nurse promised. "Lady, you have got it!"

There was a mad flurry, then. The doctors came in, like a herd of amazed trolls, poking and prodding and pushing and shoving and taking blood pressure. Looking in her eyes and down her throat, looking up her nose and at her fingers.

"I don't know what everything is supposed to *do!*" Swoosh panicked again.

"It's okay," Frances said and the doctors and nurses thought she was talking to them.

They took the needle out of her arm, they unhooked the machine at the side of the bed, and finally, they gave the nurse permission to bring in the promised cup of coffee.

"Here, dear," the nurse said gently, "I'll just get you sitting up a bit and we'll put these pillows behind you . . . that's it."

"Ahh," Frances sighed. "That's better."

The coffee was perfect. Swoosh had never tasted coffee before and even if she couldn't really taste it, but only tap into Frances's experience, Swoosh decided coffee was delicious. Frances slept for a while, then they came to wash her and change her nightgown.

Dan and Laura arrived first, then Caroline, who brought flowers and a big box of chocolates. Dan hovered, nervous, unable to believe that the woman they had told him would never come out of her coma was not only out of it but sitting up in bed and talking, even if one side of her face was slack and the arm and leg on that side didn't want to do anything.

"Daniel," Frances said clearly, "I am not incompetent. And I will never give permission for you to sell the land."

"Momma . . ."

"No," she said. "And if you say one more word about it I'll have the lawyer cut you out of the will altogether."

After they left, the nurse brought supper and Frances and Swoosh enjoyed every sip of soup, every bite of potato, and every morsel of chicken, even if it was ground to a paste. "Tell the doctor," Frances managed, "that my teeth work fine."

She hardly slept that night. Swoosh was busy, and needed Frances's help. "What does this do?" Swoosh asked.

"Moves my toes."

"All of them?"

"All of them."

"I only want to wiggle the big toe on your right foot." There followed a series of jerks and twitches, toe after toe, until, finally, the big toe on the right foot wiggled. "Good," Swoosh sighed with satisfaction. "Good, now I know how *that* works!"

Swoosh lifted the left arm, then the right arm. Swoosh clenched the left fist, then the right fist. She wiggled fingers, she made thumbs move, and then went to work on the sagging side of Frances's face.

"No," Frances said softly. "No, the hair is not supposed to *do* anything. It just is."

"I can make it wiggle. I can make it wave and. . ."

"If you can make it curl," Frances said hopefully. "I always wanted curly hair."

They noticed. As soon as they walked in the room they noticed the mop of curls. Question followed question, and Frances played it to the peanut gallery, vowing she had no idea what had happened. No, the nurse hadn't given her a perm. No, she had no idea. Nobody had touched her hair.

When the company left, the nurse came in with an aide and they began getting Frances out of bed.

"Be careful," she muttered, to them, and to Swoosh. "Easy on, now."

"I'm not sure what to do!"

"Easy on. Let's just wait a minute, now. Sit us in the chair is all, girls, please."

They sat her in the chair, then tied a safety belt around her so she wouldn't slide onto the floor. They stripped the bed and changed the linen, then put Frances back to bed. "All I need," Swoosh insisted, "is a couple of seconds with someone who can *do* it."

"Pick a young one," Frances sighed, "They walk better."

It was scary. She knew the precise second Swoosh left her. The greyness was back again, and the numbness. She couldn't move her arms or legs, she couldn't wiggle her fingers or toes, she couldn't open her eyes or make a sound. Just before she panicked, Swoosh was back, and so was light, and feeling, and sensation.

"I missed you," Frances admitted.

"It's very complicated." Swoosh sounded excited. "You wouldn't believe what all has to be done just to get one foot in front of the other without the entire body tip-tilting sideways!"

"I believe you," Frances smiled. "I've watched children learning how to do it."

That afternoon, when the nurse and the aide came back to get her out of bed again, Frances could do more than sag between them.

First one foot, then the other, her arms around their waists, her eyes squinting with concentration, even though Swoosh was doing the work. Step by unsteady step, as far as the door, then back again.

"We'll have you doing the hundred-yard dash in no time," the aide encouraged.

"Dancing," Frances managed. "I'm going to go dancing."

Nobody could believe it. The doctors were in and out and in and out and in and out all day, taking blood pressure, taking blood, looking in her eyes, listening to her chest. They loaded her into a wheelchair and took her down into the basement to where they kept all their expensive toys and they hooked her to this, hooked her to that, hooked her to something else. They flashed lights in her eyes, they asked questions and watched graphs while she answered, then they put her back in her wheelchair and took her back to her room.

"No more," she said.

"But," they protested.

"No." She shook her head firmly. "No X-rays. I don't need the radiation. No radioactive dye for you to follow through my veins and arteries. No. No more."

"But."

"Just accept the miracle, please." She patted his hand. "There are things you are never going to find with your gadgets and machines."

On the third day, they walked her to the elevator, then took her down to the rehab section.

"Easy on," she said. "We're not as swift as we'd like to think we are."

"You're doing wonderfully well."

"Yes, but we'll do better."

They helped her into the water, then stood on either side of her, two young women in swim suits, supporting her head, ready to help her.

"I have to think about this," she told them. "I have to think how it used to be. A bit like walking, I think."

"You take however much time you need," one woman said gently. "If all you do is float like you're floating now, you'll have done wonders."

"And miracles," Frances added.

She thought about being sixteen and lying on her back in the big pool just below the lower Nanaimo River Bridge. Swoosh helped.

The memory came back so clearly, so totally that Frances could smell the dust on the road, the tar on the bridge, the berries hanging on the bushes. The water lapped against the rocks, a kingfisher darted, scolding and yelling. Six dark-skinned dark-haired kids from the reserve sped past her, riding on a big inner tube from a logging truck tire. They grinned and waved and Frances waved back at them, then moved her legs gently, guiding herself towards the shore where her mother was sitting on a blanket, unpacking the potato salad.

"Way to go!" whispered one of Frances's helpers, sounding as if what she wanted to do was jump and yell and cheer and holler. "Way to *go!*"

They moved with her, but they weren't supporting her or helping her, they were just there with her, speaking encouragement, willing to wait until they were needed.

"How's that?" she asked, breathing heavily.

"That's just fine," they assured her.

"We'll do better tomorrow," she promised. "It's just . . . it's like if you had an electric train and something was wrong with one section of the tracks. You'd have to find a way to go around where you used to go through."

"You're doing wonderfully well." They helped her into a dry nightgown, then helped her into a wheelchair, to catch her breath and rest. She wanted to walk back to the ward, but she knew they were right when they said she'd had enough. Even Swoosh was tired.

They had meat loaf for supper. And the nurse did not bring it to her already ground and turned into paste. Swoosh thrilled to the tastes, to the texture, to the intricate process of chewing and swallowing.

"Don't you chew and swallow?" Frances asked. "Don't you taste?"

"No. We just . . . are."

Daniel, Laura, and the children came to see her before they left to go back to the city. The children argued over the chocolates and complained there weren't enough cherry centres. "Oh, shut up!" Frances snapped. "My God, does nothing suit you?"

"Kiss Grandma goodbye," Laura said hastily, "she's very tired."

"Grandma isn't tired at all," Frances replied. "Those kids are a pain in the ass. Put the chocolates down, you've been pigs enough for one day!"

They left without kissing or cuddling her and she didn't care. She was tired. Tired of ingratitude, tired of bitching, tired of more things than she wanted to waste time putting names to.

"We'll come and see you in a week or two," Daniel promised.

"Don't bring those children unless they've learned how to behave," Frances said clearly. "They are old enough to be civilized company. If they can't be nice, leave them at the kennel."

Caroline and Tobee came to see her, and that went better. Caroline sat staring at her mother as if she had never seen her before in her life.

"Are you going to ask me about my curly hair again?" Frances asked.

"No. No, I guess I can get used to that. It's just. . . I thought you were going to die. They said you would. . . and now. . . ."

"It's like magic," Tobee said clearly.

"It *is* magic," Frances agreed.

She went home a week later. The doctors would have loved to keep her in hospital for more tests, but Frances wanted to go home. She had to agree to have a homemaker come out every day to check on her and do the housework. Swoosh didn't have things exactly right, yet: Frances still walked with a bit of a limp, and sometimes one arm or the other would sort of flap out sideways.

"There's a lot to keep track of," Swoosh admitted.

"You sure it isn't too much for you? If you get tired. . ."

"No. No, it gets easier every day. And I love it! Without you I don't *feel* things, I don't taste them, I. . . just am."

"How do you mean?"

"Well, I just. . . wouldn't last very long. . . the air here is different and I don't think I could live without your lungs to do the breathing. And even if I did, I couldn't. . . move around. . . because the gravity is so different and. . ."

"You're sure?"

"Even if I could go back home, I wouldn't," Swoosh said quietly. "Things here are just so. . . green, and clean, and. . . cool."

Frances limped her way down to the pond and sat on a sun-warmed rock, watching the small trout dart and zip and zoom in the shadows. "Wanna try?" she offered.

"Would you mind?"

Frances got off the rock and lay down on the grass, where she knew she couldn't fall any farther. For long minutes she was paralyzed, just caught in the grey limbo, and then Swoosh was back, laughing breathlessly, and before Frances could ask even one question, she knew what it was like to be a small trout, moving through water, gliding and darting, fins moving quickly.

"Magic," she breathed.

People talked. Said it was a shame how sometimes you'd see Frances just sitting on a chair, face blank, her spell on her again. The homemaker nearly had a heart attack the day she found her lying on the grass, face up, eyes closed. But before the homemaker had her back to bed, Frances was fine again. "Don't worry," she insisted, "Don't worry, please, it's all right. It's just. . . a little fainting spell."

But it was worth it. Worth it because as soon as the homemaker left to phone the doctor and tell him Frances had fainted, Swoosh was in control and Frances was soaring high above the treetops, seeing the world with ten-power eyes, knowing what the hawk knows, the wind whistling through her pinions.

"We're just fine," she told the doctor. "We really are just fine."

Daniel had wonderful plans for the place. Each time he came to visit, he stood on the front porch and looked at the forty acres of trees he would sell to the logging company as soon as Frances died. He looked at where the trailer park was to go and smiled, spending his money before he had it.

And the years went by. Daniel's hair went grey, his face became lined, the children grew up, finally, thank God, and became decent human creatures, polite and even interesting. Caroline stayed Caroline. She put on weight, her hair began to streak with white, she had to get glasses, and Tobee went off to university. Still Daniel made his plans.

"Not while I'm alive," Frances laughed. "Not while there's a breath in my body!"

It was amazing, they said. Just amazing. There she was, riding a two-wheeler down to the store for ginger ale or coffee or to get her mail, then riding back home again, as if she were thirty-eight years old. You'd see her, summer, winter, spring, or fall, out walking the dog, which she hadn't even got until the year after she had her stroke, and the way she just stepped out and strode off you'd think she was younger than her own children. Hard to believe they'd all been shining shoes and pressing their good suits, ready to go to her funeral.

Frances sat on the porch watching the tall fir trees bending in the soft evening breeze. If second growth is like this, she thought, what must it have been like when this was all virgin timber?

"How long do you live?" she asked Swoosh.

"I don't know," Swoosh laughed happily. "Near as I know none of us has ever died."

"Eat your heart out, Daniel," Frances chuckled. "Eat your heart out."

"What if they start wondering? Asking questions?"

"I'll tell them," Frances decided, "that I owe it all to yogurt."

Doreen

❦

Graduation no longer loomed on the horizon, it was speeding towards them with ever-increasing abandon, followed by all those things the students had tried so hard to ignore: responsibility, self-determination, and the need to find a job and become self-supporting.

Doreen knew she was going to graduate with honours. Doreen knew her marks were higher in every subject than anyone had the right to expect or even hope. She knew she would probably win a special award, and she knew that she would be named valedictorian.

She had expected to go to university. She had expected to pocket her bursaries and scholarships, pack her little karazinka, and head off to crack books, win more scholarships and bursaries, and come out the other end with all the degrees and qualifications needed to open a high-priced law office in the city. Doreen even knew she was going to specialize in constitutional law, where she could deal with the fine points of interpretation, spend her days cracking the brain teasers, and never have to deal with scorned spouses, abandoned children, or the low-lifes and losers who come into conflict with the law. She expected to make wads of money, live in an apartment like the ones in the glossy slicks, and make sure Eva had absolutely everything the world could provide.

Then she hurt her knee and stayed home from school, and got hit in the face by an undeniable truth. Graduation seemed unimportant. Choosing that previously important grad gown seemed frivolous. Going to university seemed stupid; economic reality bashed her between the eyes.

"What do you mean you aren't going to go?" Molly challenged, her voice dangerously calm.

"I mean I'm not going to go," Doreen answered dully. "I'm not spending all that money on a dress, especially when I know we don't have the money. And I'm not spending any other good money on the little shoezies, or the glovezies, or the visit to the hairdresser, or. . ."

"You are so," Molly said softly.

"I am not!"

"Child, if you've got sorrow to work out of your heart, go out on the woodpile and hammer at next winter's fuel. Go dig a garden. Build a new hen pen. Use it to do something constructive and positive. Don't use that sorrow to break your momma's heart."

"Molly, *look* at her! She's. . ."

"That's right," Molly agreed. "That's right. Eva's dying."

"And you want me to go to a. . .party?"

"I want you to go ahead with your life. It's her is dying, not you. It's her life coming to an end, not yours. And you aren't going to make it a sad time. By God, child, you are not going to make it a sad time!"

"What else can it be!"

"You're so smart. But you don't know anything. You think those books tell the truth? You think it matters one snap who won the war of eighteen-twelve-fourteen? You think it matters a rat's ass when which province entered Confederation? You think the world will be a better place if we all learn about the sum of the angles bein' equal to whatever in Christ it is they're supposed to be equal to? There's more important things than any of that. And most of those things are written all over your momma's face. What ought to have been the best part of her life was shit. And the best thing that's happened to her in a long time is that she's just about out of this mess. And you aren't turning that into something gruesome just because she's made sure your life has been nothing but jam and cake!"

Molly glared, turned on her heel, and went into the kitchen to fuss over Eva's tiny supper. Doreen left the house, limping slightly, and went out to the woodshed to follow Molly's advice. Every whack of the splitting maul strengthened her resolve. She would not waste money on a fancy dress! The fanciest dress they could afford would still look like a tired feed sack alongside the dresses the doctors' daughters, the dentists' daughters, and the psychiatrists' daughters would be wearing. Spend months' worth of grocery money to wind up looking like the charity case she had always been.

"Uh, excuse me." The voice behind her was unexpected. Doreen turned, put down the chopping maul, and stared suspiciously at Alice Odgers.

"Yeah?" she growled, not the least bit interested in the social amenities.

"Could I talk to you for a few minutes?"

"Do you have to?"

"Uh, yeah, I think so."

Doreen put down the chopping maul. If she'd been in a better mood she might have welcomed Alice's visit. Alice wasn't the feather-head so many others were. Alice had been well on her way to being the town's all-time tomboy until she managed, somehow, to get a job in Madame Estelle's Boutique. How a rag-tag torn-tail had pulled that one off was one of the all-time surprises. The bigger surprise was the difference the job had made. Grubby Alice Odgers had gone in for a job and suddenly the dusty jeans, worn sneakers, and ball glove were gone, replaced by class. The matrons of Bright's Crossing gasped, gaped, then decided if Madame Estelle could work that miracle on a brat like Alice, there was hope for them. Madame Estelle's Boutique became the place to shop. The wealthy even gave up their trips to the city and, instead, put the transportation and hotel money into the exclusive little numbers Estelle imported. It wasn't Estelle's fault if the matrons and daughters of the upper crust had convinced themselves "imported" meant London, Paris, and Rome. It wasn't any of Estelle's concern if the well-heeled perceived things as they might not quite be. Estelle imported her exclusive designs from South Wellington and Egmont. No foreigner was involved in the designs, and no starving piece-workers sweat over the construction of these award-winning wonders. Hippy women and working class housewives set up sewing machines in basements and living rooms, and cut loose with creative imaginations otherwise stunted by diapers, peanut butter cookies, and measles. The international acclaim rolled in, nowhere near as welcome as the money. Estelle took fifteen per cent and willingly handed over the rest of the loot. It was to everyone's advantage that anonymity was assured. Nobody is going to pay astronomical prices for something designed by an artist and sewn by someone you might meet in the vegetable market. No, by God, if we're going to be conspicuous consumers, we want our money going to people we'll never see or speak to, someone who might wind up starring on television. How can a garment be an envy-inspiring conversation piece if it was made by some woman in a spare bedroom in the Cowichan Valley?

"Something you wanted?" Doreen tried not to sound as grumpy as she felt.

"Estelle would like you to please go down to the store just at closing time tomorrow, to talk to her about a dress."

"What dress? Why should I? How come she sent you?"

"I don't know. To all three, I don't know."

"I'm not going to grad," Doreen blurted.

"That's what I said, too," Alice laughed. "Personally, I think the whole fuss is stupid. But it would appear I owe it to my mother."

"Huh?"

"That's what they told me." Alice shook her head, then shrugged, all sign of class gone, Grubby Urchin herself revealed to be still alive and well in spite of her job at the boutique. "Personally, it looks to me like the one night a year dedicated to wiping out one helluva heap o' kids. Cars, booze, parties, ambulances, laughter, and plans for the future coming to a swift and gory end as the basketball team goes off the road and into the trees."

"But you're going anyway?"

"Maybe my parents hate me worse than I thought," Alice laughed. "Maybe they're hoping I'll be riding with the basketball team. Yeah, I'm going. After all, who would want to be held responsible for breaking her own mother's heart, right? I mean, face it, mine has survived marriage, childbirth, and suburbia. Who am I to do what none of that could do?"

Doreen grinned, made a pot of tea, and brought out the cookie jar. They sat talking together about how stupid everything was. Then Eva came from her room and moved slowly to the table, smiling that heartbreakingly beautiful smile.

"I am so glad you came to visit!" she said.

Alice believed her. There wasn't the slightest hint of falseness in

Eva, and there wasn't much in the world could give Eva more pleasure than evidence that her beloved Doreen had friends who would take the time and trouble to come and visit.

"Hello, Ms. Globilchuk," Alice smiled. "I don't think we've met before. I'm Alice Odgers. I'm in Doreen's homeroom class in school."

"Then you, too, are graduating?" Eva's smile lit the room again, she sat on the chair Doreen pulled out for her, accepted a cup of tea. "Are you excited?" she asked.

"Excited?" Alice couldn't bring herself to tell Eva the whole idea of graduation was a toothache. "Well, my mother certainly is."

"Such an honour," Eva breathed. "To think that my Doreen will walk in front of the townspeople and get her certificate! All these nice people who all these years have welcomed us, helped us, and been so kind! Many times I have wondered how I could ever thank them, how I, with no skills or specialness, could repay these people. And now my Doreen will show them that their kindness was not wasted. She will show them that their money was not wasted!"

"Momma. . ." Doreen opened her mouth to say she wasn't going to the graduation ceremony or the party following it, but Alice Odgers kicked viciously under the table, Doreen swallowed her yelp of pain, and Alice leaped courageously into the conversational breach.

"And are you going to be there, too?" she asked.

"Me?" Eva blinked, then blushed. "I want to be," she said finally.

"If you need a ride," Alice said stoutly, "you just let me know. We'll come and get you, take you there and bring you back home again."

Doreen glared at Alice, but Alice didn't care. She smiled at Eva, who sipped her tea and nodded happily.

Doreen knew she couldn't tell Eva there would be no graduation goings-on, no frantic fuss, no dithering over the dress and fretting over the shoes. Some things are just too cruel for words. So she went to see Madame Estelle at the boutique. Doreen never did understand the whys and what-fors of Estelle's offer, but it was an offer she did not even want to consider refusing.

Molly and her mother drove Eva to the graduation ceremonies, settled her in her chair, then moved to stand against the back wall. Nobody paid any attention to them. Few people paid any attention to Eva. All eyes were glued to the stage.

The doctors, lawyers, psychiatrists, and lottery winners vied viciously with each other, each wanting his graduating student to be the most expensively dressed, the most elegantly gowned. But even the fondest parents had to admit Alice Odgers' dress was the second most gorgeous creation at the ball. Doreen Globilchuk's dress was the undisputed show-stopper.

Doreen collected her awards, her bursaries, her scholarships, and the applause of the audience. She walked forward and got her certificate, and gave her valedictory address with the poise of an experienced public speaker. She had her picture taken, and even managed to smile for it. Then she went home with Eva, Molly, and Molly's mother.

"Are you sure you don't want to go to the party with your friends?" Eva asked repeatedly.

"I'm with my friends," Doreen said softly. She hugged her mother gently, wanting to squeeze fiercely. "You're the best friend I ever had in my life." And she meant it, every word of it.

She sat in a chair by Eva's bed, with the lamp draped to cut the glare, watching her mother drift into sleep. Doreen had no idea how old her mother was, and Eva herself did not know, nor did she understand the concept of age. But the simplest arithmetic suggested Doreen, at eighteen, was already a year or two older than Eva had been when Doreen was born.

Ordinarily, Doreen had no trouble putting herself in other people's shoes and empathizing with their situation in life. But sitting next to that small bed, watching her tiny mother sleeping, Doreen found it impossible to begin to imagine what life in the camps must have been like. It was easy to see what the horror had done to Eva physically, but no way to tell what it had done to her mentally, emotionally, spiritually. She wanted to be angry. She wanted to be filled with white-hot rage, to come off her chair and go out into the world fired up with determination that such awfulness never happen again. Instead, she felt sorrow, compassion, regret, and a hint of bowel-wrenching fear. She knew it could happen again, was already happening again, and would, in spite of her best efforts, continue to happen, no matter how many constitutional amendments she helped fashion.

Doreen went to her bedroom, took off the incredible creation, folded it carefully, put it in its box, and tied the box shut with string. Then she put her shoezies in their box and her glovezies in theirs, and took off the silver pendant and earrings Molly and her mother had given her as a graduation gift.

She had a bath, washed the expensive set out of her hair, then pulled on jeans and a faded tee shirt. She went back to her room and stared at the hand-carved silver pendant, the silver earrings, and the ring Eva had given her, which she had left on her finger. Hot tears scalded her face, dripping from her chin to her tee shirt. Raven. The trickster, the transformer, who can suddenly turn into HuHu the killer. She knew the legends, knew the songs and dances, knew, too, that Molly and Molly's mother had their reasons for choosing the design. Knew Eva had asked them to help her choose. And knew she, herself, was too mind-wrenched to be able to understand the symbols.

She went into the kitchen and sat at the table, watching Molly at her endless game of solitaire.

"How come you never married?" she asked.

"Why would I do that?" Molly smiled.

"Why does anybody get married. To have a family, I guess."

"I've got family." Molly put a red six on a black seven and nodded satisfaction. "I've got so many people in my family I couldn't write a letter to each of 'em if I tried."

"You know what I mean."

"Yes. Do you know what I mean?"

"No."

"There you have it, then," Molly agreed, as if everything were explained.

"What about . . . love?"

"I've got love by the bucketful and people in my life who will let me love them."

"Well, what about sex?"

"I'm all in favour of it myself," Molly smiled. She dealt three cards, studied them, dealt three more, and placed two of them.

"I feel really brain-buggered."

"Of course you do," Molly nodded. "It's part of growing up and taking your place in the world. Always figured it was a helluva price to pay, but there you have it. What can't be cured must be endured, as Sarah used to say."

"All the stuff I thought I knew and . . . I don't know anything!"

"That's a start."

"What good does it do to . . ."

"You shut your mouth!" Molly hissed. "Don't you dare indulge yourself with any of that navel-gazing shit. There's more to your life than the moss that grows in your belly button! It might not do much good, I'll grant you that. But doing nothing does harm to everyone."

"Do you really believe that? I mean *really?*"

"Yes, I do." Molly swept up all her cards and shuffled them rapidly. "I've been sitting on the fringes all my life, watching. Not because I wanted to, but because that's how they decided it would be. I did as much as I could inside the cage they said I had to live in. And the cage is still there, for sure. But it's bigger than it was when I was a girl, and there's more room in it now than there had been for two hundred years. And that's because we did what we had to do, and we never once let them make that cage smaller. I expect you to do the same, Doreen Globilchuk! A lot of people expect you to do your very best, and, in doing it, to make life better for some other people."

Hesitantly, Doreen pulled out her doubts and fears, her realizations and her worries. Molly listened, hands busy with the game of solitaire.

"And so," Doreen finished, "all that awfulness could happen again tomorrow. We haven't learned a thing."

"No?" Molly laughed. "When I met your momma the first time, I knew almost nothing about any of that particular thing. But I learned. And I remembered what my grandmother told me about how it was here when she was a girl. And I put two and two together. Now, when I watch the TV or hear a radio program, I recognize that stuff for what it is. I've learned a whole helluva lot. And you've learned more than I knew at your age. After all, if you sit on your ass with your head in your hands, you make it easy for them, and if you make it easy for them, you help them, and if you help them, you become them. Look! Aha! Second time this week I won!" She leaned back, surveyed the neatly arranged cards, grinned happily, then scooped them together, shuffled them twice, and put the deck on the table. "Doreen," she said softly, "you're gonna do okay. And you're gonna *be* okay, too. I promise you."

The bursaries and scholarships made university financially possible, and Doreen left home determined to fill every expectation her little mother might have. And Estelle found Doreen and job and a place to stay. Two very good friends of Estelle's, both of them old, one of them with half an arm missing, had retired some years previously and were living in a lovely house set back on a large yard full of flowers and shrubs. But time marches on, fuelled by our energies, and we are all of us eventually diminished. The lawn, the flowers, the shrubs, the flowering and fruit trees were too much, the house was becoming a burden. The failing eyesight of the two old women convinced them they were keeping abreast of the dust and grime, but the truth of it was the walls were no longer spotless, the paint and wallpaper no longer bright, the windows far from sparkling clean.

"You'd be doing me a big favour," Estelle told the two aging women. "The kid has a mind to make you weep with joy, but..." and she outlined the story, paying particular attention to Eva's time in the camps.

"You'd be doing me a big favour," Estelle told Doreen. "They're two wonderful old tarts, but..." and she made sure Doreen knew about the amputated arm, the failing eyes, and the aching knees.

Doreen moved her things into the spare bedroom, set up her books on the old desk in front of the big window overlooking the wild tangle of yellow climbing rose, and life for everyone concerned took on new meaning. The windows shone, the walls regained their colour, the basement became something other than a concrete hole beneath the house, and the spiders had to find other accommodations. Flower beds were weeded, the lawn was fertilized, mowed, and trimmed, the roses practically sang with joy. The first eight months passed so swiftly Doreen could hardly believe she had finished her first year. She went home for the summer, got a job in a fish-processing plant, and worried about the two old women. Would the housekeeper remember, would the twice-weekly nurse pay attention, would the student hired to stay overnight think to check...and every evening she helped Eva from her big chair to the front seat of Molly's car, and drove them to the beach. She carried her mother from the car to a big log, sat her on the sun-bleached wood, then sat beside her, holding her hand.

"So pretty," Eva said. "So clean."

"You comfortable? Warm enough? I brought your jacket if you need it."

"You are so kind to me," Eva smiled and Doreen felt as if her own throat would burst open with sorrow.

"Momma, I love you."

"I'm glad." Eva moved slightly, leaning against Doreen's shoulder. "I've been very lucky," she said happily. "I have good friends, we live in a beautiful place, my life is comfortable, and I have you. I don't know why I've been so lucky. I don't even really know what luck is. Do you?"

"Oh, Momma."

"Really. Do you have any idea what luck is? Someone was on television not long ago, being interviewed. She had won more money than you could believe. And it wasn't the first time! She said she always goes to Bingo and wins nearly every week. She enters all those competitions in the magazines, and usually wins something. She has won trips to all sorts of places. And now she's won all that money. Luck, she said. And I wondered what it is and why some people have it and other people don't."

"Maybe it's God," Doreen evaded. "Maybe God likes some people better than others."

"I don't know what God is, either," Eva laughed softly.

Doreen looked at Eva and swallowed the lump of tears. She could see her mother's face, but behind her, faint and shadowy, Doreen could also see images of the pictures she had seen in books. All those people. Any one of them could have been Eva. Any one of them could have been Molly. Or Alice. Or anyone else in the world.

"Whatever you've got now," she said firmly, "you paid for it, Momma."

"Yes," Eva admitted, "but we won't allow ourselves to become obsessed with that."

"It isn't something we should forget!"

"Forget?" Eva shook her head. "Doreen, you weren't there. There are some things people can never forget. And some things we should insist be remembered. But we can still look at the nice things, too." She lifted her daughter's hand to kiss it, and Doreen felt the soft splash of Eva's tears on her skin. "I know words don't mean the same to everyone. And I know sometimes I don't speak this language well. But it is a victory. Oh, not a victory with flags and banners and an army of liberation and guns and tanks and glory! But it is a victory that we are sitting here tonight, watching such beauty, and loving each other. They tried everything they knew and killed what seemed at the time to be everybody in my world; and still, they did not destroy my love. If we get obsessed by what they did, we might help them do what they wanted to do. We might destroy love."

"It makes me angry, Momma."

"I am glad. Angry means you care. Angry means you will not just stand there, ever, without protesting and trying to stop it. Just do not get so angry you forget to love. And now, I must go home, my heart. I am so very tired."

Doreen lifted her mother, carried her back to Molly's car, and drove her home. Molly was waiting, sitting on the back steps with the newspaper and a cup of tea, and while Doreen got the bathtub ready, Molly helped Eva undress. They bathed her, and put her in bed with the curtains pulled back so she could watch the sunset colours above the western mountains.

"I picked berries," Molly bragged, "and we've got blackberry grunt with fresh cream from Ferguson's cow. I might be persuaded to dish it out and even hand some over . . ."

"What do I have to do?" Eva said, her voice as thin as a child's.

"Bribe me," Molly teased. "Cost you a kiss."

"It is a pleasure," Eva reached up with her little-girl-sized arms, hugged Molly and kissed her cheek. "I love you," she said, nodding and smiling.

"I love you." Molly kissed Eva's cheek, then laughed softly. "Blackberry grunt coming up right away." She looked at Doreen and winked. "Give me a hand?"

Not three minutes later, when they walked into the bedroom with the tray, Eva was dead. She was lying back on her pillows, face turned to the window, eyes open and sightless. Molly knew before Doreen did. She put the tray on the bedside table, then grabbed Doreen's arms, just above the elbow.

"Easy girl," she said firmly. "You grab hold, now."

"What?" Doreen paled. She looked at her mother, sank onto the bed, and reached for the parchment-skinned hand. One long agonized shudder passed through her body, and her tears poured freely. "Oh, shit," she said hopelessly. "Oh, shit, Molly!"

The funeral was attended by more people than Eva knew had known her. Molly took care of everything, especially Doreen, who moved like a sleepwalker for days. She might have moved like a sleepwalker for weeks, or even months, but her friends wouldn't allow it. They pulled out all the stops and laid on every manipulative sentence they could think of, and it worked. Doreen heard "Eva wouldn't have wanted you to grieve" and "Eva would want you to enjoy your life" and "Eva was so proud of you" so often she put her sorrow aside and went back to the ins and outs of living, with such dedication it would have made Eva smile from ear to ear.

"You take the furniture," she told Molly. "It isn't much, and it probably wouldn't bring ten dollars at a garage sale, but it's good stuff and you're the one kept it clean all those years."

"If ever you want anything. . .a lamp, a dresser, you just say so."

"Sure," Doreen looked through the doorway into Eva's bedroom. "I just don't know what to do with her clothes. . ."

"We burn them," Molly offered quietly. "We light a fire, say prayers, and burn the stuff of the dead. And if anyone wants to give them anything, that goes in the fire, too. Money, books, pictures, stuff like that."

They built a fire on the beach. The Old Woman said the prayers, and one by one they fed into the fire Eva's clothes and the things she had cherished. When Molly nodded, two strong young men lifted the old stuffed chair and put it in the middle of the fire. As the flames began to lick at it, Doreen was able to smile. She took a deep breath for the first time since Eva had died, and a great lump lifted from her breastbone. Next into the fire was the box with the graduation dress inside, and then the box with the shoes and the box with the gloves. "I hope," she said, trembly-voiced, "that wherever she is, there are beaches and sunsets and pretty things to watch."

When classes started again, Doreen was back in the city, looking after the two aged women, mowing the lawn, pruning the rose bushes, and attending classes with a commitment and dedication that made her professors feel justified in their position as teachers. The truth was, Doreen didn't need teachers. If she had been left alone in a library she would have learned what she needed to know without any help from anyone.

The scholarships and bursaries became routine. Every summer, Doreen went back to work at the fish plant. She lived with Molly and Molly's mother, and nobody ever asked how come a Shamass was living on the reserve. During those summers, she learned more than she learned in university. She learned about law from the other side, about the Constitution from those not protected by it. Most of all, she learned what happens when the law is not seen as justice, but used as a measure of political and social control.

Silas had always been wild, everybody knew that. He was kicked out of school for a month in grade two, brought home by the police for shoplifting firecrackers when he was nine, and sent to juvenile court for setting fires when he was eleven. From twelve to seventeen he was in juvenile court almost every month, and after that, he was in adult court for everything from drinking in public to urinating against the plate glass window of the Social Credit candidate's election headquarters.

All of it ankle-biting stupidity. Nothing serious, nothing dangerous, nothing for anyone to get their shirt in a knot. But then Silas grabbed a fourteen-year-old girl, hauled her into his car, and somewhere up the Lakes Road, Silas raped the child.

"Phone the police!" Doreen insisted. "You don't just allow things like that to happen. Turn him in!"

"There's enough Indians in jail already," they said. "Won't do any good to phone the police, they'll just use it as an excuse to come on the reserve and search everybody's house, search everybody's car, count the number of fish in the smokehouse, and drive everybody nuts with questions about hunting deer in and out of season."

"But . . ."

"No."

Doreen went back to university with tattered illusions. And that Christmas, she did not go home, she stayed and spent the holidays with the two old women and Estelle, who arrived on Christmas Eve on the ten o'clock ferry with presents, a hamper of delicacies, several bottles of very good booze, and news of the folks back home.

"There was an awful accident at the reserve a couple of weeks ago," she said, looking directly into Doreen's eyes. "One of the young men ate a plate of cooked mushrooms. Actually, he started eating, but he never finished. They rushed him to hospital, but . . ." She shrugged. "The coroner said somehow he'd managed to slice up a Destroying Angel, and there was nothing anyone could do. If he'd been in the hospital itself when he ate it, or even one bite of it, there wouldn't have been anything anyone could do."

"Silas?" Doreen asked, feeling as if she were riding in the back seat of a car when it went over a hump in the road.

"I don't know his name. Bit of a rangy-tang I understand."

"Yes," Doreen nodded, then smiled. "Yes, if it was Silas, he was a bit of a rangy-tang, all right."

She went back after New Year's and had a wonderful week visiting with the old people, taking Molly's mother window shopping, eating smoked salmon and garlic prawn, staying up late telling jokes and making fun of the programs on television.

"Some things," Molly said quietly, as they walked the beach at low tide, "take care of themselves, given a bit of time."

"Other things," Doreen insisted firmly, "need a bit of a push." She waved her hand in the direction of the sawmill. "When I was a little girl that sawmill mess was a good three miles back down the beach. Everybody knew the reserve went all the way to the spit."

Molly shrugged. "We went to see a lawyer."

"And?"

"Use your eyes."

"What did he say?"

"You should go see him. You'd understand his fancy words. All we understood was we couldn't do anything without permission from the Federals, and the Federals are the very people who gave the mill permission to take over that three miles."

"You're kidding."

"Wouldn't it be nice if I was? 'Course you shouldn't take what I say too seriously, I have it on the highest authority that I'm one of a group of people who can't take care of themselves."

Doreen went to see the lawyer and she understood every word of his fancy talk. What she understood made her angry. She went back to university fuming mad, and hit the books with renewed determination.

There had to be some other alternative. There just aren't enough Destroying Angel mushrooms.

One of the few advantages of growing up in a small town where Kulturni means amateur theatre presentations of *Pirates of Penzance* is that euphemism has little place in the vocabularies or lives of the people. There is no such thing as self-chosen downward mobility, there is only hitting the skids. Nobody talks of deciding to retain the status quo, there is only holding on or, in some cases, going nowhere fast.

City people, raised in the midst of art galleries, movies, symphony orchestras, and professional theatres, learn early that entertainment and distraction are only a bus ride away from cable television and forty (count 'em) channels. City people grow up with libraries full of the latest books and more movie theatres than you could shake a stick at. And city people all too often get distracted, which may well be the overall intent of all that glitter and glitz. The small-towners with ambition gravitate to the bright lights, spend a year or two feeling out of place and awkward, then take a couple of night school courses so they, too, can talk that funny talk. But few of them make the mistake of starting to think that funny way. They focus in and they take over, having learned from history that it is, inevitably, the barbarians at the gates who wind up owning the best corners of a conquered city. The only ones apt to do better than transplanted small-towners are those who were raised in the rotting inner core of the city, allowed to drag themselves up as best they could among the dumpsters and empties, in the hallways and on the stoops of large, crowded, smelly tenements, or in those instant ghettoes the city fathers proudly call planned housing projects. Any kid who is able to haul herself out of this seething mess and focus herself in on what she perceives as the way out and up, is sure to know from an early age how to go for the throat and collect the prizes. All she has to do is learn how to walk, talk, dress, eat, and pretend.

Doreen learned how to do all of that. Estelle taught her clothes, the old tarts taught her deportment and charm, she had always known how to listen, and the people back home all knew she was going somewhere, that girl; she had her eyes set on the rungs above her, took no sass from anyone, and was a real go-getter. Which in polite terms means being upwardly mobile.

With her marks she had no trouble finding a good law practice. She finished her articling period and quietly continued working for the prestigious firm, going out of her way to be involved in as many different kinds of cases as possible, and when she was ready, she left to open her own firm.

Her offices were not large or fancy, but they were hers. She had an opening party, complete with smoked salmon, potato salad, and beer. Molly arrived with Estelle, the two old tarts dressed to the nines and bringing along a still-awed high school graduate from Molly's reserve, a slender, big-eyed young woman who had her sights firmly set on social work.

Three years later, they had another party, with only one of the old tarts attending. Doreen did it up right, and Molly grinned widely as she toured the huge suite of offices, looked at the computers, the telephones, the large expensive desks, the waiting rooms with their furniture at least as good as anything most people had in their homes.

"Very nice," she said approvingly. "Very nice and very couth."

"I approve totally," Estelle agreed. "Some plants, though, I think. A dumb cane, perhaps, and some ivy to go up the brick wall."

"I wish Momma could have seen this."

"She can."

Constitutional law, domestic disputes, adoption appeals, legal aid cases, Doreen took them all. She could have made more money if she had agreed to defend cocaine importers and rapists and child abusers, but money wasn't all she was after, and lines have to be drawn somewhere. In drawing her lines she made sure land claims were on the side of the angels, and that, more than anything, proved money wasn't the entire reason Doreen Globilchuk had chosen law.

Some thought there was no progress being made, but those who were most closely involved watched as the mill moved its heaps and stacks of lumber back down the beach to the other side of the spit. There was satisfaction in that, deeper satisfaction than in the size of the cheque the band manager deposited in the bank. A road was closed, and the railway company was allowed to continue to use the tracks but required to slow the trains when they crossed reserve land, and, more importantly, the company had to pay substantially for the right-of-way it had used for years without real permission. A four-mile section of beach was returned. Two hundred acres which had been cavalierly claimed and turned into a provincial park were signed back to the band and became a tribal park, and the money the tourists paid to park their RVs went to wages for the band members who cleaned the sites, cut and stacked the firewood, emptied the garbage cans, and did security and fire patrols. Nothing earth-shattering, nothing that would make the front pages, nothing that would be noticed by very many people, but the blood smiled. And Doreen's office wall was graced with a button blanket, which twice a year the museum tried to buy, increasing their offer substantially each time. Wealthy collectors who found their way to her office invariably asked if she would be interested in selling the bentwood box on her desk, or the talking stick hanging on the wall, or the collection of spruce root baskets on top of her filing cabinet. Doreen smiled, said no, then asked if they would care to examine the carvings on the bottom shelves of her bookcases; and she made sure the collectors went home with an assortment of business cards printed by the band, advertising the carvers, weavers, basket makers, and painters who had incorporated themselves as an artists' co-operative. An artists' co-operative represented at no cost to the artists by none other than Doreen Globilchuk, the lawyer who had skipped so many rungs on the ladder of success that to some it seemed she had vaulted up it the way Superwoman spanned the Grand Canyon.

When the second old tart died Doreen was visited by one of her professional colleagues and informed she was the sole heiress of what proved to be a substantial whack of money and rental properties. She could have moved out of her apartment and into any one of several houses, but she wasn't sure she wanted to take care of a lawn, a roof, flower beds, and other eternal concerns.

But there were kids coming to the city to go to university, and they needed a place to stay. One of the kids was winning scholarships and bursaries in Business Administration and Doreen turned the whole shooting match over to her.

In spite of everything that was happening, in spite of the matching of wits, the honing of fine points, the researching and presenting of fact and precedent, in spite of the winning and the proving and the righting of past wrongs, life was flat and getting flatter. Doreen couldn't work up any enthusiasm for anything except work, and there's a limit to how long that can sustain a person's soul.

Molly waited for Doreen to fall in love; all the fairy tales held out that promise for those who had fought the good fight and done well. Failing that, she waited for Doreen to fall on her head and concuss herself into a different frame of mind, but Doreen was as well co-ordinated as she had ever been. In the end, Molly left it all in the hands of the Old Woman. She, at least, has never been known to fail. She might take her own sweet time about things, but sooner or later, she weaves the strands, and things work out properly.

Doreen didn't know her life had been handed over to Old Woman. She just kept on with it, living it as best she knew how. Springtime, summertime, and into fall, she worked from first thing in the morning until last thing at night, going home in a cab to her comfortable apartment.

She seldom used her car. Driving in the city is a way to become an accident looking for a place to happen. All those neon signs blinking and flashing, the same shades of green, amber, and red as the traffic lights—you never know whether to slam on the brakes or slide past. Was this an intersection or another video outlet, a stoplight or a motorcycle repair shop? On TV, no matter what hour of the day or night, people tool cars up and down streets without trouble or confusion, move in and out of conveniently vacant parking spots. Well-dressed and calm, they step out, close the door, take a brief look around, and then, leaving the car doors unlocked, they walk directly to the building they want, unconcerned about thieves, vandals, joyriders, or parking tickets. In real life, you wind up blocks away from where you want to be, fumbling for change for the meter, then you walk to your destination, knowing that when you return your car will have been towed away, stolen, or so badly schmucked that a rented limo would have been cheaper.

On rainy nights, however, cabs are as scarce as rocking horse shit, and Doreen had given up trying to get one. All she really wanted was a belly full of Szechuan, and if she had to walk through the rain to get it, fine, she would walk through the rain.

Street lights a sickly yellow in the gathering dark, fluorescent storefronts bright, and people hurrying, collars up-turned, scarves wrapped comfortingly, heads pulled down, shoulders hunched. Just before the door to the restaurant, an alley, barely wide enough for two people to pass each other, and in it, garbage cans, overflowing, a few cardboard boxes with who-knows-what stuffed in them, a kid waiting for her mom, God, some people didn't deserve to breathe oxygen, all the kid had on was a thin summer dress, sagging cotton socks, a pair of blue canvas sneakers, laces knotted and grey. She looked miserable, anxiously searching the faces of passers-by, none of whom, obviously, was Mom.

Doreen opened the glass door and went inside, shivering in the sudden heat. Three paces, then another glass door, beyond it the stairs leading up to the restaurant. Suddenly, she was hungry, almost frantic, as if she hadn't eaten a decent meal in months. The smell of ginger and hot peppers, of soy sauce and spiced orange, of garlic and black beans, of chicken, pork, and fish rushed down the stairs to greet her.

The window was steamy, the neon from the storefront across the street diffused at the edges, made softer, almost beautiful. People laughing softly, talking together companionably, voices blending into one hum. Mohair sweaters and cashmere sweaters, fine wool pants and high boots, gold chains glinting, jewels glittering, and from every table the tantalizing odours of spices and sauces as the well-fed enjoyed another meal.

Doreen sipped her tea, consciously trying to relax, but her brain was busy, twisting and turning, planning and reviewing. Sharon Joe, twenty-six, mother of four children by three different men. Oldest daughter living in eastern Canada with the putative father's aged mother. Second child living with its father and his third wife. Two youngest children living with Sharon, their father in jail on a twenty-year importation charge. Sharon herself a product of the provincial fostering system, twelve foster homes in fourteen years. Apprehended at age four, mother an alcoholic and drug addict, ten siblings, living in the grottiest end of the city, Sharon hadn't known much of anything except anger and misery.

Somehow, Sharon had realized one or two things. The realization sent her looking for help. But you don't take your kids with you when you go off to dry out. So Sharon went to her social worker. Wonderful. We'll do everything we can to help. Wonderful foster home, wonderful foster parents, just sign here and the wheels will start to turn.

Three months of treatment and Sharon is back in the city, her habits and addictions behind her. The smiling social worker shakes her hand, congratulates her. Wonderful, just wonderful. Have you thought about upgrading your education? You have? Wonderful. You've done so well and it's been such a difficult time for you, maybe you should take a couple of weeks to get yourself set up, get a place to live, get yourself registered in school. A few more visits, a few more cups of tea and then the boom gets lowered with a thud. The children will remain in foster care. After all, with your history of personal instability, and let's not forget your alcoholism and drug abuse. And what's this about counselling with a feminist group? You're part of an incest and sexual abuse survivors' group? What incest? What sexual abuse? Our foster parents don't do things like that and it isn't going to look good on my report if you're hanging out with a bunch like this, most of whom are lesbians anyway if the truth be known as it one day will be.

Finally the sexual abuse survivors' group had contacted Doreen. Sharon no longer seemed able to make decisions, let alone reach for a phone to implement them.

The meal arrived and for all of five minutes Doreen managed to concentrate on sight, taste, smell. Then her brain went back to other things and she ate almost automatically. A hearing, of course. As many people and letters of support as she could line up for Sharon. Some facts and figures would help: your honour, a federal commission has established that ninety-five per cent of all people raised in fostering situations are so affected by the experience they are unable to find and retain steady gainful employment. Your honour, seventy-five per cent of all juveniles who come to the attention of the court are from families living on welfare. Eighty per cent of all children in foster homes come in conflict with the law before the age of fifteen. Sharon herself is a product of this system, are we to perpetuate the tragedy into other generations? Any mother, your honour, whatever her failings and weaknesses, is better than no mother at all.

In the bush the rain falls on living things and makes them greener, in the city the clouds sit on the tops of the buildings and seep on concrete and cement, making pale walls grey, turning grey walls black, making streets look like bottomless cracks and not all the artificial light in the world can make things truly bright.

The hot and sour soup loosened her sinuses. She sweated lightly, fully warm for the first time since she had left her office. She'd ordered too much supper, somehow she always did, but as the old joke said, the good thing about Szechuan was that two hours later you were ready for more.

Doreen had to get her mind away from Sharon. She had to stop this chasing around like a mouse in a maze and let her brain do some real work. Get the student to research the records of the worker involved. How many of the living breathing people who comprised his caseload had been manoeuvred into the same kind of position, how many families were now separated "for their own good"?

The waiter packaged up the leftovers and Doreen left the restaurant. As the second glass door began to swing shut behind her, there was a sound, a sound that cut into her thoughts. A sound very much like the mewling of a homeless kitten. How many cats were born to brief lives in the dumpsters, breeding in the garbage, giving birth to litters of slinking scavengers like themselves? And what would she do if she found it? The last thing she needed was a cat.

But it wasn't a kitten, it was that kid again. Sitting against the wall of the building, not even crying, just sitting, shivering, lips blue. Every few seconds the mewling sound overriding its breathing.

Before Doreen could think about what she was seeing, her legs were taking her into the alley. She hunkered down, unzipping her heavy Cowichan sweater. "Hey, punkin," she said softly, and the child looked at her, eyes dull. "Put this on," she said. The kid stood, took a step, moved towards Doreen and, instead of putting on the sweater, reached out and wrapped her arms around Doreen's neck, put her cold face in the warm curve of Doreen's throat and sobbed, only once. "Hey there, it's okay," Doreen lied, wrapping the sweater around the skinny little form. "Come on, let's get out of here," and she stood, lifting the child.

So what would anybody do? Standing at the mouth of an alley, a half-frozen kid clutching desperately, a bag of take-out in one hand, and not a cop to be seen. Do you go back into the restaurant and ask to use the phone? Stand on the corner hoping a blue-and-white will cruise by so you can wave it down? And then what? Down to the station, forms to fill out, contact the welfare, probably. Another little person to become one of the ninety-five per cent.

Just like that, for the first time in who knows how long, a cab came down the street, cruising for a fare. Doreen stepped out, arm lifted, and to her total amazement, the cab pulled over and stopped, the door opened, and the driver grinned. "Where to, lady?"

Six dollars later, Doreen was in her apartment trying to decide whether the kid should eat first or have a bath first. The little girl was shivering so badly she probably couldn't get the food to her mouth or keep it there if she did manage a bite. And she smelled. No doubt about it. Sour, stale, disgusting, unnecessary stink. Doreen hung the Cowichan sweater over a chair and took the kid to the bathroom.

She sat in the hot water, up to her shoulders in suds. Maybe she'd had a bath before or maybe she was sitting so passively because she didn't know what else to do. Or maybe it was just so nice to sit in something so warm it made your skin go pink. Doreen scrubbed her from the soles of her grimy feet to the top of her head, and even when water was cascading over her face, rinsing away the grey shampoo suds, the kid didn't cry. Nor did she laugh. She just let it all happen as Doreen scrubbed, lathering the little head again, rinsing it and starting all over until she knew the stink of old urine was gone, and any vermin had drowned. Then she pulled the kid from the tub, wrapped her in a thick towel, and took her to the kitchenette.

The microwave had everything warmed in seconds. The little girl sat on a chair, clean and dry, warm and comfortable, even if she did shudder from time to time, enormous body shivers that seemed to come from her very belly. And she stared. But when the warmed-up food was put in front of her and the smell reached her nostrils, the apathy was gone, the scrawny little hand was reaching for pieces of chicken, green string beans coated in sauce, grains of rice. Not gobbling, not slobbering, she ate with a mechanical determination, one hand after the other, absorbed in what she was doing, like a puppy from the pound who is just going to eat until he sees the bottom of the food bowl and if he explodes in the process, well, that's a nicer death than slow starvation.

Doreen could phone the police now. The child was at least warm and fed, and would probably fall asleep in the time it would take all the gears to start to mesh and the system begin to unfold for the poor little thing. A bed in a hospital for a few days, most likely, until some kind of arrangements could be made for in-home care. Probably a crib on the kid's ward, with clowns on the wall and toys and a television. A crib with bars, like they use when they build a jail, and the staff changing every eight hours, one strange voice after another, one strange face after another, and someone sure to tell her to relax, everything would be fine.

And what good would it do? Even after she had been there a few days, even after she had been there a few weeks, even when she was no longer terrified by all the uniforms and the sharp smells, even if someone took a chance and became human for a few minutes, maybe sat down and held the kid on her lap while she changed the nightie they had put on her less than twenty-four hours earlier, it wasn't the same as being comforted. One graduate of the system had said that her bones ached at night, not because the mattress was hard, although it was, but because there were no snuggles, no cuddles, no real concern for that inner part that can't be soothed by mere backrubs or warm blankets.

The take-out containers were empty and the little hands were smeared with sauce, grains of rice still sticking to her fingers. Her nose needed wiping, her eyes were already drooping shut, the blank stare of mindless panic was gone. Doreen took the child back to the bathroom and wiped the sticky hands and fingers. A quick, efficient dab with a piece of toilet paper, and the nose was clean. Then a face cloth to remove the last of the smeared sauce. "There you go," she said, "all clean." The little girl nodded.

Well, Doreen thought, we could always wait. If they ask why, just say you figured the welfare would be closed at night so you just kept the kid until office hours, then phoned for an appointment. They'd go for that. Even the duty worker didn't enjoy being hauled out at midnight to drive through the rain to the police station, sign forms, then arrange to have a stinking kid taken to the hospital to have more forms filled out and signed. And all of that could only delay the time before the kid could get some much-needed sleep.

"Come here, little button," Doreen smiled. The kid moved quickly, and again the scrawny arms were wrapped around Doreen's neck, the little face pressed into the curve of her throat.

She went to her bedroom, sat on her bed, kicked off her loafers, then swung her legs up onto the blankets. She pressed the remote and the television popped on, the late news bringing another day's worth of catastrophe to the viewing audience.

Another graduate of the system had told Doreen that just about the time a kid started to feel things were no longer terrifying and unfamiliar, just about the time a kid could start to feel at ease, just about then was when they drove you off to a new place where nothing was the same and you were back at square one, frightened again, every noise in the middle of the night making you feel as if your entire body was weighted with lead and you would never be able to move to safety.

"Sssshh," she soothed, stroking the bare little leg. She moved carefully and managed to get the corner of the blanket out from under them. The kid reached out to grab Doreen's finger, holding tightly. "Easy on, old girl," Doreen crooned, "gimme a half a mo' here."

The child fell asleep, and Doreen stared at the television but saw nothing. Her mind was calmly and contentedly sifting and sorting, beginning to compose the sentences and paragraphs she would present on Sharon's behalf. She no longer worried. She knew it might take two, possibly even three sessions in the courtroom, but Sharon would get her kids back, would keep them, and would never again have to walk in fear of them being apprehended.

Doreen switched off the television, got out of bed quietly, went to the bathroom for a quick shower, then went back into the bedroom. The kid was sprawled as if boneless, a faint sheen of sweat on her upper lip. Szechuan, Doreen grinned, it'll do it to you every time.

One of the workers had looked at her once, across a desk, and for a moment he had dared to let his self show through. The pain and confusion in his eyes had hurt Doreen, made her wish she had never seen it. Life, she knew, would never again be quite so black and white.

I know those statistics, he said, his voice thick with something that went past sorrow to some other place, and they're probably right. But Jesus Christ, Ms. Globilchuk, look at the wrecks and ruins they give me in the first place. By the time I get them there's already so much damage done that sometimes I think God himself couldn't heal the sores.

You only hear one side of it, he continued, and hearing is nothing, really. It's the seeing gives you cramps down low in your guts.

She had sat there, poised, casually elegant, the epitome of success, and watched as his hands moved of their own accord, picked up a two-dollar ball point pen, and started turning it, turning it, turning it.

We can only deal with what we see when we get a call and go, he said to the desk top, unable to look at her, and at the time she had thought it was shame. I went to this one place, one of your clients, in fact, and what I saw, what I have pictures of, isn't in any of your briefs or interview transcripts. I saw empty booze bottles on the floor, on the table, on the counter, on every surface they could be scattered on . . . and the door kicked in . . . and an axe—not a hatchet for cutting kindling, but an axe—lying on the living room floor. The place looked as if the Mongol hordes had just gone through on a bad day, and in the back bedroom, the kids. We had to take the door off the hinges to get into that room because they were so scared they'd pushed beds, dressers, and whatever they could move up against the door. We couldn't shove the door open, they had so much stuff piled there. And even though they'd seen me before, even though they knew me, they were terrified of me. Uncle Darren was drunk, they said, and he got mad because Mommy was smoochin' with Uncle Fred, and then there was a big fight.

He looked at her then, shook his head and shrugged, even tried to smile. And what does that do to a kid? But I bet you come out of court a lot better than I do. And maybe it will never happen again, and maybe your client smartened up, maybe she'll clean up her act and her life and maybe she'll become the happy homemaker and the supermom, but . . . it happened, and I couldn't do anything until after it happened, and we have to find a way to intervene before it happens, but, of course, there's the matter of civil liberties.

There wasn't much in the way of food in the apartment. Doreen ate most of her meals somewhere else. But there was cereal, and coffee cream, some fruit juice crystals which only needed to be stirred into cold water to approximate something a kid would enjoy. Half a bunch of grapes, an orange that had seen better days, and a bowl of yogurt which the kid seemed to recognize. When the kid was seated at the counter in what the real estate agent had called a breakfast nook, Doreen pulled on her clothes and slipped from the apartment.

Everybody knew you weren't supposed to leave a kid alone for a minute, but Doreen figured she had fifteen or twenty minutes, maybe even a half hour before the kid finished the food and started prowling around looking for death traps. There was a Salvation Army thrift store not three blocks away, and if God was truly in her heaven the store would be open for business.

The first morning rush was over and there were good smells coming from the bakery. Already there was music playing in the bar on the corner. She hurried past the shoppers and browsers, waited impatiently at the light, then raced across the intersection, as tunnel-visioned as any city dweller. The store had just opened and she moved quickly to the tables piled with used clothing.

The child wasn't a baby, or a toddler either, she had to be either a good-sized four-year-old or a small five-year-old. Jeans, size six, that ought to do it. If they were too long the bottoms could be folded or rolled. At seventy-five cents how could a person go wrong? A warm flannel shirt for fifty cents. A heavy sweater for two dollars. A pair of hardly used sneaks that looked to be the same size as the filthy ones Doreen had pulled off last night. Underwear in a bin, socks in another bin, and for seven dollars she had everything the kid would need and none of it smelling like a store or a transport van.

The kid was sitting on the bed, eyes wide, nervously twisting the tufted edge of the chenille spread, and her relief when Doreen walked in was so obvious it wiped out most of Doreen's growing sense of fun.

"Hey," she chided softly, "I'm here, aren't I? Would I take off and just leave you? Gimme a break here, okay? No woman in her right mind goes looking for stuff for lunch in her altogether." She handed over the brown paper bag. "Here, have a look. This is why I was gone."

The girl opened the bag, looked inside, pulled out the clothes, then looked questioningly at Doreen.

"Try them," Doreen urged. "What doesn't fit can be replaced. We just couldn't go sauntering into Marks'n'Sparks with you as naked as the day you were born. Need some help?"

"Nice," the kid said, then began pulling on a sock, getting one heel twisted on top of her foot.

"Here, lemme help." Doreen sat on the bed, "That's it, get this straightened around and. . .okay, stand up now. Put your hand on my shoulder so you don't tip over and fall. Right foot first, that's it. Now the other. Okay, haul 'em up, Sapphire. There you go, you're the girl with the yellow duckies on her underpants. Pick 'er out in any crowd. Now the jeans. Okay, same as before, one hand on the shoulder to stop the falling-over routine. . .right foot first. Now the left. . .that's it." She had to keep talking to stop the tears, she had to keep talking in a quiet voice or she'd shout with rage. Seven dollars. Less than the cost of a case of beer. And the kid looked as if it was Christmas time all over the world.

"Doesn't it ever stop?" she said aloud, forcing a smile. "The houses get fancier, the cars get bigger, jet travel holidays in the sun, money all over the universe, and guess what, we still have kids shivering in alleys. Well, never mind, sit down here and we'll ram on these sneaks. Hey, by God, they fit! I'll do the laces for you. How's that? Stand up and wiggle your toes. No, on the floor this time. Wiggle again, chicklet. Not too tight? Feels fine to me, but I'm on the outside of them, not the inside, so how would I know, right? Okay, here we are, you and me, and both of us have thick sweaters. Haul it on, do up the zip, and here we go, out into the rah rah rah of Saturday morning in the city."

The kid was too busy grinning to talk, her skinny fist clutched tight around Doreen's index and middle finger. Everything fit reasonably well. The jeans were a bit long, a bit loose, but nothing that would make her into a freak for other people to stare at, and now there was a bit of colour in her face she looked almost like any other kid in the civilized world. Hair a bit messy, but so what, a tidy kid is a sick kid. Big grey eyes, face too thin, but small wonder, there isn't much in a dumpster to put meat on your bones.

"Where's your mom?" Doreen asked. The kid looked up at her

and grinned. "Where do you live?" Again that smile. Well, Doreen thought, we know she can talk, after all, she said "nice." So either she doesn't want to answer questions, or she doesn't have the answers. Or maybe she's been taught the hard way not to say anything to anybody about anything.

How long had she been alone in that alley? It's all relative, anyway. An hour spent at Disneyland is nothing, an hour spent on top of a red-hot stove is forever. An hour with a full belly watching TV in a warm room is one thing, an hour in a wet alley, alone, frightened, and hungry, is something else again.

Doreen stopped at her office and made some necessary notations on Sharon's file, checked her answering machine, left a note for the receptionist and watched how the kid behaved. The kid behaved very well. She sat on the sofa looking at the magazines, waiting quietly. Obviously she was well used to waiting. Doreen phoned Kay-Lee, her occasional investigator, and outlined her problem.

"Dumpster, huh?" Kay-Lee yawned. "Well, that's not much help."

"You know the Szechuan place I mean?"

"Yeah, the best hot and sour in town. That's all you've got for me?"

"Grey eyes, shoulder-length brown hair, light brown, almost dark blond. Kind of pale, a lot thinner than she should be. Stinking little summer dress, a pair of positively rotten underpants, and you don't want to hear about the shoes and socks. I've got them in a plastic bag if you need them."

"Hang onto them. Freeze them or something if you can't stand the smell. I mean, you might want to live in that apartment, right? Okay, if that's all you've got. You can't get a name out of her?"

"Hey, kid," Doreen called, "what's your name?" The kid looked up, smiled, and looked back down at the magazine. "She grins," Doreen said, "so if she has one, she's keeping it a secret. I asked her what her mommy's name was, she grinned. Asked where she lived, she grinned."

"She simple?"

"I don't think so. Toilet trained. Walks very well. Kind of . . . tomboy, I guess they'd say. You know, not mincing or cutesy-poo. She's looking at magazines and seems interested in the pictures. She just isn't speaking. Except when I put clean clothes on her she said 'nice'. Other than that, nothing."

"I take it you aren't phoning the welfare on this one."

"Not yet." Doreen felt suddenly very uneasy. "I want to make sure this one gets handled properly."

"Yeah?" Kay-Lee laughed. "Hey, any time you want to hear how you get handled when you're a foster kid, just ask me. I've got a scar or two I could show you."

If she had been told, Doreen would have refused to believe it. The pile of pancakes looked as tall as the kid and couldn't possibly fit inside that small frame. But it fit. And fit quickly. Who was it said the stomach was the same size as the clenched fist? Pancakes, two sausages, and a glass of milk. If she'd had the chance, she'd have crammed in more food, but Doreen had no intention of trying to cope with a vomiting child.

On the way back to the apartment they stopped at St. Vincent de Paul. This time they left with clothes that fit properly. A pair of leather shoes, hardly used. A warm woollen hat and mitts. A scarf that trailed Bob Cratchit style and a warm pea jacket. Less than the price of two cases of beer and the kid was outfitted for winter. Another brief stop and they had the newspaper and a bag of groceries, including a large bunch of grapes which the kid would have eaten right then and there given the chance.

On the way back, waiting at the corner for the light, Doreen noticed the kid staring in the window of a store. Just staring. Staring at a big plastic dump truck, bright yellow and red with black plastic wheels.

By the time they finally crossed the street the kid was carrying a bag in which rested the truck, a set of Lego, and a small cuddly bear. They stopped one more time before they were back at the apartment building, and this time Doreen carried the bag with the colouring books, wax crayons, and pencil crayons. "No bloody end to it, is there?" she muttered, but she grinned and the child grinned back up at her.

Nothing in the newspaper, nothing on television, no message from Kay-Lee, just the kid sprawled on the living room floor with a colouring book and a package of thirty-six crayons.

Of course, she could always pick up the phone and call the police. And then what? Questions, forms, answers, the kid goes off to wherever it is they ship them to. Doreen could hear it now. I'm sorry, Ms. Globilchuk, it is not our policy to . . .

There was no problem about amusing the kid. When she wasn't eating she was colouring or watching TV. Or playing with the truck. Or putting Lego together and taking it apart again. Or else she was sound asleep, lying on the carpet, as comfortable as she had been when she was in bed. Doreen got a heap of work done at her desk, more than she had thought she'd get done all weekend. Then she made supper.

"Okay, kiddo, you stand on the stool here. I'm going to crack this egg and let it glup down into the ground meat. And you're going to do this. See, both hands, get right in there and mix it up. That's it. Some salt, some pepper, some spices, some garlic, and now, chopped onion. Keep mixin', girl, we'll make a chef out of you yet."

They ate supper at the counter, sitting across from each other, smiling often. Doreen cut the hamburger patties into bite-sized pieces and the kid did the rest herself, packing away a meal that would have fed an adult dock-whalloper. When supper was finished they washed dishes together. Then another bath, some more TV, and the kid was asleep, lying on several thicknesses of extra folded sheet, just in case.

Sunday morning Doreen showed the girl how pancakes got made, then took her to Stanley Park. There wasn't much to see, all the tropical critters were safely inside, but the polar bears lazed around their pool in the fog and mist, and the whales in the aquarium did their sad, imprisoned tricks. The kid thought it was all wonderful, and Doreen hoped she would never learn the truth of things.

The art gallery was a dead loss. The kid didn't even look at the pictures, she just trudged obediently beside Doreen, as if she thought it was Doreen wanted to see something in this odd place. Obviously there was no sense going to the museum. It was too damp and cold for swings in the park, and finally, they went into a Mini-Mart, toured the shelves, and went home with another bag of groceries and a matched set of Raggedy Ann and Raggedy Andy dolls.

Kay-Lee came by just in time for supper, and the kid acted as if she were used to having people just drop by and stay a while. She smiled, very carefully rolled the chicken a piece at a time in the seasoned flour, and placed the pieces on a platter for Doreen to cook.

"She have any other kitchen skills?" Kay-Lee asked, sipping beer from a long-necked brown bottle.

"You ought to see her mash potatoes," Doreen laughed. "Holds the hand-mixer and goes at it without even spraying the stuff all over the kitchen."

"You think a kid that young should have an electric egg beater in her hand? What if she gets her fingers caught or something?"

"She didn't."

"Did you see last night's paper?"

"Yeah. Why?"

"You didn't notice?"

"What?"

There was nothing in the paper about a missing child, but there, on page eleven, a very bad wallet-sized snapshot, and under the snapshot an article, less than an article, hardly big or important enough to qualify as an "item." The body of a woman was found by police in an underground parking lot. Foul play was indicated. Initial investigation suggested the woman was involved in prostitution. Name unknown. Anyone with information asked to contact...

Doreen stared at the bad reproduction of the photograph. Young. Wide, guileless smile. The picture was too dark, too blurred to tell anything else. Besides, what if the kid looked like her dad?

"You think so?" she asked carefully.

"It's as close to a lead as we have," Kay-Lee said quietly.

They didn't talk about it, but both of them were preoccupied through supper. The kid was the only one who behaved normally. She just started at one side of her plate and worked her way through to the other side, serious-faced and eager.

"She always eat like that?"

"Hey, it's serious business for her!"

"I thought they fussed about food. Kids, I mean. Whined, and had to be coaxed with games like here comes the choo-choo, open the tunnel..."

"Not this kid." Doreen realized she was bragging. She flushed, then shrugged. "I guess an overfed kid isn't hungry and has to be coaxed."

"Hell of a thing, eh? You gonna phone the welfare in the morning?"

"I suppose I should."

"Got your story ready? About why you waited the entire weekend?"

"Got three of them ready. Now all I have to do is decide which of the three to use. I think I kind of lean to the one about how I knew they were shut on the weekend and didn't like the idea of the kid winding up with the police . . ."

"Yeah. Well, whatever you say. I believe you where thousands wouldn't."

Kay-Lee left once the dishes were done and Doreen put the kid in the tub for a half hour of bubbles and splashes. When the bath was cool she lifted the kid from the water, dried her, and wrapped her in a flannel shirt, sleeves rolled back, tail dangling. Then she sat in her big recliner with the kid on her lap, not watching TV, not talking, not doing anything but snuggling.

She took the kid to the office with her on Monday morning, not because she expected to be able to keep her amused there, not even because there was nothing else to do with her, but because, she told herself, it would be more convenient for the welfare to pick her up there. She took the colouring book and crayons, the Raggedy Ann and Andy, the truck and the Lego blocks so the child would have something to do.

She would have phoned the welfare immediately except for the pile of messages on her desk and her conviction the welfare office wouldn't be any less rushed and harried than her own was and she wanted an unrushed worker. In her heart, she knew, she was stalling the inevitable.

She stood by the window, looking out at the morning streets, the traffic solid in every direction, the sidewalks choked with people. The coffee in her mug smelled delicious but tasted like stale gasoline. She heard Laura, the receptionist, come in to work, heard the low murmur of her voice, then heard the crap hit the fan. The kid yelled, Laura gasped, and Doreen whirled, nearly dropping her mug of coffee. A small body hurtled through the doorway from the waiting room, small arms wrapped around Doreen's legs, the terrified face pressed against her, the hysterical sobbing ripped at her ears.

"Easy on, old sock," she managed. She put the mug on her desk, knelt, and disengaged the clutching arms. "Hey, hey, there, easy on, now. It's okay, it's just Laura, she's a friend."

Words meant nothing at all to the child. She clung, shaking and hysterical.

"All I did was . . ." Laura's face was stricken.

"It's okay," Doreen assured her. "She's kind of shook up is all." She picked up the little girl, held her tight, patting her back gently. "She isn't used to strangers," she embroidered, lying. She knew in her heart the kid was all too used to strangers, her life had been full of strangers, her world populated by strangers.

It isn't hard to convince yourself of something you've suspected all your life. It isn't hard to pinpoint the holes in the safety net when you've watched so many people plunge through them to destruction. Laura was calm again, the kid had stopped screeching, and there was no time left for evasion or stalling.

"My cousin's kid," Doreen lied. "Things have been pretty awful for her lately." She forced a smile, felt it fit naturally onto her face, the lies clicking together in a solid wall. "You'd think people would pay attention to the statistics, right? But no, every eighteen-year-old in the country thinks she's found true and eternal happiness. And five years later. . ." She kissed the tears from the child's face. "It's okay, baby. Come on, let's make friends with Laura, okay? Come on, you'll be seeing lots of her for the next little while."

"You mean," Laura stared at Doreen, astounded. "You got stuck with your cousin's kid?"

"Well, not really stuck, but. . . yeah, it was me or the welfare. So what choice was there?"

"Wow, what a change it's going to be for you! What's her name?"

"Eva." ❦

Cheryl

❦

Nobody was surprised when Cheryl and Fred separated, then divorced. The surprise was that they had ever married in the first place. That surprise was followed by the sixteen-year surprise of them living together, having two children, and not killing each other at any point in the process.

Those who met him called Fred "charming" and "friendly," they predicted he'd go a long way and commented on how well he had already done. Those who met Cheryl said she was "spunky" and "hard-working," and privately thought she had the disposition of a snake. Some called her Mighty Mouth, some made jokes about the Fastest Tongue in the West, some said nothing but prayed to God they would never again get on her wrong side or expose themselves to the razor-sharp two-edged verbal machete she swung at the merest hint of an insult or argument.

Together, Cheryl and Fred added up to more than the sum of their parts. Individually, each had holes in their personality through which could be driven at least one Euclid truck. Together, they filled those holes and sparked each other to higher efforts. Even their families agreed he was more pleasant, she was much smarter.

Cheryl didn't dislike people, she just couldn't stand fools. Fred didn't care how foolish people were if they were useful. When these two met and got married, neither had much of anything. Sixteen years later they had two children and one house in Bright's Crossing, paid for and rented out to tenants, and they had moved to a small wart of a town on the northern tip of the island, where they lived in a badly insulated "carpenter's special" owned by the trucking company for which they both worked. The trucking company owner had suggested several times that Cheryl and Fred buy the house and fix it up, thereby convincing the townspeople they intended to stay.

"I don't intend to stay here," Cheryl said baldly.

"I'd buy it back from you," the owner bargained.

"Why bother?"

"Why do you refuse a good deal?"

"Because I don't trust the motives of people who offer me good deals when I haven't even inquired."

The boss lived in Vancouver and flew into the wart of a town when the mood struck him. He showed up unannounced and unwelcome, poked his nose in every crack, cranny, and corner, always found something to bitch about, then flew back out again after causing a tempest in the small-town teapot. Fred always grinned, nodded, smiled, and agreed with the boss, Cheryl went about her work as if nothing out of the ordinary were happening.

Fred was the manager of the trucking company and Cheryl was the office manager. That meant, theoretically at least, Fred was Cheryl's boss. Most of the time this fine distinction didn't matter to anybody; Cheryl looked after the books, answered the phone, took messages, scheduled the drivers, and handled most of the complaints. Fred gave estimates, organized the work orders and mechanics, and made contacts which might result in new business.

Cheryl also got up in the morning, put on the coffee, made breakfast, and organized the kids. While they were getting fed and ready for school, she took a cup of coffee to Fred, then, while he was drinking it and waking up, she showered and dressed for work. She and the kids left the house at the same time. She unlocked the office, put on the coffee pot, and answered the phone if it was already ringing. She organized her day, and was working when Fred came in an hour later. He went to his office, she took him a cup of coffee, and by the time she got back to her desk, the red light on the phone was shining steadily: Fred had started working.

He was busy in his office for an hour, then went down to talk to the drivers and mechanics. If parts were needed, Cheryl phoned the city and arranged for them to be sent up on the daily plane. Fred got in his company car and drove off to check on the backhoe driver, the bulldozer driver, and the truck drivers, and to look for new business. His company car had a mickey-mouse installed so he could keep in touch with the office, where Cheryl was answering the phone, making appointments for Fred to go out and give estimates, arguing with suppliers in the city, or soothing the hurt feelings of a mechanic who had been insulted by the owner on his last trip in to check on things. Cheryl never asked Fred what in hell it was he was doing when he was out making contacts, and Fred never asked Cheryl who in hell she thought she was telling the mechanic the owner was an ignorant asshole who knew nothing about the kind of work the mechanic did so couldn't be expected to be appreciative, polite, or anything but an asshole.

And then the backhoe driver brought his machine in because something was wrong with the bucket. It would lift, but it wouldn't tilt. The mechanic went over, stared at it for a long time, fiddled with this, fiddled with that, then diagnosed it.

Cheryl was upstairs at her desk, just finishing the waybills and freight records when she heard a godawful thump, a roar of pain and surprise, and the ohmigawdjesusdamn of the mechanic. She was out from behind her desk, through the door and down the stairs before the echo of the awful thump had stilled. The backhoe driver was standing where he ought to be sitting, leaning forward, his hand stuck in the middle of the mess of pneumatic tubes and gizmos in the shaft of the arm that regulated the bucket. His face was dead white, his lips blue, and his eyes threatened to bug right out of his head. The mechanic, breathing curses, was busy with his tools. All he said to Cheryl was, "Get Fred back here with the car."

She went back up the stairs two at a time, grabbed the mickey-mouse, pushed the button and shouted, "Shop calling Fred, Shop calling Fred. Accident. Accident in the shop. Come in Fred." When there was no answer and she had tried so many times she was getting frightened, she changed her call to "If anybody sees Fred tell him to get his ass back here right away."

A voice she knew she ought to recognize answered her. "I think I know where he is, I'll go find him." Cheryl dropped the whole rig and raced back down the stairs.

The driver's fingers were still jammed in whatever it was had jammed, and the mechanic was cursing frantically. Cheryl climbed onto the step, then into the cab, got behind the driver, bent her legs under him, and lifted and pushed him forward, taking the pull from his arm and hand.

"Got 'er," the mechanic gasped. The driver's fingers came free, the glove leather startlingly white, all dirt, water, and grease squeezed out of the two leather digits. He sighed deeply and sagged. Cheryl hauled him back into the cab of the machine, got him on the seat, loosened the buttons on his shirt, and wiped the oily sweat off his cold face.

No Fred. No company car. No calm person to drive them to the infirmary. The mechanic's licence was under suspension for impaired driving, so it was Cheryl got behind the wheel of the gravel truck and somehow, nobody ever knew how or believed it was possible, she got the man to the hospital.

They weren't sure they could save the fingers. The operator was half frantic, and the nurse was totally occupied with the damaged hand, so it was Cheryl who had to calm the operator, soothe his fears and even make him smile.

"Will he be able to play the guitar?" she asked anxiously.

"Oh, yes, of course," the nurse soothed.

"Good," Cheryl cracked, "he never could before this happened."

The young operator grinned, shook his head and managed to say "Corny groaner."

Two minutes later, Fred came in. The doctor and nurse took over. Cheryl backed out of the room and moved wordlessly to the waiting room where the ashtray beckoned. She lit a cigarette and puffed nervously until her hands stopped shaking.

Fred was at the desk talking to the receptionist, and Cheryl watched him as if she had never seen him before in her life. When the forms were filled in and the operator was on his way to the small surgery, a driver arrived to take the gravel truck back down to the shop, and Fred told Cheryl he'd drive her back to work.

"Take me home," she said coldly.

"Home?"

"Just take me home. I feel sick."

"But . . ."

"You can do it," she flared angrily. "You're the goddamn expert, you're the know-it-all, you're the boss! You do something for a change."

"What in hell is the matter with *you?*"

"Where were you?"

"What do you mean?"

"Where in hell were you? You're either supposed to be *in* the office or let me know where you are in case you're needed. Or be in the goddamn company car with the effin' radio receiver turned *on*, Fred."

"I was busy!"

"You're supposed to let me know *where* you are and *when* you leave and where you go *next.*"

He asked her who in hell she thought she was to talk to him like that, after all he was the boss, and she said the boss was supposed to be a responsible person and tell the office where he was at all times and he said she was just trying to be a typical wife keeping tabs on her husband and she said bullshit and he yelled he was *busy*, for God's sake.

"Busy my ass!" Mighty Mouth yelled. "I just bet you were effin' busy!" and it was the red rising from his collar to his forehead gave it all away.

"You bastard," she said quietly. "You *were* effin', weren't you? You were busy, all right, busy . . . you shit."

He dropped her off in front of the carpenter's special, neither of them speaking to the other, and he went back to the shop to unsnarl the mess. The mechanic had phoned the owner in the city, and the owner was on his way up by charter plane to find out how in hell come the manager had been unavailable and the office manager hadn't been told where he was or what he was doing. Fred could just about see the balloon going up, and knew he was going to have to work overtime just to keep his job.

The owner arrived and the yelling started. Fred sat in his big black leather office chair and nodded a lot. He heard the last plane leave and knew the owner was going to be stuck overnight in the little wart of a town, and Fred wondered how in hell he was going to calm Cheryl down enough to convince her she should save his job by cooking up a first-rate supper and making up the spare bed so the owner didn't have to spend any money on a hotel room or a lousy meal. The owner screamed and screeched and let Fred know that he already knew exactly where Fred had been, with whom, doing what, during work hours. Let him know the whole goddamn town at this point knew what Fred was doing while Cheryl was holding the whole goddamn show together and driving a badly injured man to hospital in a goddamn gravel truck while the company car had been parked beside the wrong house. And, he let Fred know, the husband who had been on dayshift at the sawmill was at this very minute screaming his version of everything and the owner wouldn't be surprised, by God, if Fred wound up with two black eyes.

But when Fred got home there was no problem about what he would say to Cheryl to persuade her to cook supper and be pleasant. She was gone. So were the kids. And their clothes. And the cat. And the turtle. ❦

Joanne

❦

The noisy cars and unmuffled pickup trucks thundered up the drive less than half an hour after the beer parlour closed. One by one the engines roared, then stopped; doors opened, then slammed; and the guys from work yelled their way to the back steps, up onto the porch, and through the back door into the kitchen.

Joanne Duncan crawled deeper under the covers, pulling the quilt up past her ears, trying to hide in the darkness. The noise came through the thin walls so clearly she could see, as well as if she were in the kitchen with them, everything they did.

The fridge door opened and closed, opened and closed, opened and closed, and each time there was the rattle of bottles being put on the racks, the clatter and click of food being shoved back out of the way, making room for more important things, like Carlings Black Label and Molsons Export.

Payday Friday night. Loud voices, laughter, and the sound of the phone dial clicking as someone phoned the order in to Hong Lee. Scrape of chairs, clunk of bottle bottoms on the table top, laughter and more laughter.

"Hey, old woman," he yelled. "Hey, old woman, you comin' out or are we gonna have ta go in and get ya?"

Joanne heard his footsteps clump across the kitchen, through the unfinished living room, to the bedroom. As the door squeaked open, he spoke only slightly more quietly than he had yelled. "Hey, darlin', don't leave me alone out here."

Her mother answered softly, he laughed, then the footstep-sounds went back to the kitchen.

"Hurry up!" Ted yelled. "If you don't get here I'll drink 'er all myself."

"Come on, Dorrie, up an' at 'em," Henry shouted. "Don't be unsociable, now."

Joanne's mother's steps moved across the bare plywood underflooring, then the noise from the kitchen went up a level. Everyone had to say Hi Dorrie, everyone had to say You're sure lookin' good, Dorrie, everyone had to say About time, what were ya doin' in there anyway, and everyone had to laugh suggestively, as if they knew full well what Doreen was doing, and considered it racy and sexual, forbidden but fair game for their fantasies.

It went on for almost an hour, then Hong Lee's delivery truck drove up and there was a scraping of chairs, the sound of quarters falling to the floor, Tommy and Fred having a long Never mind, No, it's okay, I got 'er, as Fred made change for Tommy because Tommy only had a twenty and needed a ten to put in the pot.

"Hey, you rug-rats," he roared. "Hey, all you knee-gnawing ankle-biters, you can get up now."

The bedroom doors opened upstairs and the little kids scampered for the steps down to the living room, through the living room to the kitchen where they joined the joy and laughter.

"Joanne! Come an' get it before we give 'er to the dogs!" he hollered.

Then her bedroom door was open, the light was slanting in from the big trilight lamp, and he was in the room, grabbing the quilt, hauling it aside, and reaching for her. His fingers dug into her ribs, tickling as he pulled her upright.

She pretended she'd been asleep. She knew he knew she hadn't been asleep at all, and he knew she knew he knew, but they pretended, anyway.

"Come on, sugarpie," he grinned beerily, "grab a plate and a fork and save yourself from the spectre of starvation."

She pulled her jeans and shirt on over her pyjamas. She hated the way they looked at her if she didn't. Her pyjamas were too small, the material worn thin from so many washings, and they all felt free to comment on her development the same as if she were a sow they were thinking of buying at the auction. "Gettin' big for her age, isn't she" didn't have anything to do with growing taller. "Won't be a kid much longer" had nothing to do with growing up.

She hauled on socks and sneakers because she didn't even want them to see her bare feet. She'd have covered her arms, hands, neck, and face if there'd been any way to do it. Live in a sack, maybe, with little ragged cut eyeholes to peer out of so she wouldn't bump into one of them and give them an excuse to grab at her.

She went through the kitchen to the pantry and got a pile of plates to take to the table. They pulled their beer bottles out of the way but made no move to help. They'd chipped in to pay for it, now all they had to do was eat it and digest it. Or eat it and hork it up over the side of the porch rail if the party lasted too long and got too wet.

Joanne took the lids off the containers and started putting food on plates, portions of everything. The kids waited, eyes bright, faces flushed with excitement. She could hear her mother making a big pot of tea they both knew nobody but them would drink. The men had their beer, and more out in the cars if it was needed. The kids took their plates into the living room and sat on the floor together, shovelling food into their mouths, thinking it all great fun. Joanne used to think it was fun, too. Payday Friday night, and he never came home for supper. Dorrie smiled as much as ever, but everyone knew tonight was no night for misbehaviour, no night for noise in the kitchen or wrestling on the sofa.

There was something strange in the way Dorrie behaved on Friday payday night. Supper was like something you'd expect on Sunday. Joanne didn't know if it was in case the sky should fall and he would arrive with his pay packet unopened in his pocket, or if Dorrie just wanted to assure herself that he'd missed something by going to the beer parlour with the guys. Even knowing they would all troop in when the pub closed and immediately order Chinese or Italian, Dorrie cooked big hot suppers and the kids ate as if they had hollow legs.

Well, that part of it Joanne could understand. Tension made her hungry, too. As if some part of her were saying Maybe I'm not relaxed, maybe I'm nervous, but by God my gut will be happy! Like when she'd opened that book about the war and saw all those pictures of people who had been starved so bad for so long their pelvic bones stuck out like big salad bowls, and she couldn't stop eating the whole time she looked through the book. Apples and raisins, cheese, big thick slices of bread with margarine slathered deep on top.

After supper the kids played in the back yard or kicked a ball around in the field beside the house, but nobody asked to go to the playground or spend time at a friend's house. Dorrie didn't want to be bothered with anything, she wanted to see where everyone was without having to call them or go looking. The kitchen had to be cleaner and tidier than usual, everything put away, everything washed until it shone, what could shine, which wasn't much in a house getting built a bit at a time as cash and inclination dictated.

The men waited until all the kids had their food, then they waited while Joanne filled a plate and handed it to her mother, and another for her father. Then she served the guys, one by one, and each of them just nodded, not even saying thank you. They'd all chipped in equally, hadn't they? He didn't pay any more than anyone else, even though his wife, her kid, and their kids would eat. Why say thank you?

When everyone else had a mountain of food, Joanne filled her own plate and went into the living room with the kids. She felt more comfortable there. Nobody else would have called it comfortable, knowing all those yahoos were in the kitchen, drinking themselves closer and closer to that moment when one word set off a punch-up guaranteed to bust a chair or knock the door hinges wonky.

Tommy had a common-law who sometimes met him in the pub and drank with them, showing up as part of the crowd. Tommy didn't pay any more when she was with him, nor any less when she wasn't. Joanne already knew the rules. They sat at a table and put their money in the middle, ordering rounds in turn counterclockwise, the waiter taking the money from the pile in the middle. Except the women, who weren't supposed to put money in the pot. Even if they had any, which most of them didn't.

Ted used to have a common-law but she up and left. Didn't even take any furniture, just packed her clothes while he was at work and when he came home there was the table set for supper, but all there was on his plate was a note with some words from a song: Got along without you before I met you, gonna get along without you now. Ted blew a hairy, knocked the table over, broke the dishes, wrecked the kitchen, then went out and got himself altogether shitfaced before going back to sit, bawling, in the mess of broken glass, spilled milk, and splintered chair legs. When he found out where she'd gone and phoned her to tell her to get her ass back where it belonged, she sang a passage from another song: Well you can cry me a river, cry me a river, I cried a river over you. He still cried rivers. He'd drink and laugh and joke and flirt with anything that was warm, right up to the point where he started maundering on with his own song, about how a pretty lass and an old beer glass made a horse's ass outta me. Not half a beer later he'd be leaking all over his face.

Henry's wife sometimes got a babysitter, but she didn't go to the pub, she came to the house and sat in the kitchen with Dorrie, talking softly, watching out the window as if there were any chance at all they would show up before the last dog had been hung.

Fred didn't have a steady woman, not that he wasn't always trying, and it was hard to figure out why nobody would move in with him full-time or even stay very long. He was okay-looking, and clean enough, he didn't have any disgusting habits like nose-picking or pocket pool. But they'd only go out with him five or six times and then he'd be riding the old lonesome trail again, looking as hopeful as a dog dropped on the side of the road miles from home.

When all the eating, chewing, and swallowing were finished, Joanne collected the plates and forks, piled everything neatly on the counter, wiped the table, then escorted the kids out to the crapper in the far corner of the back yard, waiting for them to pee themselves dry before she took them back to their upstairs rooms.

The beer caps were thick on the table top again, and Dorrie had a glass of suds. Joanne hoped Dorrie wouldn't fall off the wagon again. It was hell when Dorrie was drinking. Most of the time she could take it or leave it, dip her beak and join the party but stay human and nice and like her almost-always self. But every now and again the wheels would come off and she'd fall from the little red rider and land nose first in a lake of booze. Then she argued with him, and screamed at the kids. She might or might not do house-work, she probably wouldn't cook a meal or pack a lunch. The sight of someone else cleaning up would send her into a fury, and noise ruled supreme until your head just felt stuffed with it. Then there'd be hell's own fight, and Dorrie would get herself pulled together again, sometimes for so long you'd get sucked into thinking this time, for sure, she'd dried herself out and was going to stay dry.

Joanne went back to her room, closed the door, moved to her bed in the darkness, sat on the edge of the thin mattress, pulled off her shirt and jeans, and lay down gratefully, squirming a bit to get her pyjamas back where they belonged after being scrunched underneath her clothes. She drifted in and out of sleep in that half-world of wakening where every sound is magnified and conversations fifty feet away seem to be happening right inside your ear drums.

They had the radio on now, WWVA Wheeling West Virginia on the shortwave band. He was telling them all for the umpteenth time how it was music brought him and Dorrie together in the first place.

"There she'd be, just as pretty as she is now, all dressed up and laughing in spite of being there with that fuckin' loser, and it didn't matter what song anyone wanted, she knew 'er. Just tuck that cheapo fiddle under her chin and off she'd go, playin' her little heart out, singin' along with whoever had the floor, makin' harmonies and counterpoints and all that good shit, and I thought by God Frenchie, I thought, you gotta get your head outta your ass and find you a way to send that goat-blower down the road."

They all laughed and hoo-rahed. Goat-blower. That was Joanne's own dad. Goat-blower. Well, maybe so. How would she know? She hardly remembered him, except that when he was drinking there was no party and no Chinese or Italian take-out, just heavy heavy silence and ugly I-hate-your-guts looks. Big hard hands pounding learning into her ass and Dorrie sitting sullen and half-cut, glaring out the window from eyes rimmed with blue bruise.

Goat-blower.

"But no matter what I tried, that little girl wasn't havin' none of it. If she's nothin' else, my Dorrie is loyal, right Dor? I mean that asshole was the asshole of all assholes, the absolute example of fuckin' assholiness, and cheap, too. Right, Dor? I mean she was his invite, right? Who'd'a ever asked the miserable shit anywhere if it wasn't the only way to get Dor to go and take her fiddle, right?"

"Right," Fred agreed. "Right fuckin' on, Frenchie."

"And she had one good dress. Now I ask you. I mean the day I can't get a good dress for my woman is the day I stop spendin' money on some damn thing I don't need, know what I mean?"

"Too true, French, just too fuckin' true."

"Smokes or something. Hell, I'd pawn my shotgun before I'd have my woman lookin' shabby, know what I mean? But him? No fuckin' pride that man. So anyway, after a while I almost give up. I mean knock on the door and it'll be opened don't always hold true. Ask and it shall be granted? I was doin' more than askin', Christ I was on the floor weepin' like a puppy, beggin' with my tongue down to my shoelaces. But old Dor, she just smiled and said Oh, quit your teasin'. Man, I wasn't teasin'! Then the cocksucker blew 'er all to hell and did me the favour of all times. We're at this place, see, and, well, hell, you was there, Henry."

"Dave Plecas's place."

"Right. Dave, he's havin' this party, and there's some fifty or sixty people there, and washtubs fulla beer'n ice, and I got my banjo and Dorrie, she's got her fiddle and one of the Wakely boys had that tin-top guitar of his."

"Dobro, Frenchie, for Chrissakes it's a Dobro."

"Whatever. And we're havin' just one helluva good time and all of a quick, like right off the fuckin' wall, here's this squinty-eyed asshole couldn't find his mouth to eat garbage with a bent spoon, and he's yellin' at her that she's tryin' ta put the make on old Tom Chaperowski. I mean the old geezer hadda be sixty if he was a day, right? And she says things like no, honey, it wasn't like that at all, and he screams you callin' me a liar you fuckin' hoor? Well, I thought I'd freeze to death, that's how cold I went. I said to him I said, you got no call to talk like that to Dorrie, she ain't outta line, you are, and he shoves his big fat finger halfway inna my eye and says to me he says, shut your fuckin' face you frog bastard. Now I don't mind bein' called Frenchie but I do object to bein' called frog, y'know? And then he says, you can always tell a fuckin' frog in a crowd of white men because they talk with their hands, they fight with their feet, and they fuck with their faces. And Dorrie, she kind of turns away and she's about to pack her fiddle in its box and he just ups and lets fly. Shit la merde, man. She went ass over appetite there and I knew she was out cold as a clam. I mean she was *out*. And he's all set to give her punch number two, right? Now I ask ya, the woman shouldn't'a been hit the first time, and she's out for the fuckin' count for sure and he's windin' up to let fly again? There's limits, right?"

"Fuckin' right, Frenchie. Real limits."

"Right. And the fiddle, it hits the floor and Dorrie lands on top of it and I knew from the crunch it had played its last song."

"Fuckin' shame. Her old man made that one, didn't he?"

"So he did. Never knew him myself, but I seen some of the stuff he made and he was more than a fiddle-maker, he was what they call a luthier. Fuckin' genius, that man. Made his own glue but never gave nobody the recipe so when he died . . . so there's this fiddle been killed and the shithead, he's all set to send Dorrie right along with it and if I'd'a thought about it I'd'a likely just sat there because the only religion I got is devout coward and instead it's like I'm watchin' myself. Up off the fuckin' chair I come and the old boot just keeps rising, up and up until it gets him right where the family jewel is stored."

"Shit man, it was classic. Ker-thunderin-pow," Henry laughed. The others laughed with him, except for Dorrie who wasn't saying anything.

"And when he went down to the floor I just let fly another into the throat. Picked up Dorrie, picked up what was left of her poor bustup fiddle, and old Henry, there, he packs the banjo for me, and I fuckin' left the party." He laughed again, and Joanne heard the long gurgle as he sucked beer into his dry throat. "Had our own party, didn't we, hon? Been havin' 'er ever since, too, by God. That's why there's so many goddamn rug-rats in sleepin' bags upstairs. No more'n get a bed bought for one of 'em and there's two more crawling underfoot!"

"Well, Jesus, but he was mad," Henry prompted.

"Mad? Listen, that ain't the word for the shape that sad bastard was in when he finally quit pukin' his guts out on the lawn! You ever seen a man so bent outta shape he's the colour of a cooked beet? That was him, the goat-blower. Shows up at my place before noon the next day, I was livin' in that little blue trailer over at Cassidy's place, the one wotzisname's in now."

"Pearson? Parson?"

"Whatever. So you can figure how skookum it wasn't, right. And all of a quick here's this fuckin' moron kickin' at the door and raisin' supreme shit. So I called the cops. They get paid more'n a thousand bucks a month to keep shit outta my life, right? And that was shit smashin' at my door. But he was out by Monday and the fat in the fire for sure because by then Dorrie'n me we'd gone and got the kid. Paid the babysitter, the whole thing. Moved her stuff, moved the kid's stuff, Christ that little blue trailer was crowded, I'll tell you. And still the dumb shit couldn't take the hint."

"Come to my place," Henry said happily. "Thought you was my friend, he says. I'm no friend, I said, of a man who punches out his woman in front of a house fulla people."

"So by Jesus if he don't wait like an egg-suckin' coon, until he sees her alone. Comin' back from shoppin', packages under one arm, kid under the other. And be damned if he don't beat the shit outta her again. I come home, no Dorrie, no kid, no note, no nothin', and then the phone rings and it's the fuckin' hospital and aren't they tellin' me Dorrie is bein' kept overnight. I go up and it was to make a grown man sit down and bawl his eyes out. Even the fuckin' kid's been taken to the cleaners. I mean, really. Four years old and he slams her around like she was fifty years old and six foot tall and a man to boot. And I tell you, that bastard won't come closer to dyin' until the day he actually does 'er. If I coulda got my hands on him I'd'a . . . well, damned if I know what I'd'a done because I never got the chance. Fucker was gone. Gone lock, stock, and fuckin' barrel. But Dorrie, she didn't care, she signed the papers and everything anyway. Do he ever come back his ass is grass and I'm the fuckin' lawnboy, I'll tell ya."

And on and on and on, the one big dramatic event of his life, and Fred waxing fat on the reflected glory of it all. Joanne didn't know how Dorrie felt having the whole world treated to a verbal re-run, but she knew how she felt about it, she felt like if she was big enough she'd take the dirtiest, smelliest pair of summer socks she could find and ram them in Frenchie's mouth just to stop him from trotting her out naked and defenceless for all the world to peer at, like a bug in a jar or a freak in a circus tent. Hear ye year ye hear ye come one come all put down your dime, just one thin dime and see the kid who got punched out on the street, never another like it in the history of the world, ladies and gennulmen, come see for yourself, just one thin dime and you too can see where the arm was broken, you too can see the scar along the bottom jawline where they had to cut in to get the bits of shattered bone where the boot-toe connected. If she had a silver plate in her head I could charge you a quarter but all she's got are a few little stitch marks.

She drifted off, and came back to the sound of Ted blabbering on about how lucky Frenchie was. "You got you a good woman, Frenchman, and you better know, the way you know your own goddamn name, just how lucky you are. Fuck, man, if I'd'a been that lucky I'd'a been a happy man but you know as well as I do what kind of a streetwalkin' slut I hadda get tangled up with."

She wasn't any such thing. She was short and kind of square, she had laugh lines and a gravelly voice, she sewed so well you couldn't tell it from store-bought. She left for damn good reasons and everybody knew it but nobody said anything.

Frenchie tuned up his banjo and told Dorrie to get her fiddle. Then he had to tell everyone at longwinded length how it was he'd worked extra hours for months on end to get enough spare cash to go to Vancouver and get the finest goddamn violin they had in the fuckin' place. "I'd'a got her a Stradivarius if they'd'a had one. I mean it. Sell my brand new Fruit of the Looms if I have to."

When Dorrie was sober, she played any hour of the day or night. The drop of a hat and she'd be playing. When she was drinking, the fiddle never came out of its case.

"You're so fuckin' lucky, Frenchman. I hope you know how lucky you are." Ted was getting past the moaning and whining and close to the snivelling and crying. He always made out he was a first-class music lover, but if he had been, his woman might not have caught the eleven a.m. headed out of town.

Someone was clattering spoons, someone else was clapping, and the sound drowned out Ted's maundering and moaning. Joanne let the music close around her like a security blanket. As long as they were playing and singing they wouldn't be fighting and yelling.

She dreamed she was finished grade twelve and ready to go off on her own and Jessie Williams was standing at the mike telling seventy thousand people she wanted them to give a big hand to a singing fool from Jessie's own home town. And then Joanne was walking out into the bright hot lights, her old Simpsons Christmas sale catalogue guitar in one hand, and people were clapping before she even started playing and singing.

But it wasn't people clapping, it was him, hauling her out of bed by one arm, lurching unsteadily back to the kitchen, grinning that lopsided grin that said he'd had too much to drink, about a bucketful too much.

"Ted's heart's broken," he slurred, "and he wants you should do him a somebody done somebody wrong song."

He shoved her little guitar at her, and she took it without thinking. She plucked the strings, tuning automatically, feeling their eyes on her pyjamas, feeling their eyes looking through the faded flannelette, feeling all the hot red beer idiocy as they licked their lips or guzzled their beer or burped their chow mein breath.

"I don't wanna," she heard herself say. "You're all drunk."

"Play the fuckin' thing!" he snarled, that crazy do-as-you're-told-goat-blower look in his eyes.

"I don't want to," she repeated.

"Play, for God's sake, Joey," Dorrie said urgently. "Don't cause a fuss."

"I'm not causin' a fuss," she exploded. "I was asleep! And they're all drunk as skunks! Nobody is really listening."

"Fuck this!" Frenchie yelled. "I bought the cocksuckin' thing, and I paid for the cocksuckin' thing, so play the fucker for my friends!"

"No," she shouted, every bit as loud as he did. "I don't have to!"

And he reached out, grabbed the guitar and smashed it on the corner of the big black woodburner. "Then eat shit, bitch!" he snarled. "If you won't play for me and my friends you won't play for nobody at all!" He threw the shards in the corner, then turned to smile at his woman. "Come on, Dorrie, play a sad song for Ted so's he can quit cryin' the blues."

Joanne felt herself disappear altogether. Felt herself become part of the wallpaper that hadn't even been put on the gyproc walls yet. She didn't count, her opinion didn't count, what she wanted didn't count, and they could all get along just fine without her and the guitar she didn't even have any more.

She went back to the bedroom, got into bed, pulled the quilt up to her ears, and lay dry-eyed, hearing the sound of Dorrie's fiddle, knowing that the next time she woke up Dorrie would be half crocked and the fiddle would be in its case, hidden out in the woodshed, up in the rafters where he had never found it yet. They'd all tiptoe around like cat-terrified mice until Dorrie had washed whatever it was that was stuck in her throat back down into her gut where it could be ignored for a while.

One of these days she'd be finished grade twelve. One of these days she'd be setting off on her own. One of these days Jessie Williams would stand up in the bright warm lights and say Ladies and gentlemen, I'd like you to give a good country welcome to a singin' fool from my home town. Put 'em together and make a good loud noise, please, for my good friend Joanne Duncan. 🍂

California

🍒

The Elder Gods snore in their caves and barrow mounds, coming awake only briefly when swollen bladders or blocked bowels demand. Grumbling, ill-tempered, and bored to shit, they rise, stumbling, to move to the lip of the Great Abyss and relieve themselves of the inner burden of dozey millennia. It is then the earth shifts and rolls, the mountains rumble as the guts of the Elder Gods rumble, entire mountainsides slide downward, rivers are blocked, cities are destroyed.

Many of the gods return to their sleeping places snorfling and snuffling, coughing and hacking, scratching their asses or heads, then go back to sleep. Others stop briefly at the Table of Plenty and nibble or gorp, depending on their nature and personality. Some who claim to know say the food on this table is as old as the gods, bread which never goes stale, cheese which never goes rancid, wine which never turns to vinegar. Others who make claims of knowledge say there are still those who are faithful to the Ancient Vision and visit regularly, bringing roast chicken, cappuccino, and strawberry shortcake. Still others insist it is up to each of the gods and goddesses, that everything is but their vision, we are all but the dream of the gods, and that is why we live in a world at once beautiful and ugly, fertile and barren, full of wonder and horror. It depends, they say, on which part of whose dream we occupy, whether we live our lives in a dream of peace or a nightmare caused by indigestion or constipation.

The Elder Gods withdrew when the experiment of free choice proved humankind to be less than they had desired. A few of the Old Ones wanted to sweep the losers away and start again, a few others thought it would be nice to leave the earth a natural parkland, without having to bother in any way with the latest experiment, a vocal minority spoke long and eloquently of evolutionary development. "Give them some time to get their feet under them," they debated, and the elders, with nothing better to do at the time, agreed.

Evolution takes time. In fact, without time there isn't evolution. The gods, even those inclined to indulgence, began to yawn as time after time humankind opted for the bigoted and bizarre, the narrow-minded and restrictive, the oppressive and the punitive. One by one the gods shook their heads and went to their beds. One by one they closed their eyes and opted for a snooze.

Each time a god wakens, the world trembles on the lip of eternity. Each time a god moves to the brink of the abyss to shit, we all stand, unknowing, in the shadow of a temper tantrum. Just one of them can prove every theological argument null and void. Determinism can vanish in the reek of a purple fart.

Boredom alone both threatens and saves us. The Elders have been bored for so long they have begun to yearn for anything to relieve the boredom, even for a moment or two. If a thousand years are but a day in the sight of the Elder Gods, how long is a moment? How long a moment or two? Every now and again, just to relieve the tedium, one or another of the Aged Ones pulls a cutie.

California Murphy was one of those cuties.

California's mother, Barbara Murphy, hated her father, had little use for her mother, and thought her entire family the most boring bunch of dimwits ever created. She may have been correct. She ought to have included herself in her own estimate. Barbara Murphy wanted something different in her life. She wanted something exotic, something unpredictable, something she could not anticipate.

Barbara Murphy wanted a man who in no way resembled her father. She particularly wanted a man who did not have a mouth like Ed Murphy's mouth. Ed Murphy was big, Ed Murphy was powerfully strong, Ed Murphy had a temper like a dyspeptic snake and fists like the hammers of Thor. That's why nobody ever called him Liver Lips to his face, but only behind his back. Ed Murphy's mouth looked inside out. It also looked upside down. Children practised rolling their bottom lips as far down as they would go, then stretching the tips of their tongues over their top lips, almost touching their own noses, making a wet, glistening, unpleasant, rude, and still inadequate mockery of the mess Ed Murphy carried between his nose and his chin.

Barbara Murphy's mother Candace (nee Schmuque) married Ed for his body and his wallet, and managed to overlook his mouth. Besides, as she found out on a warm summer night within earshot of the rhythmic surging of the tide, a mouth like that had its compensations. She lay on the imitation Navajo blanket, watching the pale all-knowing moon, smelling the scent of thimbleberry leaves, holding her date by the ears, deciding what she would be willing to endure in return for what she was learning for the first time. Candace Schmuque Murphy did not regret her bargain.

But Barbara regretted the bargain. No need to explain to her that without Ed Murphy's chromosomes she would not be who she was. No good to tell her had Candace married someone else there would never have been a Barbara Murphy. Barbara knew what Barbara knew, and she knew every kid in town called her dad Liver Lips. Or worse.

Barbara Murphy hated her name, hated her life, and wanted a change. She endured high school because she had not yet perceived another option. She got a job in the B. C. Hydro office because it was available. She continued to live at home, paying room and board until she had saved enough to buy some furniture, then she got her own apartment in town and walked to work every morning, walked home again after work.

Barbara Murphy socked her money away with almost religious zeal. She was determined to Make Something of her life, and money was a good way to do that. She stood behind her counter, smiling coolly at the people who came in to pay their hydro bills. She took money, made change, stamped bills "Paid," and waited tensely for her life to improve.

She knew what she wanted. She knew exactly what she wanted. Nobody had ever warned her to be careful what you wish for, you might get it.

He wasn't Irish, he didn't get up every morning in the dark, get dressed in heavy work clothes, eat bacon, eggs, and pancakes, then head off with his rain gear, his aluminum lunch box, his huge thermos, and his caulk boots. He didn't sling rigging or set beads, he wasn't a monkey-wrencher or a High-Ho operator, he didn't make twenty-five bucks an hour ten hours a day five days a week four weeks a month seven months a year. He didn't have muscles hanging off other muscles, he didn't chew snuff, and he had no desire at all to go to the rodeo in Quesnel.

And he didn't have liver lips. His mouth was as finely drawn as any artist's masterpiece. He had eyes like a cocker spaniel begging for a soup bone, and a body designed for ballet tights. Barbara Murphy knew the first time she saw him that this was what she wanted.

She got him. By breaking every rule her mother had taught her, she got him. When he came in to pay his bill she learned his name and address. She looked it up in the phone book and sure enough, there he was, and it wasn't even a toll call. She watched him carefully for two months before she made her move. Then she moved into his apartment building, not caring that the rent was thirty dollars a month more than she had been paying. A dollar a day isn't much to pay for a chance to catch what you have wanted all your life.

She made sure they met in the hallway. She made sure she went down to the laundry room at the same time he went down to the laundry room. And one night, in the elevator, she asked him if he would like to come over for supper.

He did. He arrived on time, looking like a gypsy. Barbara Murphy had never seen a man wearing a red satin shirt with puffy sleeves, she had never seen a man wearing one thin gold chain around his wrist. She fed his belly, she fed his ego, and she did not make the mistake of trying to seduce him on the first date.

She bought two tickets to a concert and invited him to go with her. She took him out for Szechuan before the concert and picked up the tab as if she had no interest in saving money. She took him for drinks after the concert, and thanked him in the elevator for a wonderful evening. Still she made no attempt to seduce him.

Until their seventh date, because seven was her lucky number. This time it was and it wasn't. She had no trouble getting the very gorgeous young man into bed. No trouble turning his crank. No trouble adapting what Ed Murphy had shown her own mother. She had no trouble at all until it came to the part about to have and to hold in sickness and in health for richer for poorer till death do us part. He wasn't into that shit. Traditional marriage and monogamy were fetters around the ankles of the world. A man has to do what a man has to do. Onward and upward, excelsior.

When she began to get insistent about it, when the pages on the calendar passed unmarked one month, two month, three months, and Barbara Murphy felt the first twinges of absolute desperation, he did more than fold his tent and silently steal away; he packed up lock, stock, and barrel, and was gone some time between midnight and eight a.m. Gone as if he had never lived on the third floor. Red satin puff-sleeve shirt, shiny loafers, and little gold chain.

Barbara Murphy wasn't without her resources. She didn't know where he was, but she knew where his mother lived.

"Oh my God," his mother sighed, knowing as soon as she opened the door and saw Barbara's eyes. "Oh my God."

"Where is he?" Barbara asked.

"California, I suppose," his mother managed. "He wants to be a movie star."

It was spite made Barbara Murphy name her daughter California. Spite because one brief look at the newborn baby girl told her everything she needed to know. She didn't know one of the Elder Gods had risen for a shit and taken it into his head to break the monotony with a good chortle. She only knew her daughter's face was stamped forever with an all-time joke. There was the lovely little finely drawn mouth. And all around it, Ed Murphy. Eyes, nose, chin, cheekbones, yellow-brown down-slanted eyes, neat brows, long lashes, and wide brow. The two men in her life, father and lover, staring up at her from a cuddly pink blanket.

Neither Ed Murphy nor Candace Schmuque Murphy ever said "How could you" or "I told you so" or "Look what you've done now, you fool." They took the news the way so many other parents have taken the news, they welcomed the child the way so many other grandparents have welcomed children, and they did everything they could to smooth the rocky way.

Candace looked after California uncomplainingly while Barbara went off to her drippy little job. Ed treated California as he had treated Barbara: he made sure she had some toys, he repaired the swing in the back yard, he took her for walks and ice cream cones, and he got from California what he had never got from his own daughter. Ed Murphy got love. California didn't care if he had Liver Lips. California didn't care if he wasn't always clean-shaved. California didn't care he had callouses thick on his hands and no matter what he did his nails were always grimed. California didn't even care if he looked like a workie, walked like a workie, talked like a workie, and thought like a workie. He was her grandpa and she adored him. California didn't care her grandma was boring, she didn't care her grandma watched the soaps and worried more about the shine on the living room floor than she did about the theory of evolution. California loved her grandma, and not because of the spice cookies which came hot and soft from the oven, or because of the lunchtime soup served in a lovely thick blue bowl, or even because Candace had never believed eating bread crusts brought any improvement in morality. The kid didn't care for them and the chickens loved them, so why kick up a stink? Cut them off before you put the devilled egg sandwich in front of the child.

California drifted happily from day to day, from birthday to birthday, and then she started school. She didn't particularly care for her teacher, she detested the smells in the school, she did not enjoy sitting for long hours at a desk designed by Torquemada to be as uncomfortable as possible, and most of what they tried to teach her had no relevance to her life, but she spewed back the answers they wanted, got very good marks on all the exams, and floated from grade to grade in a chain of years linked by glorious summer holidays.

California seldom saw her mother. Barbara got up, got dressed, got California out of bed, got her dressed, fed her breakfast, then took her to Candace. California went to school from her grandma's house and came home from school to her grandma's house. She had supper with Candace and Ed because Barbara had meetings, Barbara had night school, Barbara had projects and Barbara had no real interest in California. Whenever she was finished whatever she was doing after work, she picked up her daughter and took her home to bed. Small wonder the kid called Ed and Candace's place "home" and Barbara's place "Mommy's place."

Every birthday Ed brought out his camera and took a picture of California, and Ed could have made his living with his camera if he hadn't been making a better living as a workie. Candace always got three copies of the birthday photo, one for her own album, one for

Barbara, who stored the pictures, and one for the other grandma who seldom heard from her fading son in California.

When the other grandma asked if California could spend part of the summer holidays with her, Barbara was relieved: here was someone else to help do what Barbara did not wish to do. Ed and Candace were relieved because every grandma should see her granddaughter and they were getting a bit old and stiff, they did enjoy time to themselves. And California was delighted. Someone else to visit, someone else to go for long walks with her, someone else who liked to go to the Children's Petting Zoo, someone with a house in Bright's Crossing, where a kid could spend most of the day diving off a big rock into the swimming hole, then pick blackberries for pie, or tarts, or jam, or blackberry grunt.

California finished high school and prepared for university. Ed and Candace had no trouble coming up with the money for tuition and accommodation, Barbara grudgingly shelled out for clothes and bus fare, and California's marks in school guaranteed her admission.

And then California discovered computers. This made sense where nothing else in school had made sense! Here was a kind of logic she had been denied all her life.

She dropped her psychology courses, she dropped sociology, she dropped history, and she ignored literature. California forgot she had ever enjoyed playing basketball, she turned her back on softball, she neglected to go for long walks on the seawall, and she stopped dancing to music from her radio. California dedicated herself to computers the way her mother had dedicated herself to getting California's father.

The family could not believe it was happening. The tan faded, the laughter stopped. Their darling became a frowzy mess, living in the bowels of the university hacking with the other hackers. All Ed knew about computers was they had put hundreds of people out of work. All Candace knew was California seldom came home on weekends and when she did she munched absentmindedly at spice cookies while poring over pages not even written in English As She Is Spoke. All Barbara knew was computers would probably take over the Hydro company and leave her nobody to boss around in her new position as District Supervisor, her reward for all the classes, courses, and projects with which she had replaced the gorgeous creature in the red satin shirt.

Then the other grandmother died and left her entire estate to

California. The aspiring star gnashed his perfect pearly teeth, cursed intricate and colourful curses, then decided he had always hated women anyway and didn't bother to come home for the funeral.

California was grieved to lose her other grandmother. She wished the old woman had lived longer. California even wished she had been able to buy her own computer without having to lose her grandmother to do it.

Ed and Candace sighed, shook their heads in disbelief, and told Barbara to stop bleating. It was, after all, the kid's own money, and if the kid wanted to drop the entire shiterooni into a computer system, that was the kid's business, at least she'd had the good sense not to sell the little house in Bright's Crossing.

"Who'd buy the damn thing?" Barbara raged. "It's got to be sixty years old, it sits on two acres of land, not enough for the farm tax break. The front yard is nothing but rhododendron bushes and flower beds and the back yard has been dug up for gardens so many times the weeds don't even try to grow there any more."

California quit school. She packed her few things, moved them into the little house, and started finding out more about computers than she had ever dreamed possible.

There were so many things could be programmed. Things nobody else had yet thought about programming. No sooner did California get the programs developed than somebody wanted to buy them. The money went into more and better equipment, except for the little bit she needed for food, new jeans from time to time, and a small stipend for someone to look after the yard, the rhodies, and the garden.

California was standing in line at the Bank of Montreal, waiting her turn at the teller's wicket, when her eyes fastened on a little notice she had seen more times than she could count. "All transactions at this till will bear tomorrow's date." That part of California's brain which loved computers clicked and buzzed. California stepped forward when it was her turn and moved to the wicket on which the little placard was placed. She withdrew one hundred dollars, put it in her wallet, and walked from the bank knowing she would still collect interest on her money, even though it was in her pocket. It might as well have stayed in the bank, her transaction would not take effect until the next day. "I could empty my account today," she realized, "and still get interest on it until tomorrow!"

California bought her groceries, carried them onto the bus and rode the ten miles to Bright's Crossing staring at the plastic bag of brown rice without seeing it. When she got home, she cooked the rice without thinking about it. She cut and stir-fried chicken strips and vegetables without being aware of what her hands were doing. The computer-expert left lobe of her brain was starting to interface with the creative right lobe of her brain. The hard-headed workie genes she had inherited from Ed and Candace were holding hands with the off-beat contributions of her father. The single-mindeness Barbara had donated was taking its place on line with the canny smarts of her other grandmother.

By the time supper was ready, California was past the musing and the wondering, she was into the belief and manoeuvring. She looked at her supper and grinned, she picked up her chopsticks and dove in. For the first time in three years, she was all together again. She was who she had been before she met computers, plus who she had become because of computers. She was, more or less, whole.

And somewhere in the labyrinth of the barrow mounds, several of the Elder Gods snickered at the boredom-bashing stunt one of them had pulled.

California went back to the Bank of Montreal the next day and made arrangements to leap into the wave of tomorrow. She explained to the manager what kind of computer set-up she had at home, what she wanted to do, how she intended to do it, and, in return for their co-operation, she picked a few of the bugs out of the bank's own system.

Then she went to the Bank of Nova Scotia and asked to see the manager. Less than half an hour later, California walked out through the big glass doors, grinning, and headed for the Canadian Imperial Bank of Commerce. And from there, the Royal Bank of Canada.

California caught the Islander back to Bright's Crossing, walked from the bus stop to her house, went inside, closed the door, made herself a pot of coffee, and went into her computer room. There she withdrew all of her money from the Bank of Montreal and deposited it in the Bank of Nova Scotia. Then she transferred her money from the Bank of Nova Scotia to the Canadian Imperial Bank of Commerce. She sipped her coffee and shifted her money from the Canadian Imperial Bank of Commerce to the Royal Bank of Canada. Then she drank some more coffee and snickered. She was now collecting interest on her money from four different banks.

She opened second accounts in each bank and had her interest transferred to the new files in her computer. She transferred the interest from one bank into the account for interest in another bank. She moved money from here to there and from there to somewhere else and then back to where it had originally been.

California stored everything, then turned off her computer and went for a bike ride. The next day she took the Islander down to Ladysmith and went from bank to bank opening accounts. She caught the Islander south to Duncan and did the same.

By the end of the week, California Murphy had accounts in every branch of every bank on the island. She moved her money into and out of every one of them every day. She got interest on the same few dollars from over three hundred banks.

Then California left the island and went to Vancouver. It took her three days to go to every branch of every bank in the city. Then she went home and programmed her new accounts into her computer, snickering and giggling the entire time. She set up the programs so she didn't have to sit there herself doing the transferring, it all happened automatically.

The web grew. California opened accounts in Bamberton, in Comox, in Surrey, in Cloverdale, in Aldergrove, in Pouce Coupe. She had accounts in Lytton, she had accounts in Prince George. She would have had accounts in Spuzzum if there had been banks in Spuzzum. And when California Murphy had accounts in every branch of every bank in British Columbia, she moved on. Alberta, Saskatchewan, Manitoba, Ontario, California extended herself happily. Quebec, Prince Edward Island, New Brunswick, Cape Breton Island, Labrador, Newfoundland, and each of the territories.

The interest poured in. And the computer switched the money from bank to bank, from branch to branch, from account to account, whizz brrr click.

With Canada in her pocket, California turned to our great neighbour to the south. She forged new paths and destinies across that line some have always considered to be the thin line between genius and insanity. The world's longest undefended border vanished, and California had accounts in Richmond, Virginia, in Lubbock, Texas, even in Porcupine Ridge, Tennessee.

Whizz brrr click, whizz brrr click, interest coming and interest growing. Money transferred and money shifted. The wave of the future crashed on the shore of glee, and California Murphy saw only challenge, heard only the siren song of opportunity.

The Bank of Montreal noticed it first. What in hell is this? Three and a half million dollars, vanished into thin air? How in fuck, asked the Chairman of the Board of Directors, did we manage to lose three and a half million goddamn dollars? All the books balanced. All the ledger sheets did what ledger sheets have always been supposed to do. No mistakes anywhere. But the ozone had swallowed three and a half million goddamn dollars.

They had each and every one of their employees examined. Private detectives swarmed like termites in the springtime. And still the amount of profit supposed to go into the pockets of the few was not as much as it should have been.

The Chairman of the Board of one of the major banks met with the Chairman of the Board of another major bank. They put aside their supposed political differences and sat down together with bottles of expensive booze, forgetting free trade, forgetting national identity, forgetting everything except the horrible knowledge that somewhere in the balloon of commerce there was a pinhole, through which the hot air of economic stability was leaking.

"Check your computers," suggested an underpaid teller.

The Bank of Montreal hired, at mind-numbing expense, a computer specialist who brought her own disks to work with her. It took her less than half an hour to cross-check the simplest things. You don't get to be a computer expert by being stupid, and you don't get to be a computer specialist worth mind-numbing consultant fees by being dim. The computer whiz waited several weeks before making her report.

"Nothing we can do about it," the RCMP yawned. "It's all perfectly legal."

"As long as she pays income tax on the profit it's nothing to us," said Revenue Canada.

"Better not change the law or the banks themselves will be out of business," the President of the Bank of Canada said with a frown.

"Fuck around!" exploded the Chairman of the Board of Directors of one of the major banks.

The Bank of Montreal hired a lawyer. The lawyer poked and prodded, picked nits and honed fine points, then met with the entire Board of Directors and dropped the bomb.

"Fuck around!" they all squealed.

The lawyer took the bank's Lear jet from Toronto to Cassidy airport, then took a stretch limo to Bright's Crossing.

California Murphy invited the lawyer into the house and listened to everything the lawyer had to say. Then California Murphy laughed.

"I am entirely within my rights as a citizen," she said softly.

"Fuck your rights," the lawyer smiled.

"What I'm doing is totally legal."

"Fuck legality."

"It's not immoral."

"Fuck morality."

"There's not much you can do about it."

"I could have you knee-capped."

"Even a knee-capped cripple in a wheelchair can sit at a computer terminal."

"I could have you killed."

"Ah," she nodded. "I see."

"I hope you do," the lawyer smiled. "However, we'll let you keep what you already have. And we'll give you five million dollars as a gesture of our good faith."

"Good faith," she nodded.

"And you will stop what you are doing."

"Will I?"

"You will. Or we'll cancel your accounts. We have that right. Every business has the right to refuse service."

"And if I go to court?"

"I promise you it will cost you more than even you can afford."

"Okay," California shrugged. "It's been fun."

"I just bet it has," the lawyer agreed.

The lawyer took the stretch limo back to Cassidy airport, got on the Lear jet and flew back to Toronto, took a limo from the airport to Bay Street and met with the Chairman of the Board of Directors of the Bank of Montreal.

"It will cost you," the lawyer said "ten million dollars."

"Fuck around!" the chairman said.

"That's less than a year and a half at compound interest," the lawyer said firmly, "and I suggest you look up the word 'extrapolation' in your Webster's."

The Chairman of the Board of Directors sighed.

The lawyer got paid an incredible amount of money for his services and got the five-million-dollar difference between what he'd offered California and what she actually got.

The Bank of Montreal did not advise any of the other banks. It took six months for the Bank of Nova Scotia to realize four and a half million dollars had evaporated into the ozone.

California knew the Bank of Nova Scotia was starting to get antsy. California knew because her new friend, a computer specialist who had shown up in Bright's Crossing with several very interesting floppy disks, received a phone call offering her a job as a consultant to the Bank of Nova Scotia at what can best be called an unbelievable fee.

California bought a five-dollar Miss Clairol kit at the drugstore and turned her hair from light brown to vivid auburn. She bought fashion glasses with window glass lenses, changed her style of clothing, and walked into the Bank of Montreal.

There is no law against using a name other than your own to open a bank account, as long as you don't do it with the intention to defraud. And what California Murphy was doing was not fraud. California Murphy opened an account in her new name, Nell Frazier, and deposited one hundred dollars in her new daily interest savings account. Then California Murphy, still calling herself Nell Frazier, went to the Bank of Nova Scotia and opened a daily interest savings account with one hundred dollars. Then Nell Frazier went to every branch of every bank on Vancouver Island and opened a daily interest savings account at each one.

The representative of the Bank of Nova Scotia arrived in Bright's Crossing in a Lear jet and took a stretch limo to California's little house.

"What I'm doing is legal," California Murphy said.

"Fuck legal," said the lawyer.

When the lawyer from the Bank of Nova Scotia left, California went to her computer room and deposited four million dollars in her own account and four million in the account of her very good friend the computer specialist. Then she grinned and listened to the whizz brrr click as money moved from one account to another account and Nell Frazier became richer by the minute.

Then California had a long, hot shower, put on clean jeans and a clean blue-and-white-striped cotton shirt, hauled on brand new white cotton jock socks and highly polished burgundy loafers, and got behind the wheel of her brand new Saab. She drove from Bright's Crossing to town, and parked in Ed and Candace's driveway.

Candace had roast chicken, mashed potatoes, gravy, fresh garden string beans, and hot biscuits, with blackberry grunt for dessert. California ate with the best appetite in the country, then handed her grandparents a big brown envelope. Candace opened it, stared, then blinked back tears of joy.

"All the way?"

"All the way," California agreed.

"I always wanted a trip around the world," Ed "Liver Lips" Murphy smiled. "But how can you possibly afford . . ."

"Never," California said firmly, "look a gift horse up the ass, okay?"

It only hit three-point-one on the open-ended Richter scale. Hardly worth noticing, certainly not worth reporting. There are minor earthquakes all over the world all the time. The Elder Gods were chuckling, rolling over in bed with grins on their great craggy faces, not quite as bored as they had been a moment or two ago.   🍎